DAWN OF DARKNESS

A NOVEL

LEE BRANDENBURG
& MATT ISAACS

To order additional copies of this book visit
Amazon.com

BookSurge Publishing

Or write to
Hampton Books
1122 Willow Street, #200 San Jose, CA 95125

Library of Congress Cataloging-in-Publication Data
Brandenburg, Lee.
Dawn of Darkness, a novel. I Title.
ISBN 1439234809
ISBN-13: 978-1439234808

Printed in the United States of America

We dedicate this book to the more than one million, two hundred thousand Americans who died in this country's many wars before they had a chance to live.

Best wishes,

[signature]

Harbin, Manchuria

September 1942

After dinner, the gentlemen retired to the study for brandy and cigarettes. In the lamplight, their faces gleamed with perspiration. Their cheeks glowed pink. They had been laughing for a long time, so long, that the muscles around their mouths ached. In the quiet period between dinner and drinks, as their smiles faded, a few secretly wanted to retire. Others, afraid of the unsettling silence, tried to dispel it with a few more hollow guffaws.

They were dressed in formal attire: the officers wore their decorations; the scientists, black jackets with skinny black ties. Most of the doctors had taken to wearing their hair in the military style fashionable in Japan, clipped so short it looked blue. They held their cigarettes lightly and, perhaps because of their drinking, allowed the ashes to fall on the thick, burgundy carpets belonging to Major General Shiro Ishii.

The general had invited them to his home for one of his famous parties, the talk of Japan's military and moneyed elite.

They had taken the Manchurian Railway from the port city of Dairen, north through the rolling hills of China's Liaoning, Jilin, and Heilongjiang provinces, to arrive finally in Harbin, a city of intrigue on the outer edge of the Japanese empire. Everything about the journey rang of power and mystery: the captured railroad and countryside; the cosmopolitan city sprouting like an oasis on the lip of the Mongolian wasteland. Many of the men had made the trip without their wives. There were secrets to be unlocked on this trip—whispers of comfort women and deadly concoctions. The dinner launched a promising week of entertainment and business.

Ishii ushered the men into his study with the help of his wife and a few Chinese servants. The general was a tall, imposing man. He stood just inside the doorway of the room with his hand outstretched toward a semicircle of plush leather chairs and tried to say something witty as each man entered, causing the guests to cringe through their smiles at his rancid breath and hurry forward.

After the gentlemen were comfortably settled, Ishii's wife, Kiyoko, sang for them. She performed a traditional dance with a fan and sang, accompanied by her thirteen-year-old daughter, who artfully plucked a *koto*. The sonorous throb of the instrument and the woman's fluid gestures, like fluttering birds, drained the fire from the men's cheeks. It was a sad song, which ended with the singer shedding tears for a lost child. The performance over, Ishii's wife wished the men goodnight and tried to lead her daughter from the room, but the girl resisted. "I want to stay with father," she said, moving toward a seat in the back of the room.

Kiyoko blushed, prompting Ishii to speak up. "Go now, Harumi," he said. "You can help Mother serve tea and cookies when we're finished." The women left, the girl cloaked under the arm of her mother's kimono.

Ishii pulled a movie screen down from the ceiling. "Gentlemen, I've gathered you here this evening to show you the progress I have made on a series of experiments devoted to the war effort. What you are about to see will forever change your perceptions of the role of science on the battlefield."

Ishii strode to the back of the room, turned out the lights, and flipped the switch on a movie projector. The machine began to whir and light filled the canvas on the wall. "The venerable Dr. Naito provided this footage from the facility in Mukden," Ishii said.

A sharply dressed man stood up in the front and bowed. "And I have yet to see a yen for them," he announced to a hearty laugh.

A blurry image filled the screen—a straight shot of a five-by-five-foot jail cell. A door opened and a soldier in green fatigues stumbled into the chamber. The emaciated man, blond with a patchy beard, appeared frightened as he turned his head from side to side. "That's Joe," Ishii said. "He was suffering from an incurable case of dysentery and had only a few months to live regardless of what we did to him."

"Yes, but how did he contract the dysentery?" someone asked.

"Natural causes," Naito said, and received another laugh.

The American soldier looked straight at the camera and covered his mouth and nose with his hands.

"Hydrogen cyanide smells like bitter almonds," Ishii said.

The man tried to pry open the door of the cell with his fingers, then fell in convulsions to the floor. In a final gasp, he threw himself at the glass protecting the camera, and slid down, unconscious.

"The subjects are unable to hold their breath," Ishii explained. "The gas stimulates respiration."

The film cut back to the empty chamber. A Chinese woman with a baby stumbled through the door. The mother held the infant tightly to her breast and stared straight at the camera. Like the soldier before her, her eyes began to dart around the room. The baby, wrinkled and tiny, bobbed his head away from the mother for a moment to look around with wide-eyed curiosity. The woman clutched him tighter to her chest, then laid him on the floor and shielded him with her body. Her back rose and fell with her breath, then gradually stopped moving.

Someone groaned and ran from the room, clutching his collar. The end of the filmstrip flapped against the machine. Ishii turned up the lights. The guests were slumped deep in their chairs. One man's face looked as if it were made of wax. Another sat with his mouth agape. Slowly, the gentlemen roused themselves from their seats to stretch. A few affected wide yawns and twisted their necks awkwardly.

"It looks like you've been with a woman," the dapper Naito said to a neighbor and grinned. "Your face is flushed."

The man glanced around to see if others were watching him. His collar was open at the neck; his jacket wrinkled in the back. He feared Ishii's scrutiny, but his host, he saw, was looking around wearing a smile of immense satisfaction.

Chapter 1

Fort Stotsenburg, Philippine Islands

December 1941

Leo Jimenez lay shirtless on the warm slab of rock, listening to the sounds of the Sapang Bato River below. In addition to the burble of the water, he could hear the low murmur of the women gossiping as they scrubbed their laundry in the shallows and the occasional shout from the men fishing with spears. Leo shaded his eyes and gazed up into the deep blue sky. He smiled. Though he was thousands of miles from where he had grown up, he believed he had finally come home.

The Aetas were dark-skinned like himself, but that was where the physical resemblance to his new acquaintances ended. At five foot six, Leo was no giant, but even the tallest of the tribesmen came only as high as his nose. They wore nothing but loincloths—even the women went topless, exposing their dark breasts—and they all had huge crowns of kinky black hair. The first time Leo had encountered the group gathered around a palm, he had approached them cautiously with his sketchbook and pencils, expecting them to be shy. But they quickly revealed themselves to be quite the opposite. Almost immediately, they had surrounded him and begun caressing his arms and chest, even his crotch. Then a sprightly young woman with a magnificent head of hair had leapt into his arms.

Like cats, the Aetas roamed around the base with a privileged status. They were free to come and go as they pleased, while military personnel had to show I.D. at the gates. Today they chose to frolic by the river, tomorrow they might be found digging for grubs outside the barracks. The other guys would toss them coins or cigarettes or try to coax one of the girls into the sack, but Leo was genuinely curious about them. They had led him on excursions to the top of Mount Pinatubo, an extinct volcano with a pristine pool of water at the top where they swam naked to escape the heat. When he lounged by the river after morning drills, the women would often gather around him to rub his back affectionately, as if they had known him forever. Their touch aroused him, though he could never quite gauge their intentions and he never tested them. Having grown up with three sisters, he felt more comfortable in the company of women, particularly this group, with whom he felt a stronger affinity than even his fellow Hispanics from Albuquerque.

He sat up and began sketching the same young woman who had leapt into his arms. She was beautiful and entirely unself-conscious as she chatted amiably with her sisters and cousins in a tongue that sounded vaguely of the Navajo the ranch hands spoke back home. Aside from getting away from his overbearing father, Leo had enlisted to see the world, but he had never imagined exposure to a culture so innocent. A voice behind him startled him from his reverie. "Get dressed, Leo, there's trouble."

When Leo turned, he could see his friend Jake McGriff was serious.

"The Japs are coming," Jake said tensely. He was dressed in uniform and carried a rifle, another sign that something was amiss. Since their arrival in the Philippines on the *SS Coolidge*, the new recruits had spent more time in Hawaiian shirts playing cards than training for battle. The troops in the artillery corps ran drills in the mornings while it was still cool, then retired for beer and siestas by noon. Now Jake looked nervous. "They hit Hawaii. Blew it out of the water."

Leo sat up and drank from his canteen. "You're crazy," he said, refusing to allow the news to bother him, even if it meant outright denial. He was comfortable there on the rock.

"I heard it on the radio. They knocked out all our battleships and cruisers. Took out all our planes."

"Then why isn't anyone doing anything?" Leo asked skeptically. The Aetas went about their business, oblivious to the discussion.

"Our planes have been up in the air patrolling since this morning," Jake said. "I heard from one of the pilots that there was a plan to bomb Jap air bases on Formosa, but MacArthur called it off."

"Then it's OK," Leo said, relieved. "The general knows what he's doing."

"I'm not so sure about that," Jake said. "I'll meet you back at the barracks." He began to jog away, then stopped for a moment. "Are you coming, Leo?"

"Yeah, yeah," Leo said, pulling his shirt over his head. The heat was oppressive as he began to walk back to the base. He passed a barracks window, and saw a few soldiers still lying on their bunks. Then the faint buzz of engines reached his ear. Leo turned to see two V-formations of bombers perfectly aligned, high in the sky, coming in over the mountains from the China Sea, a black storm of at least two hundred planes. As they got closer, he watched them release things that glinted in the sun like tinfoil. Next, he heard a gentle sighing sound that grew louder and carried a fluttery overtone. Then, with a deafening immediacy, the explosions began.

Leo dove into a ditch behind a bamboo revetment. The bombs began pounding the runway, boom, boom, boom. He could feel the reverberations in his gut. Huge chunks of earth flew into the air, leaving deep craters. Something hit an American bomber less than one hundred yards away on the tarmac. The plane collapsed in the middle, then burst into flame.

The Zeros came next, flying so low Leo could see the pilots' faces. One of them wore a white scarf around his neck. He was smiling. He came straight down the runway, big red dots emblazoned on the wings of his plane, then looped around and approached the airfield from a 45-degree angle, strafing the American planes from the side.

Leo heard the sound of American gunfire all around him, but didn't see any Japanese planes going down. The Zeroes kept ripping everything up and returning as if the attack would never end. The stench of black smoke and gasoline filled the air.

Leo was still trembling in the ditch long after the last enemy plane had departed. His teeth were chattering when he finally climbed out. He passed by the same barracks building and heard up-tempo big band music coming from the radio as if nothing had happened. Around the corner, he saw his first dead body. The man's face was burning, flames eating through his cheeks. A ruptured gasoline tank blazed nearby.

Leo rushed back to the base, his legs tingling from crouching in the ditch. Soldiers were slowly emerging from their hiding places, fear on their faces. Near his barracks, a car horn blared. It came from a '38 Ford, the driver, his head leaning against the steering wheel, had been shot dead.

* * *

Like a mighty boot, the Japanese had kicked over the anthill, sending the unprepared American troops scrambling to regroup. Leo struggled to assemble his rifle amid the tumult surrounding him in the barracks. "Look alive!" Sergeant Whitaker shouted at the men, as if they needed prodding. Leo cursed himself for trying to clean the rifle at the last minute; now he couldn't put the damn thing back together. The more time he wasted, the more nervous he became.

"Are you still fiddling with that thing?" Jake asked him, annoyed. "I'm going to leave without you if you don't hurry up."

"Will you help me? I won't ask you again, I promise."

Jake sat down on the bunk with a sigh. "Now watch closely this time," he said, inspecting the pieces of the disassembled Enfield. "You should have learned this months ago." Leo watched his friend's gray eyes dance over the parts, instantly absorbed in the task. Jake showed his top teeth when he concentrated, an expression somewhere between a smile and a grimace. The Philippine sun had scalded his tall forehead and bleached his crew cut nearly white.

"Get up off your ass, private," Whitaker shouted as he dashed past Leo with a box of supplies. Startled, Leo busied himself for appearances, rummaging aimlessly through his musette sack. For all his enthusiasm entering the service, he had found himself inept at the most rudimentary aspects of soldiering: cleaning his rifle, loading a howitzer. He wasn't stupid; he could do any one of these things given time to think them through, but he was helpless when rushed. In the first weeks of basic training, he had tried to transfer from the coast artillery into a medical unit, where he had intended to enlist all along, but Whitaker had denied his request. He wanted someone to pick on. Often Leo had questioned his decision to join the service at all—his father had advised him against it—but never more so than now.

"Don't listen to that bastard," Jake said. It was easy for him to say. They both hated the tight-faced little man with the pencil mustache, but unlike Leo, Jake had taken to army life effortlessly. "Buck up and show him you can fight as well as anybody."

"I can," Leo said, as much for himself as for his friend. He stood up and made an angry face at a little mirror hanging on the wall. Three months in the military had slimmed the baby fat from his cheeks, but the rest of him, while still short, had grown thick with muscle. He stretched open his eyes to show the whites, hoping to wake himself up.

"What are you doing looking at yourself?" Jake asked, incredulous. "I'm trying to help you here, and you're off in la-la land again."

"I was watching," Leo lied.

Shaking his head, Jake handed him the assembled rifle. "Here you go, dreamer. Next time, you're on your own."

* * *

Over the next week, smoke and the sharp aroma of burning flesh hung in the air as American and Filipino forces flailed blindly at the hard-charging Japanese airplanes. The Zeros seemed to be everywhere, tireless machines smashing the flimsy barracks and nipa huts.

Captain Herman, the unit's commanding officer who had spent far more time at the Jai Alai Club than on the airbase, appeared lost in the firestorm, marching from one side of Clark Field to the other, shouting orders, then forgetting his commands as soon as he issued them. Faulty equipment contributed to the confusion. The ancient Enfield rifles, relics from the Spanish – American war, jammed repeatedly. The army had designated the 50-caliber machine guns as antiaircraft mounts, but the guns lacked sights to aim, and the men consistently missed their targets by as much as fifty feet. And when the captain assigned Leo and Jake to a half-track, a cross between a jeep and a tank, which neither of them had ever driven, he failed to mention that shooting the gun while driving would strip the gears. The thing froze in its tracks within three-quarters of an hour.

For Leo, the hours passed in a series of flickering images: the Filipino girl lying on the ground, her clothes torn. He went over to help, though he wasn't sure what to do. The sky had been thick with a blanket of clouds all day, but as he approached, the setting sun ducked below the fog, casting people's faces in a bright orange glow. The girl's father knelt over her, wringing his hands as he consoled her. The girl had been whipped by shrapnel, up her legs and chest. She was so thin. With no medic in sight, Leo tried to peel off her blouse to treat the wounds, but the girl covered herself with her arms. "Let him do it," her father said in English.

Leo rinsed his hands with rubbing alcohol and meticulously picked the shards of metal from her flesh. He was at his best given time to concentrate, and at that moment, no one existed in the world except the young woman. The father contributed his shirt, torn into strips, to stanch the bleeding from her belly. Leo cradled her in his arms and carried her back to the first aid station. "Are you a medic?" one of the nurses asked, inspecting the girl.

Leo shook his head. "Artillery."

"You did a good job," she said. "I think she'll live." The nurse had the same quick eyes as his sister.

"Any chance I can get a medical kit to take out there?" he asked.

She paused. The station was under strict orders to keep a tight hold on supplies. "Here, take one," she said, and shooed him off.

Leo had turned down a future assured of comfort, even privilege, simply to prove, stubbornly, that he could take care of himself. His great-grandfather, the son of a wealthy Mexican family, had been one of the founding fathers of Albuquerque long before New Mexico entered the Union in 1912, even before the Indian wars and the coming of the railroad. Leo's family's holdings had grown during the boom years until they now owned great swaths of farm and cattle land, a minor fiefdom on the southwestern plain.

For years, Leo's father, Juan, had been passing on the lessons he had learned from his forebears: plant peas in February when the weather is cold enough to give them snap; whip a horse across the stomach with a lariat if he's bloated; use salt to stop the bleeding of a castrated bull.

Leo had enjoyed learning the folk wisdom, but the education wasn't always so pleasant. His father would bark at him for his clumsiness replacing the glass in the barn window. He had always had trouble working with his hands, which sometimes felt like foreign appendages. He lived a life of the mind, a half step removed from the ordinary world.

Why he would think army life would suit him any better than herding cattle was beyond him now. Aspiring to a career in medicine, he had foolishly believed he might receive medical training in the service, which his father, in search of an heir, would never have allowed him to pursue at home. He had enlisted, telling his family only after the fact. The confrontation was every bit as frightening as he had imagined it would be, but he had survived—with the help of Jake, whose presence had fortified his courage. He could never have guessed that he would be placed in the coast artillery, or that Whitaker, his immediate superior, would deny his request for a transfer. Of course, Japan's attack on America had come as a surprise as well, and fear itself had since assumed an entirely new meaning.

* * *

The air assaults came in waves, first Pearl Harbor in Hawaii, then Clark Air Base the next day, then Nichols and Cavite, forts south of Manila. In every case, the American planes had been parked tightly together to prevent sabotage. Now they were obliterated. Once considered inept, the Japanese appeared unstoppable. Within two weeks, the imperial forces captured three points along the northern rim of Luzon, virtually unopposed.

General MacArthur's defensive strategy proved disastrous. The large but inexperienced Filipino armies were supposed to defend the beaches, backed by American troops. But within a week the Japanese were breaching the perimeter, and soon some forty-three thousand enemy soldiers massed along the upper third of the island.

Though resistance stiffened as the enemy moved south, by Christmas, MacArthur was calling for a "strategic withdrawal"—retreat was not in the U.S. Army lexicon—allowing the regiments surrounding the capital to funnel into the Bataan Peninsula, west of Manila. The strategy, dubbed War Plan Orange, had been devised over a decade before as a theoretical precaution in case the islands were ever attacked. This defensive mind-set was among the many reasons why MacArthur hadn't taken a more aggressive stance in the critical hours following Pearl Harbor. Nevertheless, a retreat was something new and not a little dismaying for the Americans. Within five months they would surrender.

* * *

Chapter 2

Harbin, Manchuria

September 1942

Shiro Ishii's guests left well after midnight. Baron Ikeda, a cousin of the emperor, had invited everyone to share a case of vodka he had discovered in the basement of his Russian mansion along the Sungari River. Of course, Ryoichi Naito, from the prison camp at Mukden, had accepted immediately, never one to miss an opportunity to consort with royalty. He and a drunken horde of doctors had followed the baron howling like wolves in the frosty night.

The last guest to remain was the elder statesmen Colonel Chikahiko Koizumi, Ishii's closest confidant. The great man with the generous beard and belly had agreed to stay for a final bowl of broiled eel over rice, which he picked at while slumped in an enormous easy chair. Ishii sat across from him on a velvet couch. His daughter, Harumi, had fallen asleep with her head in his lap. "Ah, you must have been raised in a proper samurai family," Ishii said when he saw his friend pluck a few pieces of rice from the side of the bowl with his fingers. "I bet if you dropped a grain at dinner, you had to pick it up and eat it."

Koizumi smiled in recognition. "My father was always aware that he was able to eat without having to work the land himself."

It was familiar territory for the two, who shared a common background, though Koizumi was nearly a generation older. Both had grown up the sons of samurai who had rejected the country's headlong drive toward modernization in the final years of the nineteenth century. Ishii's father had refused to pass beneath the new telegraph lines spanning the countryside, even if he had to walk an extra mile to avoid them. He carried salt in a pocket of his sleeve and scattered it over his head if he ever came face-to-face with a Buddhist priest or a funeral procession. An isolationist to the end, he had committed suicide in protest of the Russo – Japanese War in 1905.

In addition to their similar upbringings, the careers of Ishii and Koizumi had followed parallel lines. Having observed the success of Germany's chlorine attacks during the First World War, Koizumi had founded his own country's research of poison gas. Like Ishii, he too had pushed for the continued development of scientific weaponry in defiance of the Geneva Convention of 1925 and other international accords banning chemical and biological warfare. Ishii, of course, had expanded the programs dramatically with his success cultivating deadly pathogens, and in doing so, had far surpassed Koizumi in renown and power. But the elder, who was still active in military politics, enjoyed a privileged status as the only one allowed to speak plainly to his volatile prodigy. "The films affected you tonight," he said. "You grew quiet after you showed them."

Ishii laughed as he caressed his daughter's hair. "I've been thinking about my mother," he said in a hushed voice, careful not to wake the girl. "You know, I was with my mother and Kiyoko, who was my fiancé at the time, when I saw my first movie."

"What did you see?"

Ishii hesitated to get the pronunciation right. "*Il Cuore*," he said with his best Italian accent. "*The Heart*. It was about a ship-wreck." He paused in reflection. "That was the day I learned my mother would die."

"You must have been young," Koizumi said with concern as he stretched to place the empty bowl on the ottoman at his feet. He proceeded to search his vest for fallen grains of rice.

"Not so young," Ishii said, allowing himself to fully indulge in the memory with his friend. "I was thirty-two. A graduate medical student at Kyoto University. I remember it was spring but cold. Kiyoko wore a fox-fur scarf my mother had bought her in Tokyo, and she looked lovely. I couldn't keep my hands off her."

"And here's the result," Koizumi said, gesturing toward the adolescent girl asleep in her father's lap.

"Yes," Ishii said distractedly, still adrift in the past. "The theater was crowded, so we had to sit right up front. And I remember my mother coughing incessantly into a handker-chief. But I didn't pay her much attention, I was so taken with my Kiyoko." Ishii looked into his daughter's face to make sure she was asleep, then gently lifted her hand before him. Low-ering his voice even further, he ran a finger along her wrist.

"I reached up her sleeve and began caressing her like this, touching the tender skin just below the elbow. She pulled away, fearing someone might see, but I persisted."

Koizumi laughed quietly.

"It was only after a long coughing fit that I turned to my mother, annoyed, and noticed the blackened blood in the ball of silk she held. And that's when I realized how deeply the consumption had burrowed into her lungs. She died three weeks later."

"Hm," Koizumi mumbled and sat up in his chair. "So tonight you saw the film of the mother and baby gassed in the chamber, and perhaps you felt remorse."

"Don't be silly," Ishii said dismissively. "It was the sound of the projector that reminded me of her. No, the work is an entirely separate matter. I have no doubt the annals of science will record my name with pride someday."

"Don't think of yourself," Koizumi said gravely. "Think of your homeland."

* * *

Koizumi had been the one who introduced Ishii to the concept of science in service of a greater good. When the two met in 1930, Ishii had never considered his livelihood in terms beyond the narrow scope of his ambitions. His research of biological weaponry had been productive but still widely ignored by the country's military leaders, who paid little attention to the Surgeon Corps. But Koizumi had opened Ishii's eyes to an approach, based on spirit rather than science, that tapped into the restless nature of the times. This amalgamation of spirituality and nationalism, promulgated by the great general, Kanji Ishiwara, changed Ishii's life, elevating his work, he felt, from mere research to that of a higher calling.

The first time Ishii had heard the general speak, junior officers had packed the lecture hall, making their usual ruckus. Many smuggled in flasks of whiskey. Ishii disliked the firebrands, but grudgingly respected the sway they held with the high command. Their ruddy, severe expressions were becoming the symbolic faces of a nation eager to assert itself on the world stage.

Ishiwara, a short, stocky man in an officer's uniform, stepped up to the podium, and the lights dimmed. A spotlight made his skin almost glow. He had a wide, flat nose and high cheekbones. "Gentlemen," he began. "I know many of you from previous meetings, and I wish to welcome those of you who are here this evening for the first time. You are all soldiers in the service of our emperor and of our divine nation, and so I am compelled to share with you what I feel to be the wellspring of our duty to both.

"Our nation is currently in a state of terrible confusion, a madness of sorts that's been caused by the degenerate influences from the West. In the course of our country's industrial growth, Western ideas have infected some of our people. A few have used the fruit of this growth to accumulate great personal wealth, even to the point of harming the emperor and the great nation he embodies. As a result, many have lost touch with the *kokutai*.

"I need not convince you of the importance of the *kokutai*— the spiritual force that links each of us to the emperor as his children—the essence of your training as elite members of the

Japanese Army." He paused to peer into rows of young faces as if to impress them with the gravity of the moment. Ishii shifted in his chair.

"Nichiren, the apostle the Buddha specifically sent to our nation, has unveiled a role and a duty for us all, and the *kokutai* is the universal principle by which the evolution of the world will ultimately be resolved."

The colonel described in precise detail Nichiren's prophecy of the final confrontation between the soulless forces of the West and the divine moral principles embodied in the Japanese empire. "This Final War looms on the horizon," he thundered. "The restoration of the world's moral order cannot be consummated except by the triumph, under the leadership of our emperor, of our divine Japanese nature over the West. The inevitable conflict, long foretold, is imminent. Specifically, it is in our hands. Nichiren said there was only one fundamental truth, the truth written in the words of the Buddha.

"And we who know the truth must exert ourselves tirelessly. We must be ready in the moment of the world's greatest need, to draw our swords, as Nichiren commanded, and spur the triumph of righteousness. The outcome of the Final War is assured, but we must each struggle to fulfill the divine imperative. There is no time to be lost!"

Ishiwara went on to quote Napoleon, Frederick the Great, and Helmuth von Moltke. He spoke of a divine imperative. Indeed, the coming conflict would be no ordinary war. Such a clash would require the deadliest of weapons, the very sword of righteousness. The general had called for modern weapons—invoking even the visionary hope of developing bombers capable of circling the globe. Though the general never said so explicitly, Ishii understood him to mean biological weapons as well.

At the end of this speech, the audience rose and applauded riotously. Ishii stood as well, surprised at how moved he was by the general's words, and he recognized that the young men in the audience shared his enthusiasm for this new spirit. The vast, universal approach to war, gave him all the reason he needed to sell his superiors on the idea of creating the ultimate weapon. The timing couldn't have been better.

* * *

Only a few months after that speech, in the autumn of 1931, the country was jolted awake when Ishiwara and a handful of other rogue officers from the Kwantung Army blew up a section of the South Manchurian Railway just north of Mukden. They blamed the Chinese for planting the bomb, giving the army a reason to advance into Manchuria. Within weeks, the imperial army brought three provinces of Manchurian China under Japanese control. Japanese forces went on to take Harbin. Before long, the territory was declared a new state and renamed Manchukuo.

The lightning strikes of the northern Kwantung brigades, numbering no more than ten thousand men, stoked national pride and inflamed a new breed of young officers who were eager to vault the country onto the world stage. Many of the firebrands had joined radical secret societies like the Black Dragons dedicated to this adventuristic spirit. In this way, a coup was set in motion that would require a decade to complete. The Cherry Blossom Society, one of hundreds of such organizations fomenting revolution, conceived of a plan to wipe out soft Japanese government officials with an aerial bombardment of a cabinet meeting, paving the way for a military takeover. Officials only narrowly diverted the plan, later dubbed the "October Incident." A Nichiren sect called the Blood Brotherhood Band, however, declared war on the "capitalist-internationalist" order, and murdered a former finance czar as well as the chairman of the Mitsui Corporation.

As the gutters ran with blood and Japan's leadership fulfilled its dreams of continental dominance in China, Ishii and his mentor Koizumi found their wings. Koizumi became dean of the Tokyo Army Medical College thanks, in part, to his affiliation with Ishii, who had captured the army's imagination with an ingenious water filter to be used on the field of battle. The filter, which he named after himself, had earned him thousands of yen. Meanwhile, using his filter research as a front, Ishii had been making huge leaps in his cultivation of bacteria, developing new strains of plague, more powerful than the epidemics that had wracked entire European civilizations. His operation grew so rapidly he soon needed a larger facility, someplace remote where he could farm the bacteria and test its potency.

"Manchukuo," Koizumi said over drinks one night. Everyone in the city now wanted to escape to the wide-open spaces of the north country.

"Manchukuo," Ishii repeated, wrapping his lips around the word as if it were an exotic delicacy. "But how will I get there?"

"I have no money to give you, Ishii."

"I didn't ask."

"No, but I know you."

Ishii rolled his cup of sake between his palms as he considered his options. "Then I'll ask the minister of finance," he said with confidence.

"Takahashi?" Koizumi asked, his mouth full of tuna. "You're knocking on the wrong door."

"As you said, you know me." Ishii said.

* * *

The next day Ishii appeared at the minister's home, dressed in his finest military outfit. He found the wizened old man, sitting at a low table, drinking tea. An extra cup was set next to the pot. Behind him was an alcove hung with a large watercolor of a branch covered with pink plum blossoms. The major bowed until his forehead touched the floor. "I am Ishii Shiro, director of the Epidemic Prevention Department at the Army Hospital."

"Your reputation precedes you, sir," the elderly man said and inclined his head. "What can I do for you?"

"I have come to ask you for financial assistance," Ishii said humbly.

Takahashi's eyes widened in surprise. "There are proper channels—"

"I understand, sir. But after much consideration, I decided that this channel would be most effective."

"I'm afraid I don't understand," Takahashi said. The houseboy poked his head into the room. "Is there anything I can get for you before I leave, sir?"

Takahashi smiled serenely. "We're fine, thank you." He turned his attention back to his guest. "You were saying?"

"I come to you, sir, with the best interests of our country at heart," Ishii said. "As you may know, for a number of years I have worked on water purification techniques and vaccinations to strengthen the effectiveness of our fighting forces. I wish to expand this program, to build a modern facility in Manchukuo, but to do this, I need your assistance. Such a project could, of course, serve your cause as well, for as we all know, our country needs to bolster the military."

"I appreciate your interest," Takahashi said with more than a little sarcasm. "But I have already committed to a number of valuable military programs. Anything more would take money from other priorities."

"I can promise you, sir, that my facility would create thousands of jobs," Ishii persisted. He was beginning to lose patience. "It would provide a springboard for expansion in the vast region, for mineral and oil exploration, for farming. You laugh, sir, but my plan makes simple economic sense."

Takahashi was indeed laughing but shaking his head. "I am afraid I must decline."

Ishii joined in the merriment as he reached into his military jacket and removed a metal flask; then he quickly cut the hilarity short. "Let me put it to you more simply, sir." He banged the vial on the table. "What I have here is a bottle of cholera—"

* * *

The northbound train flew by the countryside of mainland China, past the sprawling open-air markets, the soybean farmers knee-deep in mud, curious, blank expressions on their faces. Ishii spat at them from the open window. They were dark skinned, these people, with pinched expressions like crab apples. He had left his wife and three children at home, and brought along a young girl, as strong and limber as a mare, as a companion. The major rode her in his private car, day and night, past the prairies. As he bucked, he saw the mountains towering in the distance, so large they dwarfed his memories of Mount Fuji.

Traveling in secret, he chose the alias Togo in honor of the majestic leader who had defeated the Russians in the naval battles at Port Arthur and Tsushima. Ishii felt like a conqueror himself. These rivers and valleys, these peasants with their muddy complexions, spoke of Nippon's military might. The Manchurian Railroad Company was an imperialistic force in its own right, employing some of the greatest minds in Japan to help unlock the potential of this new land.

Takahashi had spurned Ishii's request for funding—even after he had threatened to dump the contents of his vial on the table, killing them both. It was not until two of the finance minister's grandchildren came down with mysteriously high fevers, followed by severe bouts of vomiting and diarrhea, that Takahashi changed his mind. As if by magic, an item appeared on the following year's budget for the creation of a "water purification" station at Harbin in the upper reaches of Manchukuo, at a cost of ten million yen. Ishii had known the right men in the legislature to ensure the project survived the budget hearings. Unfortunately, the finance minister's grandchildren did not fare as well. Takahashi would know better next time.

Ishii eventually brought his own family to Harbin, settling in the exclusive part of town reserved for a few rich Chinese families and the Japanese who arrived with the occupation. At a crossing of the great railways leading south and east, the border town fashioned itself as the last great city before the hinterlands of the Soviet Union, with its pistachio-green train station built in the art nouveau style, its neoclassical cathedrals and synagogues, its symphonies and homegrown circus.

Ishii's family lived in a huge, Russian-style mansion, with elaborate arched windows and wrought iron trim. The house had a magnificent mahogany staircase and fireplaces in all the bedrooms. Black, shiny chandeliers hung from the ceilings. The outer walls were made of chiseled sandstone, covered with ivy that turned blood red in the fall.

In the years leading up to the war with the United States, Ishii laid the foundations for his laboratory, a massive block of concrete he would call Ping Fan. As the ripe fields of wheat rattled in the breeze, Ishii ordered the earthmovers to roll through before the farmers could harvest their crops for the coming winter. The natives scattered like ants and attempted to brave the winter in nearby caves. But the doctor drove the Mongol peasants from their land, wiping out ten villages in his path. His mercenaries spread sorghum across the floors of the houses and set them on fire. They executed anyone who offered resistance. Ishii personally drove one of the bulldozers through a line of huts.

In place of the crude wooden structures, Ishii built a brick monolith. His heart lay in every block. As thousands of Chinese laborers toiled in the desert, the buildings sprouted like regenerating cells, one upon another, all with the same white, square-tiled facades. The property consumed almost four square miles with its dormitories and barracks, jail, and power plant. It might have been a prison camp with its wide moat, high dirt walls, and barbed wire. To keep up appearances in Harbin, Ishii instructed his men to call it a lumber mill. Occasionally the whine of a buzz saw could be heard in the compound.

For the families of the Japanese guards and scientists, Ishii created Togo village, complete with a Shinto shrine, an auditorium, and a swimming pool. He built a library, a brothel, a school for the children. His brother Mitsuo ran the local prison; another brother, Takeo, raised the laboratory animals. Mercenaries, hired from his hometown of Chiyoda, in their reverence called him "War God Ishii."

* * *

When the compound was completed, Ishii addressed an assembly of elite scientists in the oak-paneled conference room. From his position at the podium, he could observe the vast main laboratory below, where hundreds of researchers toiled like worker bees, manufacturing their own brand of honey.

"At last we are underway," Ishii announced with pride. "I believe you will find the laboratories here to your liking. If there is anything you need for your work, just ask. Money is no object. Now, for the business at hand," he said. "Our research will depart from the principles you learned as doctors. Believe me, I am aware of this. Nevertheless, I ask you to pursue this line of inquiry, one as scientists probing for the truth in natural science and, two, as military men, seeking to build a powerful weapon against the enemy."

Ishii led the scientists on a tour of his masterpiece, intro-
ducing them to a few of the busy researchers. Dressed in green
and blue coveralls, "anti-disease suits" made of rubberized silk,
they were covered from head to toe, with zippers down their
fronts and drawstrings at their necks. Every worker had a little
basket of red apples at his side. After every possible exposure,
the researcher would quickly pull off his mask, bite the apple,
and spit out the pieces having been told that the germs would
be absorbed in the meat of the fruit.

The main laboratory, as wide and airy as an aircraft han-
gar, was devoted to the study of pathogens: anthrax, dysentery, plague, cholera, and gas gangrene. Squat one-ton boilers
stewed meat bouillon until a brown skin formed on the top.
Chrome autoclaves, their surfaces shining like warped mirrors
in a fun house, sterilized the culture mediums. Typhoid bacillus gathered like pearls on the agar, while anthrax was muddy.
The scent of cucumber hovered over the vats of dysentery.

In Takeo's animal warren, fifty thousand chickens pecked
at each other, laying eggs for the production of Rickettsia
prowazekii, an epidemic form of typhus. Fifty thousand rats
churned in a sea of bodies good for the extraction of Rickettsia
mooseri, another lethal typhus strain.

Of all the creatures, Ishii loved his fleas most, particularly
the *Pulex irritans* for its lightning-quick legs and marvelous
durability. He kept a photograph of a flea, vastly magnified,
on his wall. He bred the creatures in big glass jars, gluing a
rat's feet to the bottom of the container to feed his lovelies.
Through a microscope, he would watch plague bacteria mul-
tiply in a flea's shiny, black stomach a few days after it bit an
infected rat. These germs would engorge and finally clog the

flea's esophagus. He could count on his messenger surviving perhaps a month.

An expert pilot, he tried spraying the fleas from a high-compression hose attached to the wings of his plane. In addition, he developed a delicate porcelain bomb called the *Uji*, filled with oxygen, rice, and fleas, which would spare the insects on impact. Released from high altitudes, the ten-quart projectile would explode into tiny fragments on contact, leaving no trace except a swarm of hungry fleas. He dropped the bomb among prisoners shackled and bound to wooden stakes. Each time, at least one became infected, but Ishii needed more impressive results. He tinkered with the altitude, with the thickness of the porcelain, with the number of fleas, until he achieved ratios as high as thirty percent. Still he was not satisfied. To further his studies, he would require more prisoners.

* * *

Dust swept across the plains, covering the green Dodge trucks as they bounced down the dirt road to Ping Fan. All but the front windshields were painted over to prevent anyone from viewing their cargo. When the trucks arrived at the plant, men wearing surgical masks and goggles, white coats flapping in the breeze, quickly unloaded long objects wrapped in straw, carrying the mummified forms on gurneys. When one of the forms fell off its bed and began writhing like a caterpillar, the men converged on the wriggling mass and wrestled it through the wide doors of the plant.

They threw the bundles into individual holding cells and untied them. There were eight captives in all: three thieves, an opium smoker, two Chinese intellectual dissidents, and two young women, one Russian, one Chinese, believed to be prostitutes. The men in white coats offhandedly called the prisoners *marutas*, or "logs," a joking reference to Ping Fan's supposed purpose as a wood mill. Eventually, they would cut many of the "logs" into little pieces like so much timber.

A hole was cut in each cell door to observe the prisoners inside. The men in white coats carefully marked the symptoms on charts clipped outside the cells. They observed a variety of conditions: black abscesses from anthrax rotting the forearms and calves. Bones poking through skin. Night sweats from fever. Dry, pathetic coughing. The men in white coats were free to explore the outer reaches of science. They injected the thieves with plague—except one, whom they injected with horse piss. This prisoner convulsed violently for a few minutes, then expired. They shot air into the opium smoker's veins to chart his chest pains and watch him black out.

They connected one man's heart to his intestines to observe the blood circulate through the fecal tubes. The legs and arms would jerk spasmodically when the scientists touched the brain with a scalpel.

They took the Chinese intellectuals out to a field and tied them to stakes at various distances from a shrapnel bomb filled with gas gangrene. They protected the prisoners' upper bodies with metal shields and thick blankets to prevent them from immediately dying from the blast, but they left the legs and buttocks exposed. The prisoners screamed when the shrapnel struck their hindquarters, but that was nothing compared to their shouts the following week as the gangrene set in, leading to a quick expiration.

The Russian woman showed signs of having lost her virginity and was deemed a prostitute. The Chinese woman, nineteen, still had her hymen intact. Following these private inspections, the men in white coats led the women naked into a deep freeze unit and set up a camera so they could observe the effects of frostbite. The temperature in the room was reduced to forty degrees below zero. Through the two-way mirror, they watched them dig their nails into each other's flesh, seeking warmth. Frost gathered first on their eyelashes, then on their lips and nipples. The veins under their skin turned bright blue. They clung to each other silently until the film ran out.

* * *

Chapter 3

East Coast of Bataan

May 1942

The men limped north through the dust like a loose column of ants, hungry and mute. The line stretched for miles— some sixty thousand Filipinos, another ten thousand Americans wading through the ninety-five-degree heat. The soldiers walked with their shirts open, their dog tags bouncing off their bony chests. In the eyes of the weak there was only a vacant stare; in the strong, a grinding resignation. Their shallow steel helmets offered a little shade, but not enough to keep their heads from smoldering. None of them had ever dared whisper a desire to yield, but less than six months after the Japanese had pulled them into war, more than a few were glad to surrender. Hunger and the jungle had beaten them. We're out, they wanted to say. Unforeseen circumstances. Play on without us.

The sturdier prisoners shouldered the injured, desperate to keep them moving. Faltering led to certain death. Many couldn't wear boots, their feet were so swollen, and after a few miles, they were bloodied from the hot, sticky road. Others hobbled forward on crutches. Stay on your feet—or die. One Filipino who had lost both legs tried to paddle through the dust using only his arms. He slithered on his belly for a few yards before a Japanese guard stabbed him in the neck with a bayonet.

Jake muttered as he walked. His ears were still ringing from a blow he had taken to the head. He had been minding his own business when something came down on his helmet so hard the shock nearly sent him to his knees. When he turned around, a little shrimp of a guard was standing there, proudly pointing to the dent he had made in the steel. Down the road he went, the little bastard, still laughing. Jake thought his neck might have been broken. If the cocksucker had stuck around, Jake would have taken him out, damn the consequences.

All night, the guards screamed at them. When they called for a halt beneath the sweltering sun, the men instantly collapsed in the dirt and tried to sleep. Half an hour later they were back on their feet, up, up, up. Then some jackass would decide to change direction. The guards didn't know what the hell they were doing. Christ, they made the U.S. Army look like a finely tuned machine. It was just common sense to stop for a few hours at Cabcaben, where the men could rest on the benches and refill their canteens. But that would be too reasonable. Instead, the guards called for a halt about a mile north of the base, smack-dab in the middle of nowhere.

The prisoners had to sit in the road, choking on the dust from the passing tanks and jeeps.

Jake had dodged the debilitating gut bugs going around. He didn't need parasites to feel queasy. Just looking at the men around him made him sick to his stomach. Their bodies were racked with disease, their flesh riddled with sores. Leo had adopted an awkward gait, having lost sensation in his feet. A medic said it was beriberi, brought on by the lack of vitamins. No thiamine. Whitaker was afflicted with the condition as well. The two walked along like exotic birds. Larsen, the cook, marching a few rows ahead, had picked up something nasty. Dysentery of the worst kind. The poor guy wanted to lie down and die, but the others wouldn't let him.

If anything, Jake was constipated. He hadn't crapped in nearly a week. Leo's chlorine tablets, plunked in the canteen they shared, helped him avoid the bugs, but not the constant abuse of the Japanese soldiers. Marching four abreast, Jake was at the end of the row, closest to the passing vehicles traveling back and forth to his right. The guards seemed to have it in for him. Maybe they didn't like his mug.

Leo, on the other hand, breezed by with nary a whack. After days without food, he was still strong, thanks to his naturally thick physique. He had turned inward, losing himself in his thoughts, so that he appeared almost sanguine. While others criticized Leo's dreaminess, Jake admired his friend's ability to escape into his own world. He could learn from his friend, who seemed to have a knack for reminding Jake of things he knew deep down, but had forgotten.

They had met playing on the same baseball team in their last year of high school. Jake, a pitching prodigy, had led the team to the state championship series, with the help, in no small part, of his catcher Leo, who, simply through proximity, had become his friend. As battery mates, the two invented a secret language of hand gestures and shrugs, transmitted almost telepathically, over the sixty feet between the mound and the plate. At the start of the season, Jake had decided what to throw next, shaking his head until the appropriate sign appeared. But as the season wore on, he came to trust his catcher's judgment. He sensed something different in Leo, a wisdom.

The two exchanged few words on the trail. Talking made them tired. Jake might have been more chatty if not for the raging parade of Japanese trucks and cars passing by, which kept him vigilant. He watched the guards patrol up and down the line, two escorts for every hundred men. He studied their sweaty whiskered faces as they argued over tattered maps. Charged with transporting the men sixty miles northward in no more than a week, they were in over their heads and growing increasingly violent.

He had seen one of the officers hack off a prisoner's head for no reason. It happened so fast, the body had remained standing for a moment, the hands gripping spasmodically, while the head wobbled in the dust. A few miles back, they had forced a man to kneel as if they were about to execute him, then shot his leg instead and laughed as he limped down the road. At times like these, Jake wished he could pull out the picture of Angelina, Leo's older sister—anything to distract himself for a few moments—but he didn't want his friend to know he had it.

The night before they had shipped out, Angelina had surprised him with a kiss after the farewell party, though she was engaged to a banker's son. The girl had a wild side. One kiss led to another and soon Jake was driving up to the water tank where they could be alone.

A wooden platform, a few feet across, had provided a perch a few inches over the dark expanse. Jake lay his sweater across the boards for them to sit on. She had shivered and turned away when he tried to kiss her. He leaned toward her again and this time she kissed him passionately. Slowly, she lay back under his weight. When he paused to study her face in the dim light, she sighed, reaching out to touch the placid water. With a laugh, she splashed him, then ran her wet fingers through his hair. Angelina had given herself to him, but not completely, which made him pine for her all the more.

Leo didn't even know that the two shared feelings for each other. The photo was Jake's good luck charm.

One foot in front of the other, Leo told himself. Keep walking until you see another caribou, until you round this curve, until someone tells you to stop. It sounded simple, but every step felt like an ember burning through his boot. Every step raised a puff of pale dust, a blend of earth and air as fine as cooking flour that settled on his pant cuffs and whitened his sweat-soaked beard. At twilight, the dust swallowed the sun in a choking, purple morass. Ashes to ashes. He imagined falling into the powder as if it were a feather bed. Bathing in the earth like an elephant on an African plain.

A range of dun-colored mountains ran along the western horizon, painted in yellows and ochres with patches of green. Massive bulls grazed in the irrigation ditches. Little wooden crosses poked above the tops of the round haystacks lining the road.

The guards stopped the men beside a spring in a grove of floppy-leafed banana trees. The water gushed clear and bright from a four-inch pipe. It sang as it spattered on the rocks covering the bottom of a ditch. The prisoners stared at it, no more than ten feet away. None of them dared approach the water.

A handful of Japanese guards filled their canteens at the gurgling pipe while the prisoners stood dry-mouthed in the sun. The guards poured the water into their mouths and over their faces.

After the baseball season, Leo's father offered Jake a job picking fruit, and even gave him a room at the house. Jake never spoke about his own parents, and never invited Leo to visit his home. Leo knew only that his friend's father was gone, and that his mother was often sick in bed. If he ever asked questions, Jake unfailingly evaded them, until, over time, Leo quit asking.

Like brothers now, they worked together in the apple orchards, Jake on the ladder, Leo on the ground with a basket lined with egg pallets to prevent bruising. Leo instinctively knew where his friend would toss the fruit based on nothing more than a wink or a nudge. Sometimes, Jake would swing from limb to limb like a monkey. The other hired hands would gather to watch him clamber to the highest branches, a cigarette dangling from his lips. They immediately took to him, though he didn't speak their language. He simply had a way of winning people over, including Leo's father, who embraced him as a second son and proceeded to teach him the same lessons he taught Leo.

Unlike his friend, Jake could fix anything. And in time, Mr. Jimenez called on him first to help lay new piping in the

irrigation ditches or build a new holding stable to brand the
cattle—tasks Leo had always considered laborious. Leo took
more interest now that Jake was receiving so much attention,
and often volunteered to do chores he would have performed
only begrudgingly in the past.

Leo took pride in teaching Jake how to ride a horse that
summer, one thing his friend didn't master with ease; he tried
too hard to control the animal. But in time, he learned. The
two explored the gray miles of tableland, the horses forging
through the bleached grama grass. They followed the *acequias*,
filled with turtles and minnows and bullfrogs as big as dinner
plates. Or they traced the Rio Grande, barely a trickle in the
summer, over the black tongues of basalt, utterly free.

Suddenly, one of the prisoners hurled himself at the spring
and began lapping like a dog. The water slicked back his hair.
He gasped with pleasure, then returned to drinking. The
guards watched the man aghast. Then one of them stepped
forward and belted the prisoner across the face with his rifle
butt. The man's jaw dropped as if it had come loose from its
hinge. The rifle came down again and opened his head. Blood
muddied the sparkling water. The guards made everyone start
moving again. The man lay in the ditch, the water rinsing his
face clean.

One foot in front of the other. The dead joined the fire-
gutted tanks and overturned trucks littering the ditches along
the side of the road. The corpses looked like bundles of rags.
The talahib grass grew lush and thick around them. Three,
four days dead and the weeds were already sprouting around
their collars.

Leo fixed his eyes on the back of the prisoner in front of him. He could see the man's spine poking through his shirt. All his fellow soldiers wore grim, unchanging expressions that hid their emotions from the guards. When Whitaker's buddy Paul DeLillo had fallen facedown in the road, unable to take another step, the guards had torn him up with their bayonets within minutes. Whitaker had shown no anger, no feeling, but kept walking, his face pinched in a tight grimace.

The "buzzard squads," as the men called them, were always there to finish off the stragglers. These were the dregs of the imperial army, the goons with heavy brows and missing teeth. The longer the march went on, the more vicious they became. When the hike had begun, death was still sacred, even for the goons. Days in, however, it had become a muddy, bloody habit. For the prisoners, death became part of the landscape. Nothing could shock them anymore. The sight of a young Filipino man, disemboweled on a barbwire fence, his guts hanging in bluish, purple ropes, hardly made the men turn their heads. A body was a temporary garment. Those walking were not much different from their brothers along the roadside. A little more air in their lungs. A little less dust in their mouths.

* * *

One foot, hot like iron, in front of the other. Men from the same platoon tended to stick together, even if they had hated each other before. Whitaker, for example, had softened toward Leo after months of picking on him. They suffered from the same ailment, and more important, the surrender had wiped out their differences. As tough as a steel rivet,

Whitaker had little patience for dreamers when shrapnel was whistling through the air. Now a prisoner, he had only to worry about himself, and from this selfishness emerged a gentler, more generous man.

Peter Larsen, the company cook, marched ahead with a forlorn expression, stripped of everything he owned, his mess kit, even the meat on his bones. His skin hung in folds like an ill-fitting suit. Bundles of rags they were, all of them, the living and the dead.

The men showed little loyalty to strangers. Jake flew into a rage when Leo allowed someone a sip from their canteen of sterilized water. "What's wrong with you?" he asked. Jake's face was thinner now, almost skeletal. "Do you think we have enough water to just throw it away?"

"But he needed it, Jake," Leo said.

"He *needed* it," Jake sneered. "What that guy needs is a punch in the nose."

The man's name was Charlie, a cabdriver from New York, walking just ahead of Jake in the parade. He never stopped complaining. "Jesus Christ, I'm thirsty," he kept saying in a nasal twang. "What I would do for a goddamn glass of lemonade. Jesus Christ, I'd kill for a sip! Just one sip!"

He was a rawboned man with square shoulders and a nose that sloped to a sharp point. He had a wild mane of hair. "When the fuck are we going to get off this road?" he'd exclaim, as if someone could give him the answer. "Where are they taking us anyway?"

"They ain't taking us anywhere, pal," Jake finally piped up. "We're taking them. And if you don't shut your trap, we're going to leave you here."

"Fine by me. Just show me to the nearest steak house, Jackson."

He called everyone Jackson. The conversation died there. The men's strength would allow for only so much banter or even rancor. A sudden chorus of shouts rang in the air. Someone had wandered out of line. Judging from the way he wobbled on his feet, the man was delirious. A column of tanks was approaching on the right. A Japanese soldier grabbed the man and flung him into the tanks' path. He stumbled forward, then tripped over a rock. He was too weak to get up. The tank treads pushed him into the earth. Bits of bone stuck in the treads. Another rolled over him, then another. The metallic smell of blood filled the air. Leo covered his mouth. There must have been a dozen tanks in the line. By the time they had all passed, there was nothing left of the soldier but his clothes. A dust-covered sleeve lay outstretched as if pleading for help.

* * *

A soldier hanging off the side of one of the tanks rapped Jake across the nose with a bamboo pole. The blow brought tears to his eyes. He clenched his fists and chased the tank for a step or two before slowing from exhaustion. "Jesus, motherfucking jackass son of a bitches," he cried. "Why me?" He tore his helmet off his head, suspecting it drew their attention. "Anybody want to trade places?"

The men kept walking in silence.

"Aw, c'mon," he said halfheartedly. "It ain't so bad."

"Oh, yes it is," said Charlie, the wild-haired New Yorker, directly ahead of Jake. "It sucks eggs. So shut up and quit trying to weasel out of it, Jackson."

"Mind your own business, pal," Jake growled. "You're asking for it."

Just outside of Lubao, a few Japanese soldiers loitered next to a ramshackle chicken coop. They were passing around a big jug of red wine. Jake could see they were drunk by their blotchy cheeks. As the prisoners walked by, the intoxicated soldiers jeered and spat at them. One was noticeably smaller than the others. Maybe five feet tall. His wet hair stuck straight up like a child's after a bath. Just as Jake was observing him, the imp came charging into the line of prisoners. With a running leap, he flew onto Leo's back and held tight. His companions on the side of the road slapped their caps against their thighs and hooted like cowboys. Leo lurched forward to keep his balance. "Get him off me, Jake," he said quietly.

"Hold tight, buddy, we don't want to piss him off," Jake whispered. "Steady as she goes." Jake grabbed Leo's arm to lend him support. A spill could lead to disaster. "We could use some help here," Jake called to the men. They nodded in acknowledgment when he looked around, but no one stepped out of position. The guards lurked nearby. The prisoner next to Leo, Tommy Buchanan, was too sick with malaria to do anything. He could hardly keep himself upright. "Get him off me," Leo begged.

The midget pumped his fist in the air, whooping and hollering as he left his drinking companions behind. A passing guard noticed the show, laughed a little, and then walked on. Jake wasn't worried about Leo's muscle. He knew his friend was strong enough to go on, but he had to make sure Leo didn't anger the little bully. "Watch for rocks," Jake warned. "Steady now."

Leo grunted and bumped into Tommy, causing the frail prisoner to take a few staggering steps of his own.

Jake checked up and down the line. The nearest guard was a good distance away. Quickly, he looped the strap of his canteen around the man's head and garroted him with an audible snap of the neck. In a matter of moments, two men stepped up from the rear and pulled him off Leo. They tossed him into a weedy ditch where he tumbled in a heap. Instantly, they fell back into their places in case the guards were watching. "What was that about?" Leo asked.

"The little guy saw too many Westerns," Jake said.

"He was strangling me."

"Shit, you think that's bad," Jake spat. "I've been carrying you since the first day we landed on this island." The words came out unexpectedly. The killing had brought Jake's blood to the surface, and suddenly he was furious, at the surrender, at MacArthur for abandoning him on Bataan. He couldn't stand being the one responsible for holding everything together. He could take care of himself, and everyone else around him, but he didn't have to like it.

* * *

Tommy Buchanan looked pale, almost green. Every couple of days the fever hit him, first the teeth-chattering chills, then a blazing temperature that drenched his fatigues in sweat. When the spells struck at night, he could ride them out, shivering on the ground. Leo tried to comfort him during these episodes, covertly giving him sips of water from the clean canteen. When the chills hit during the day, Tommy shook and shivered. He moaned as he walked. "Mama," he would stutter through his chattering teeth. "Mama."

He never ate on the rare occasions when the Japanese guards distributed balls of rice. His bones showed through his skin. When his voice gave out, he still kept pursing his lips: "Mama, Mama." Somehow, he remained on his feet for five days, whimpering to himself, until he finally tripped over a rock and went down for good. Leo tried to pick him up.

"Leave him, Leo," Jake commanded. "Drop him and move on."

Nobody stopped to move the body off the trail. The rear ranks stepped over him with hardly a glance. New York Charlie, however, noticed the opening and quickly took the dead man's spot to get away from the roadside traffic.

"What the fuck are you doing?" Jake hollered when he saw Charlie make his move. "I'm taking that place."

"Finders, keepers," Charlie sneered.

Jake pushed the wild-haired man. "Get the fuck out of here."

Charlie swung back with a punch that landed just above Jake's ear. The two fell to the ground in a jumble of pointy elbows and knees as the procession marched over them. "Guard!" someone hissed. "A guard's coming!"

Jake scrambled to his feet and slipped into the vacant position. Charlie stumbled when he arose, limping with a badly twisted ankle. He faltered, then fell out of line. A passing guard punctured his side with a bayonet. He managed to hobble forward for a few paces before the guards miraculously called for a halt. One of them grabbed Jake by the wrist and pulled him aside. "I didn't do anything!" he protested. "Why are you messing with me? I didn't do anything."

"Jake!" Leo cried as he watched the guards drag his friend away. He dared not chase them.

Meanwhile, Charlie crawled through the group of men sitting on the ground. "Somebody help me," he said. "I got a hole in my side. If someone don't help me, I'm finished." The prisoners avoided his eyes. "Please," he begged. "I'm bleeding."

The guard blew the whistle, signaling the men to rise. Leo reached down and with one arm pulled the injured man to his feet. "I can carry you a little ways. Get on my back." Charlie draped his arms over Leo's shoulders, and the two began walking.

Leo was worried about Jake but he had heard no gunshots, nor the anguished howl that often accompanied the thrust of a bayonet. He tried to find comfort in that, though he knew they might have disposed of Jake in any number of ways. The thought was too painful to hold in his mind. He hardly noticed that Charlie had passed out on his back. He was heavier than the Japanese soldier, but not by much. All bones, Leo thought as he inhaled his passenger's stale breath. In the purple light, he could see little drops of blood falling on the dusty road.

They stopped that night in a field, the grass clipped by horses or cattle. The bushes along the edges displayed a misty pink. Squinting, Leo could make out a few gnarled tulip trees with flaming red blossoms. As dark fell, he watched the stars. The sky seemed so much lower than the high clear heavens of New Mexico. Charlie groaned in his sleep. Leo felt feverish himself. He heard the sputter of a machine gun in the distance, but that was nothing unusual.

Daylight was at least an hour away when Jake, Leo, and his father had sat crammed together in the front seat of the pickup as it bounced down a rutted dirt road. Insects flashed in the headlights, then disappeared. Leo leaned his face against the glass and listened to his father talk about how they used to break horses in corrals made from logs of mesquite. His father's baritone filled the cab. "We'd build the pens right out there on the mesa," he said.

"How'd you get the saddle on them?" Jake asked.

"Slow down, *hijo*," the rancher said with a laugh. "Breaking a horse isn't easy. You can't rush it. Leo learned that."

"I know how to break a horse," Leo protested. His father was alluding to the time the roan mare nearly trampled him. These were the things his father remembered. "You said I had a soft touch with the horses."

"Too soft," his father answered. "But Leo is right. You must be gentle with a horse. Treat her as you would a woman. Do you know how to treat a woman, Jake?"

"I know a thing or two."

They both burst out laughing, and Leo joined them, his voice ringing loudly in his ears. They stopped on a sandbank by the river. The air felt especially cold after the intimate warmth of the truck. His father and Jake gathered the pump-action shotguns and duck calls from the truck bed. Jake had borrowed Leo's old hunting jacket.

There were only two guns, so Leo had brought his pencils and a sketchbook. The flats were home to a tremendous population of waterfowl. The last time he had come here with his father, they had heard blue cranes whooping to each other across a pond. It had been just the two of them, and Leo had brought down a large mallard.

The men found a thicket in which to hide. There was nothing to do but wait until dawn. His father had moved on to telling Jake about the summer that he and a local veterinarian had set out to fix an entire herd of bulls. Jake listened, nodding, as he smoked. "On the first day, I did about two hundred alone," Leo's father said. "The vet did about thirty-five—and he lost three." He chuckled. "I lost none. I told him, 'I trust in the skill of my hand. I trust in my eye. I trust in the knife.'"

"How much salt did you use that summer, Papa?" Leo asked, but his father didn't hear him. He was describing how, with bloody fingers, they threw the *cojones* into the ashes of the fire to roast like potatoes.

As the sky lightened, the murmur of birdcalls began to swell. They could hear the honking of geese now, thousands of them. The hills began to take shape. Beyond them, the purple Oscura Mountains emerged against the brightening horizon. Suddenly there came a shuddering of air, muffled at first, then louder: the thrumming of wings. Snow geese, rising in a massive armada, wheeled upward in a slow tornado. Tens of thousands of white, long-necked birds lifted into the air just as the first rays of sun shot from behind the mountains. Slowly they rotated, gathering altitude as they widened their unwinding circle. The sound of their honking was almost musical until the blast of shotguns filled the air.

Flying so close, they were easy picking. The two men shot and reloaded repeatedly from behind the blind. One by one, the big birds fell from the sky. The shells knocked them sideways on impact. Leo crouched near his father's side. "Papa, let me have a shot," he said, but the rancher didn't hear him beneath the roar. He touched his father's shoulder, and spoke more loudly. "Can I try?"

His father turned to him with a bewildered expression and shooed him away. "Not now."

The birds were still wheeling skyward as Leo backed away and began hiking up the trail. He knew his father was punishing him for all his little failures as a man. It was a cruel game, playing friend against friend. Leo wondered how he could possibly have been born the son of such a monster.

It took him half an hour to reach the paved road. He could still hear the shotguns, though most of the birds had already headed upriver. He decided to follow them on foot. To the east, where the sun already burned hot, the Jornada del Muerto desert stretched to the mountains. A loose formation of surviving geese flew overhead. Their melancholy cries sounded almost human. "Gone," they honked. "Gone, gone, gone."

* * *

The guard shepherded Jake down the line at a quick pace, stinging his back and thighs with a switch if he slowed. The prisoners barely raised their eyes as he passed. The guard kept jabbering at him. He couldn't think what he had done to draw their attention. Just because he had scuffled with Charlie?

Away from the road, a group of Japanese soldiers stood in a cane field with shovels in their hands. Ever since he had fallen into the hole on Bataan, Jake had hated the sight of shovels. The guard lashed his back again with the switch, and Jake hurried toward the soldiers, who were obviously waiting for him.

As he drew closer, he realized they were standing over a body. It was so small it looked like a child, until he drew closer and recognized the sunburned face of the short soldier who had been riding Leo.

One of the soldiers handed Jake a shovel and motioned for him to start digging. Jake struck the blade into the hard dry earth, locked within the shallow roots of the sugar cane. The bamboo switch cut across his neck when he failed to pry loose a sufficient pile of soil. Jake dug in again, harder this time, and leaned on the spade for leverage. The Japanese soldiers gnawed on cane stalks as they watched. He cut a five-foot channel, long enough to hold the body, and began to dig deeper, but one of the soldiers motioned for him to extend the length.

They were forcing him to dig a grave for himself, not the little soldier. He chipped at the ground again. He would die soon. He wondered what would happen if he simply refused to go on. If they were going to kill him, at least make them work for it. But that would only draw out his suffering. Surely they would torture him, slash his throat, or simply bludgeon him with the shovel. The guards spoke quietly among themselves as the sky turned purple. They laughed at times, obviously enjoying their rest from the long journey on foot.

Jake considered making a run for it, but he couldn't bring himself to do it. He was utterly at their mercy. It wouldn't matter if he begged for his life or offered to suck them off or kissed the ground at their feet. He had no say.

The guard lashed him again, and he struck the earth with greater force. The trench was deepening. The sun ran red along the tops of the hills. The soldiers made him kneel at the foot of the hole and put his hands behind his back. He wanted it to come quickly now, to be rid of this sense of powerlessness. One of the soldiers began calling out something in a slow cadence, then shouted. A shot rang out and he felt someone kick him. He fell face down in the hole. It was black and silent. Then he heard laughter. It grew louder until it filled the air. Someone pulled him to his feet, but he was still in the hole. He could see the peaked caps of the guards. One of them pulled him up and led him to where the prisoners were sleeping at the side of the road. They kept laughing.

* * *

The guards blew their whistles at dawn, a signal that the men had five minutes to get moving. Leo ran his tongue over the dry roof of his mouth. He usually drank a sip of water to start the day. That's when he remembered that Jake was gone. The air already felt warm and moist. Charlie lay sprawled on the grass. Leo shook him awake. "What? What happened?" Charlie mumbled.

"It's time to start walking," Leo said. "The guards blew the whistle."

The field was almost empty as the men gathered in formation on the road. Charlie stood up, then immediately fell to his knees. A black circle of blood, the size of a dinner plate, covered his left side. There was a hole in his shirt where the guard had stabbed him. His frizzy hair was filled with little twigs. "You got to help me, pal. I can't make it alone."

"I'll carry you," Leo sighed. "Get on my back, but hurry up." Charlie climbed on his back and Leo began walking with the others, bent slightly to accommodate his burden. Charlie felt heavier than the day before. Leo kept looking to his right, where he was accustomed to seeing Jake's lean form.

One foot in front of the other. Charlie slept all day. A guard came by that afternoon and shouted at Leo. He pointed at his passenger and then pointed to the ground. Leo could barely see the guard's face. The sunlight was so bright it stung his eyes. All he could make out was the square top of the soldier's cap. Leo smiled as if the two were exchanging pleasantries, then he turned and kept walking. If he simply chose to believe them to be good, sensible people, they would behave accordingly. Somebody said they were approaching San Fernando, a town he remembered from what seemed like a lifetime ago. He and Jake had stopped there for a Coke on one of their last trips to Manila. They had been walking for nearly a week.

He was relieved to see the guards ushering the prisoners into a large shed to rest, until he entered and saw how crowded it was. The heat was unbearable. Everyone was jostling for space, kicking up the dust. The sun shot spears through the cracks in the corrugated metal walls. Along the floor were sandy patches encircled by rocks. They looked like cockfighting pits. Crooked bleachers and chicken feathers floating through the fetid air confirmed the impression.

Leo dropped Charlie in a bare spot on the dirt floor and fell down beside him. There was no room to breathe. "You have to sit up, Charlie," Leo said. His companion lay motionless. Leo patted him on the cheek. "Wake up, Charlie." He pressed his ear to the man's chest, then held his finger under the fellow's long nose. Charlie was dead. When he searched the body, Leo found a little leather-bound Bible tucked into the man's back trouser pocket. In his shirt, he discovered a piece of peppermint candy.

His fingers were so deadened, he could barely tear the wrapper off. The candy burned his mouth with an icy sweetness. He suddenly felt light-headed from the burst of sugar. He knew the fever would pass, but the thought provided little comfort in the moment. The warehouse echoed with explosive bursts of flatulence. The guards had barred the men from digging latrines, forcing them to defecate where they sat. Soon the floor ran with feces. Leo nursed the last sip of water from Charlie's canteen and, clutching the Bible, fell into a fevered sleep.

The men's moaning continued through the night. Leo dreamed of roosters with golden plumage pecking at each other's throats. The birds stalked each other around the ring with razor blades tied to their claws. They struck quickly, savagely. Leo woke up. He was freezing. He heard a ghastly cry and saw a man squatting nearby. "Lord have mercy," he cried. "God help me."

The guards huddled around a kerosene lamp at the far end of the building. They cast towering shadows along the walls. Leo held fast to the center of himself, a pillar of stone, unmoving. Embracing this core, hard and cool to the touch, prevented him from combusting altogether. Stay firm, he thought to himself, his teeth chattering. Solid and unmoving.

* * *

The next morning a coppery glow filled the metal shed. Leo folded Charlie's arms across his chest and left him there when the Japanese soldiers marched everyone to a rail depot. After enduring a night of chills and sweats, Leo could barely stay on his feet. The welcome sight of the train depot drew him the last few hundred yards.

An engine pulling a long line of boxcars entered the station. When the guards rolled open the doors, a fierce heat rushed out. The cars had been baking in the sun. Leo was one of the first to cram inside. The men kept coming, packing the box tighter and tighter, until Leo's arms were pinned to his sides. Then the guards slammed the door shut. No light. No oxygen. The smell was unbearable. The men shouted for the guards to open the doors, but their pleas went no farther than the suffocating walls. As the train started moving, the men began to wail. "Oh, no, not again," the soldier next to Leo cried. "I'm sorry, guys, but I can't hold it in."

The floor began sloshing with bodily fluids. Leo could feel the liquid running into his boots as the train accelerated. He felt the chills coming on. His spine turned to ice. His legs were giving out, but it didn't matter. The men were packed in so tightly he remained standing.

The next thing he knew, something was poking him in the ribs. He was stretched out on the floor of the boxcar. A Japanese soldier was jabbing him with a pole to see if he was alive. He lifted his face from the muck. A few other bodies lay motionless around him. He got to his knees and crawled to join the other men sitting in a big group on the ground. They were taking off their boots to drain the filth, which spilled out in long, viscous strands. "Where are we?" Leo asked a man with a grizzled beard.

"Capas." The man glanced at him up and down. "You look like you've come back from hell."

"Not sure I'm back yet."

The man nodded solemnly. A guard circulated through the crowd, counting heads. When he had completed his task, he ordered the prisoners to return to column formation. Leo teetered to his feet. As the line began to move, he reached for the shoulder of his newfound friend. The man pulled away. "I'm sorry, pal. I ain't strong enough to carry your load. I have to fend for myself."

Leo felt too weak to go it alone. Soon the column was well ahead of him. He led a smaller group of stragglers. In an act of mercy, the buzzards allowed the weak to drag themselves to the prison camp, no matter how long it took. From the top of a rise, Leo saw a maze of broken-down buildings surrounded by barbwire entanglements and guard towers. A seagull wheeled in circles overhead.

* * *

Chapter 4

New York City

May 1942

Quiddick's Saloon was thick with smoke when Murray
Sanders pushed his way to the table where he often met a few
colleagues. Max Sampson, the head of Columbia's microbiol-
ogy department, usually came along with Maynard Cox and
Boris Glasounoff from the Rockefeller Institute. They were a
competitive bunch. Murray, who had not yet turned thirty,
played a junior role within the circle. He was also the hand-
somest, with a thick crop of chestnut hair and a strong jaw.
The others often teased him for his appearance, as if his good
looks belied his intelligence. "Hey, Sanders, how about fetch-
ing us another round?" cried Sampson, Murray's boss. "I'll have
a martini, dry."

"And I'll have a vodka straight up," said Glasounoff.

"Whiskey and water for me, old man," said Cox.

Murray repeated the orders to himself on his way to the bar. He returned a few minutes later, nervously balancing a tray of glasses.

"Hey, I said dry," Sampson said. "This is as wet as your wife."

The men laughed when Murray's face turned red. The barb demanded a response. "Well, at least I have a wife," he said bravely.

"Don't dump your problems on us, old boy," his boss retorted and moved on, a cat grown weary of his hobbled plaything. "You still having trouble getting those cancer cells to take, Sanders?"

"Mission accomplished," Murray said, glad for the reprieve. "I raised the temperature a degree, and, bingo, they filled the dishes."

"So you helped them along a little bit," Sampson said with a wink. "All in the name of science, right?"

"Actually in the name of the Rockefeller Institute. They were getting antsy to see some results," Murray shot back. He didn't mind playing the rogue if it won his boss's approval. They all knew the game. He raised his glass. "Drinks are on old man Rockefeller!"

"Hey, did you hear the Japs are injecting cancer cells into Chinese prisoners?" Glasounoff asked. He was a short man from Brooklyn with rough hands and the chatty disposition of a mechanic. "I read about it in the *Daily News*."

"Don't believe anything you read in the *News*," Sampson said. "The Japs wouldn't know cancer from franks and beans."

"Oh, I wouldn't put it past them," Glasounoff said. "I'll never forget how that Jap tried to weasel some samples out of me at the lab when I first got hired. That's when I knew the war was coming, two years before Pearl Harbor."

"Here we go again," Sampson said. The story had become the stuff of legend.

"I'm running late for work," Glasounoff said.

"And it was pouring rain," Sampson said with a grin. "Sorry. Go on."

Glasounoff continued, unfazed by the irritant across the table. "It's pouring rain and I have to check the numbers on the goddamn monkeys. Well, just as I'm parking, this Jap approaches me."

"How'd you know he was Japanese?" Cox asked.

Glasounoff shrugged. "Funny thing is, the guy knows my name. He doesn't bother to introduce himself. Just walks up and gets in my car. He's about forty, wearing a brown derby and a trench coat. A real smooth character. Barely an accent. Well, we get to talking and he tells me he's from Brazil of all places. But he looks distinctly Asian, so I'm suspicious. Then he springs it on me. His lab is working on something big and he needs a culture of the yellow fever virus, an unmodified *Asibi* strain."

"That's the most virulent type," Murray cut in.

Glasounoff nodded solemnly.

"So what did you do?" Sampson asked.

"I refer him to Dr. Sawyer, of course. But he says he doesn't want to get him involved. He doesn't want to alert the competition."

"That's us," Cox said indignantly.

"So then he offers to pay me a thousand dollars. A thousand frigging dollars. Of course I turn it down, so then he offers me three thousand, a grand up front, and two more upon delivery."

"You should have taken it," Sampson said.

"I tell him the cultures are locked up in an icebox and I don't have the key. Which is the truth. So then, he asks me to bleed a goddamn monkey to get the shit that way. I swear to God. He's a pushy sucker. It's pouring down rain and the windows are steamed up. I'm wondering where we're going with this, you know what I mean? Well, the next thing I know the guy grabs my arm and I just go nuts. I grab the son of a bitch by the collar and start shaking him. Knock his hat right off his head. While we're scuffling, I somehow manage to open the door and push the son of a bitch into the rain. And that was the end of it."

"Did you report it?" Murray asked.

"Sure I did. Sawyer nearly shit his pants. He called the feds, for god's sake."

"That's the biggest crock I've heard in a while," Sampson said.

"It's not a crock, and I can prove it."

"How?" the men asked. They leaned in with interest.

Glasounoff reached under the table and produced a brown derby. His drinking partners gasped. "Fits perfectly," he said as he donned his prize.

The men grinned in admiration. "You bought it at that little haberdashery across from the university," Sampson said. "I saw it in the window."

"The hell I did," Glasounoff responded with a grin. He flipped the hat and pointed to the interior where, upon closer inspection, they could see something written along the rim in an Asian script.

* * *

Murray Sanders had considered joining the service when the United States entered the war, but his wife, Molly, had convinced him to wait so they could start a family. So he stuck to the study of pathogens and caused a minor stir when he discovered a novel way to track the airborne transmission of infectious diseases. He began playing with Micrococcus prodigiosus, harmless bacteria with a bright, visible red color. One day Murray stashed a handful of clean culture plates around his lecture hall and then scooped a dollop of the bacteria in his mouth before morning classes. After a long day of talking, he collected the plates and put them in an incubator overnight. By morning, new colonies of Micrococcus prodigiosus appeared on the plates like mushrooms after a spring rain. If the bacteria in Murray's mouth had been smallpox, hundreds of his students might have contracted the disease.

The experiment impressed the administration, yet Murray was not happy—Sampson's bullying affected him more than it did the other researchers. A few days after the gathering at the bar, he accidentally stumbled into his boss. He'd been daydreaming. Sampson laughed and slapped Murray's face hard enough to sting. "Where in the hell is your head, Sanders?"

Murray could feel his boss's hand on his cheek all the way home. Steam billowed from his mouth as he walked. Germs, he thought to himself, watching the clouds rise and disappear. The world is filled with germs. As soon as Molly greeted him at the door, however, he forgot his irritation. She took his coat and hat. "Where's your scarf, silly?"

Murray ran his cold palm over his neck. "Did I take one this morning?"

"What am I going to do with you?" his wife asked, holding his face in her hands, then whispered in his ear. "My father dropped by for dinner. He says he wants to talk with you about a project. Some big secret."

Jim Hallstrom was already seated in the living room, visible from the door. He smiled broadly, showing the gap in his front teeth. "Ah," he said. "The king returns to his castle." Though he had lived in Baltimore for a decade, teaching bacteriology at Johns Hopkins, Hallstrom remained a Minnesota Swede at heart. His folksy manner, however, belied an agile mind. As an adviser to the National Institutes of Health, he maintained a wide network of influential contacts in government, and had opened doors for his son-in-law at Columbia.

Murray sat down on the couch across from him and tried to appear at ease. At times, he felt as if he were still auditioning for the job of siring progeny. "Molly mentioned a project, something you wanted to talk about."

"You don't mess around, do you, Murray?" Hallstrom said. "I like that. No small talk." The big man slapped his hand on the table. "How would you like to move down to Maryland, my boy?"

Murray paused. "Sir?"

"Can you keep a secret?"

Murray nodded.

"I know you're trustworthy. I trusted you with my daughter, for god's sake. Well, between us, a number of academics have been meeting down in Maryland to discuss how biology might be used as a weapon. At the military's request, of course."

"As a weapon?"

He nodded. "Something to throw back at the Germans. But vaccines as well. This is cutting-edge stuff, son, and we've got some money to play with. The brightest minds of the Ivy League have been attending these meetings—Jim Sherman from Cornell, René Dubos from Harvard. The best. Your boss, Sampson, would give his left nut to be included in these ranks."

"Then why don't you bring him on board?"

"He's an asshole, that's why," Hallstrom shot back. "We don't have time to deal with assholes."

"I'm flattered," Murray said, excited. "It sounds intriguing, but I would have to talk to Molly, of course."

Hallstrom lowered his voice and leaned over the table conspiratorially, cupping the side of his mouth. "Does she make the decisions around here, Murray?"

"I didn't say that," Murray protested.

Hallstrom chuckled as he stood up. "My daughter sure knows how to pick 'em."

* * *

Murray mentioned the conversation to Molly that night in bed. They lay together, spooned front to back, under a mountain of blankets. "Your father offered me a job," he said,

"I knew it was something big," she said excitedly.

"The military has asked the universities to research using bacteria as a weapon. Your father said he could find a place for me in the program. The contacts alone would be worth it. Not to mention the fact that we'd live closer to your folks."

His wife flipped over to face him. "Wait a minute. Slow down. Closer to my parents?"

"We'd move down to Maryland."

She sat up, slightly agitated. "And what's this about bacteria?"

"I don't know, honey. But it would give me a chance to get out from under Sampson. You know how important that would be for me."

"My father never said a word to me about this," she said, surprised. "But what do you mean when you say *weapon*? I've never heard of doctors attacking anyone. Isn't that one of the first rules or something? To 'do no harm'?"

"I'll be working on *defending* us against these weapons," Murray explained. He could never guess how these conversations would go with his wife, such a cautious soul. "Please, honey, don't make this too complicated. It's a good thing, believe me."

* * *

A steady light rain was falling when Murray arrived at Camp Detrick for his first day and showed his identification to the guard at the gate. Soon a short, balding man in a drab three-piece suit came trotting toward the car. Water droplets covered his spectacles. "Murray Sanders?" he asked and stuck his hand through the car window. "Ira Baldwin. I'm the director here. Don't mind the security, we'll get you set up with a badge, and I'll show you around."

After Murray signed in, Baldwin led him outside, where they picked their way over a makeshift sidewalk made of wood planks that sank under their feet. "As you can see, we're still in the process of making this a modern facility," Baldwin said, gesturing to the low-slung barracks. "Watch your step."

The fog was too thick to see farther than a few feet as they followed the path of unstable slats. But soon Murray saw a tall, dark building emerging from the mist. As he got closer, he realized the two-story edifice was covered with black, tar paper. The structure looked hollow and cold. "The men call this Black Maria," the director said as he unlocked a gate to the barbwire fence surrounding the building. "It doesn't look like much more than a glorified chicken shack, but for now it's home."

A sentry with a pistol guarded the door to the building. Baldwin nodded as he passed, showing his badge. "Our first order of business is to deliver approximately seven pounds of dried Clostridium botulinum to the British government. I assume you are familiar with the strain?"

"Of course," Murray replied as he marveled at the plump chrome tanks packing the room. The organism was one of the deadliest toxins known.

"Here we refer to it simply as 'X,'" Baldwin said. "We're making a vaccine as well as an offensive weapon, to counterpunch if necessary."

A man wearing a lab coat and goggles was standing nearby, inspecting the contents of a glass flask. Baldwin introduced him as Arvo Thompson, a veterinarian by trade, turned toxicologist.

Murray extended his hand to shake, but his new acquaintance recoiled. "We keep contact to a minimum around here," Thompson said apologetically.

"The flask Arvo is holding contains the starter culture," Baldwin said.

"Hall 57, to be precise." Thompson spoke with a faint Boston accent. "From this we get something strong enough to use in the field."

Murray scratched his head. "But I was told I'd be working on defensive operations."

"Oh, you are, you are," Baldwin said quickly. "You'll focus, 'principally' and 'primarily'"—he gestured in the air with his fingers—"on vaccinations. But don't forget we're fighting a fire here, Murray, and sometimes we have to get dirty as well as burned."

* * *

Murray began manufacturing botulin with Thompson and a wild-eyed Scotsman named Henderson from Britain's secret biological weapons program in Porton Downs. Henderson was a man who had spent a bit too much time with a flock of sheep on Gruinard Island, an abandoned rock off the coast of Scotland. Tall and gaunt, he refused to shave and had little patience for safety precautions; on Gruinard, he had poisoned his first flock of sheep, pouring suspended anthrax spores into a bombshell, with no more protection than a bandanna wrapped around his nose and mouth. When the experiment was finished, he pushed the dead sheep off a cliff with a bulldozer without any thought to the consequences.

Despite his rough manner, Henderson had earned his doctorate at London University. His research was crude, but it was years ahead of the American program. Thus the man made periodic visits to Camp Detrick as a consultant. He disdained Americans, particularly Ivy Leaguers, and never tired of digging his spurs into Thompson. "I don't care if the machine is leakin', man, keep her runnin'," he shouted at the soft-spoken scientist when one of the valves began to ooze toxin. "You've got all this fancy equipment, and you're worried about a few drops. We used to make the stuff in milk cans, for shit sakes."

When Baldwin heard of Henderson's cavalier attitude, however, he kicked the Scotsman off the base.

"Good God, man, you can't move an inch around here without gettin' your beard stuck in the gears," Henderson protested. "I've worked with these materials long enough to know what I'm doin'."

Baldwin simply pointed toward the door. The director never left any doubt who was in control. He was a kind, sensible man, an agricultural bacteriologist from the University of Wisconsin, and Murray and the other scientists all respected him. His convictions were as plain as the large mole on his nose. More important, he was a confidant to George Merck, chairman of Merck Pharmaceuticals and the golden figurehead for the American biological weapons program.

As Murray became better acquainted with his new surroundings, he realized he had gained entrance to something bigger, more important, than he had imagined. New scientists were showing up every day from Yale and the University of Chicago. Murray felt as if he had come home. Gone were the petty squabbles of university life. Baldwin made him a section chief overseeing the development of botulin and anthrax.

There were minor scares. Baldwin quarantined the entire Black Maria building when one of the cultivators burst.

On another occasion, a reactor tank overflowed with anthrax foam, which entered the air vents and began pouring out of the building like soapsuds from a washing machine. The stuff began to puddle and flow toward a storm sewer. Three guys from engineering quickly dug a dirt wall around the bubbly substance to contain it before it could do any harm.

Murray made sure Molly never heard about the mishaps, but one night in bed she discovered a rough spot on his elbow, a minor reddish-brown discoloration. Murray tried to downplay the patch, though he knew it could be a sign of an anthrax infection. A few scientists at work were already treating reactions of their own. "That's funny," he said. "It might be eczema. I'll have the staff doctor check it out in the morning. It's nothing a little antibiotic can't clear up."

"Are you sure?" Molly asked. She lay on her side, her face flushed, her silk nightgown clinging to her round hip. "You look a little nervous."

"Nervous?" He laughed.

"You're breathing funny."

"I just had a workout, in case you forgot."

"You're not trying to hide anything, are you?"

"No." He laughed again. "Don't be silly." Murray never could lie; he laughed whenever he tried. "It's eczema, darling."

"We're making a baby, and you come home with spots on your elbow. Now you're laughing, and that can only mean one thing."

"Stop—it's nothing," he said, covering his mouth with his hand.

"You're going to bring a baby into this world, and you're not going to even be alive to see it. And look at you. You think it's funny."

"Anthrax isn't even contagious," he said into his pillow.

"Anthrax? What the hell is anthrax, Murray?"

"Nothing. Nothing at all."

The wound healed with a penicillin treatment, but Molly's trust wasn't so easily restored.

* * *

As a section chief, Murray gained access to the army's intelligence briefings. One report confirmed the story Glasounoff, his former drinking companion, had told at the bar. Apparently, a Japanese agent calling himself Naito Ryoichi had tried to acquire the yellow fever virus many times from the Rockefeller Institute. More recently, another Japanese operative had called on the Rockefeller laboratory in Brazil, inquiring about the same disease.

More disturbing, American agents in Asia had discovered solid evidence of Japanese germ warfare attacks on the Chinese in Manchuria. "We think they've killed a lot of people," Murray's stony-faced commander told him as he tossed a thick file on the table. "They've been poisoning the wells and reservoirs over there."

Murray opened the folder. The mimeographed pages were dog-eared, and little handwritten notes had been scribbled along the edge of the text. The case concerned the city of Changteh, a town of about fifty thousand in the province of Hunan, outside Japanese-controlled Manchuria.

An American woman by the name of Mrs. Bannon, a nurse at the Changteh Presbyterian hospital, saw a Japanese airplane pass overhead while she was on her way to work early one morning. She thought she might be killed. To her surprise, however, the plane dropped no bombs. Out of the sky came scattered wheat, rice, and little scraps of wadded paper. The woman refrained from touching them. She had heard about suspicious viral outbreaks in other towns, and, sure enough, when the authorities brought a few items into the hospital for testing, they were covered with plague bacteria.

Within a week, an eleven-year-old girl was brought to the hospital with a high fever. She died two days later. An autopsy uncovered the presence of plague on her stomach lining and intestinal tract. Other victims followed, until the death toll reached five. Just as a special investigation team arrived in town, another farmer succumbed to the disease. The man had lived on the street where Mrs. Bannon had seen the plane drop the light debris. The medical specialists confirmed that the deaths had been caused by bubonic plague and began an investigation to determine the cause. The lead examiner found several suspicious circumstances relating to the outbreak. First, the town had never been afflicted by plague. Second, all the victims of the disease contracted it within fifteen days of the aerial drop. Most suspicious, the town's citizens came down with the illness before the local rats, which normally carried the disease first.

Murray slapped the report back on the table and shook his head. "Who else has seen this?"

"Merck, Baldwin, a few others," the officer said. "What do you think?"

"I think we're in serious danger."

* * *

Chapter 5

O'Donnell Prison Camp, Philippine Islands

May 1942

"Sure as shit, he's got give-up-itis," the Kentuckian said when someone asked about the Mexican kid. "Has anyone been feeding him?"

No answer.

"I got his boots," the Kentuckian said.

"I got his Bible," said another. "I'm out of rolling papers."

Leo heard the men staking claim to his things as if he were already dead. Bluebottle flies crept over his net. He had stopped eating, stopped getting up to relieve himself. No one bothered to move him when the rain fell on his face through a hole in the roof.

Lying in the dirt, he lived in a dream state. When the temperature rose, he returned to his mother's kitchen, a child again, clinging to her apron. The red clay tiles felt cool beneath his bare feet. The kitchen was always dim in the summer, so dark the chilies hanging from the ceiling looked black. Leo would retreat there to escape his father. Mama was stirring pinto beans in a big pot. She stuffed a warm tortilla into his mouth. She always fed him when he felt down. *Come, mijo. Mi gordito. Come.*

Gracias, Mama.

"Who the hell you calling mama?" the Kentuckian asked. The man was shoving rice into Leo's mouth. "I ain't your mama," he said. "I'm just givin' you a little rice so nobody thinks I sent you to an early grave on account of your boots."

* * *

The hours of digging had set Jake back in line. He'd traveled in the last boxcar and staggered into Camp O'Donnell a day after most of the others, long after the first settlers had claimed the prime locations. Not that there was much to distinguish the crude bamboo barracks with their leaky thatched roofs and dirt floors. It was a wide, sprawling encampment in the shadow of wooden gun towers. A barbwire fence stood between the squalor of the camp and the rolling plains of cogon grass stretching to the horizon.

Before the retreat into Bataan, Allied troops had tried to render the former airbase inoperable by sabotaging the water supply. Now their effort was coming back to haunt them: only two working water spigots survived to serve thousands of prisoners. Those strong enough to stand spent hours in line waiting to fill a few canteens from the dribbling faucets. As Jake searched for Leo and the others, he saw men either standing mindlessly in line or stretched out on the ground. He had ailments of his own. A high-pitched hum echoed in his ears from all the blows he had taken to his head. The purple signature of a rifle butt marked his bony ribcage.

His morale improved immeasurably when he found Captain Dyess and a few others, including Whitaker and Larsen, but not Leo. They had scoured the camp in search of absentees, but nobody had seen Leo since the hike. Jake was beginning to worry. While most officers had busied themselves finding the driest nipa huts available, Dyess had stuck with his men and banded them together to look after each other. Within the first week, the captain encouraged everyone to join work details. "You stay busy, you'll stay alive," he told them. Though wobbly, Jake dug ditches until the guards assigned him to the burial team.

There were the diggers and then the mules who carried the dead. Jake was a mule. His job was to circulate through the dilapidated barracks looking for corpses. They were easy to find. Twenty to thirty men—sometimes as many as fifty—died each day from disease and lack of nourishment. Bodies piled upon bodies. The mules wrapped each corpse in a blanket and tied the ends to a bamboo pole, which they carried between them. The graveyard was nothing more than mud pits. The men called it Boot Hill, named after the burial grounds in the Old West where men died with their boots on. The Filipino soldiers called the place *sa sabungan ng Uwak* or "where the Uwaks fight," referring to the carnivorous black birds constantly skulking about.

When they had first arrived in April, the tail end of the dry season, the ground had been too hard to penetrate very deeply, so the pits were shallow. But as the wet season began to soften the earth, some of the bodies floated to the surface, a stiffened leg or arm rising from the muck. The cool of the mud pits had lowered the body temperatures of a few poor souls suffering from malarial fevers, returning the lifeless to consciousness. They had emerged from the earth to live another day before falling down for good.

The job got to Jake's head; it made him so crazed he sometimes found himself cackling uncontrollably as he stuffed a dog tag into a dead man's mouth and slid him into the mire. Sometimes, in a semi-delirious state, he talked to the corpses, like the time he recognized a familiar face among the bodies. Big Louis, his body contorted and no longer so big. "What are you doing in there?" Jake whispered. "Come on out of there. Come on, quit teasing." Of course, the cardsharp couldn't answer him. The diggers always tried to cover the bodies with soil, but the swampy muck rarely held for long.

As Jake made his rounds, he took on the job of doctor; it was up to him to decide whether a man was ready for the grave. Before he turned a corpse over to the diggers, he'd try to straighten it out. More fit in the pit that way. "You might as well take this one here," someone said, catching his attention. The speaker was lying on his side, his head resting on his hand, reading a leather-bound pocket Bible. Next to him lay a curled up brown body. "He's a goner."

Jake checked the prisoner for signs of life. He put his ear to the soldier's chest and heard his heart faintly beating. Maybe another day, Jake thought to himself. He grabbed the chain around his neck and peered at the dog tag. Jimenez, Leonardo, it said. Catholic.

Jake gasped. Sure enough, those were Leo's thick eyebrows. "I tried to keep him going," someone nearby said. "He had nobody to look after him."

Jake groaned. He scooped up his friend and carried him back to his barracks. Once as dense as an anvil, Leo seemed almost to float in his arms. "I found Leo," Jake said as he entered. The men struggled to their feet to make room for his cargo.

"Little Jiminy?" Dyess asked. "Poor kid. Is he alive?"

"He looks like shit," Whitaker said.

"Yeah, well so do you," Jake said.

"Give him some of your water, Whitaker," Dyess said. The noncom made a sour face. "That's an order, Sergeant. And tonight at dinner, I want everyone to contribute one bite of rice to the Leo fund. We've got to get some food into him." Dyess felt Leo's forehead, then pried open his eyelids. "He's jaundiced to the gills."

* * *

A week after Jake found Leo, the Japanese moved the men to a prison camp near Cabanatuan, about forty miles northeast. To get there, many of the prisoners had to hike back to Capas and board the boxcars, but Jake escorted Leo in a truck along with the other invalids from camp. The vehicle was packed with bodies, and the road was bumpy, but the ride was heaven compared to the trains. Leo slept the entire trip, his head lolling against Jake's shoulder.

It had been Leo's idea to enlist all along. Jake had no reason to leave; he had everything going for him. There was Angelina, of course, which might have led to something. And he had a real job at the ranch. Mr. Jimenez was grooming him to run the show someday. At first he relished the rancher's attention, even as he realized it was hurting his friend. But over time he grew increasingly uncomfortable, especially as the favoritism became more obvious. What nourished him in the beginning began to feel like he'd drunk too many egg creams. So when Leo floated the idea of joining the army, he jumped at it without thinking twice. Even now, he was glad for his decision, perhaps more so.

Like O'Donnell, Cabanatuan was a former American fort, in this case, a farming station in the middle of an open plain. The nipa-thatched barracks, with their wooden walls and floors, offered more shelter than the previous camp. Better yet, it had bunks. The new arrivals joined a large group of captives who had only recently surrendered on Corregidor. These men, mostly officers, were in much better shape than the prisoners from O'Donnell. Before surrendering, they had eaten three squares a day, sometimes with ice cream for dessert. They had slept in cots every evening. The men on Bataan, in contrast, had been reduced to one-third rations, and began the march already starving. Even after their capitulation, the Japanese had spared the Corregidor men the horrendous trek. Jealous, the Bataan troops called them "tunnel rats."

Captain Dyess soon organized a series of efforts to improve his men's living conditions. The relocation seemed to breathe new life into the officer as he strode about their barracks barking orders. The flecks of copper in his eyes began to glimmer again. He instructed his men to patch the holes in the thatched roof and widen the walkways to keep the mud out. He ordered others to dig deeper drainage ditches. He initiated a fly-swatting contest. Anyone who killed one hundred flies or more received his choice of a hard-boiled egg, stolen from the camp chickens, or two smokes. An officer from Engineers oversaw the construction of a makeshift septic tank out of scrap lumber and salvaged tin. The swarms of flies soon diminished.

Dyess's barracks seemed a little brighter than the others in camp. The men appeared sturdier on their feet. The captain made sure everyone gave Leo a tiny portion of their meals. The menu rarely varied—rice three times a day, with the odd half-rotten camote thrown in. Maybe a few mongo beans and a little flour. The Japanese turned over the cooking operations to the Americans, who boiled the grain each day in fifty-five-gallon drums.

The tiny but life-sustaining meals infused Leo's cheeks with a little color, but he needed something else. He still spent no more than an hour a day with his eyes open, drifting in and out of sleep the rest of the time. Iridescent green bottle flies buzzed around his head. "He needs quinine," Dyess said as he ran his fingers beneath Leo's ribs. "His liver and spleen are swollen, working double time. Quinine's the only thing that'll save him. In the meantime you have to keep him awake."

"C'mon, buddy, snap out of it." Jake lightly patted his friend's cheek. "Wake up."

"No, I mean shake him like you're raising the dead," Dyess said. He twirled a bamboo cane between his fingers like a baton. "He doesn't need your sympathy, Jake. What he needs is rage. It's the only thing that'll keep him alive. You have to make him feel hate." Dyess suddenly belted the soles of Leo's feet with the rod. Leo moaned and Dyess struck him again. This time, Leo cried out and opened his eyes. "Survival is in the mind. It's all upstairs," Dyess said. "If he quits, he's finished." He struck him again, leaving a pink welt.

"Stop!" Leo cried weakly.

"You're hurting him," Jake said. He stepped between the captain and his friend.

"You understand me now, son? Kindness has no place here." The captain's high forehead was polished with sweat, his eyes round and bright. "Make him hate with a passion. If he wants to kill you bad enough, he won't die. Get him to hate you, then find some quinine."

"Fat chance getting anything from the infirmary," Jake said dejectedly.

"I heard that the Japanese received a shipment," Dyess said. "Maybe it hit the black market."

Jake sighed. "I guess I'll go talk to Moe."

Moe Gardner was a National Guardsman from New Mexico's very own Two Hundredth Coast Artillery. Jake had never met the guy until he ended up next to him in the back of a chow line. The two discovered they both came from Albuquerque. Jake had even pitched against him. Struck him out, of course. When they stumbled upon this coincidence, they whooped and embraced each other. They were comrades. Like Jake, Gardner was an easy talker; a cutup with a shock of red hair. His weak chin gave him the profile of a sea turtle. For the remainder of the march, they tried to recall every old haunt, every pretty girl. As soon as they landed at O'Donnell, however, they went their separate ways, Gardner to his card-playing partners, Jake to Dyess's barracks.

The last time Jake had seen him in the chow line, Gardner had offered to help him out if he needed anything. He knew people, he said. Jake found him in a barracks on the southern edge of the camp near one of the water spigots. The line for the faucet stretched and curled like a snake: at least fifty men were waiting, holding their canteens limply at their sides. Guys were known to die standing in line for water.

Gardner reclined on his bunk, a cigarette dangling from his lips. He smiled when he saw Jake. "I was wondering when you were going to show up."

Jake noticed that Gardner was wearing fresh fatigues. "What's shaking, Moe? You practicing your swing?"

Gardner chuckled. "I've been thinking about taking up golf when I get back, actually. Make friends, influence people." He looked at Jake through a haze of smoke. "What brings you to these parts?"

Jake scratched his head nervously. "I'm looking for some quinine, Moe. I have a buddy who's really sick. Another kid from Albuquerque. He's got it bad. He ain't going to make it if I don't get him something."

"What are you offering to trade?"

"To trade?" Jake scratched his head again and laughed quietly. "I'm not exactly flush at the moment, but when we get back—"

Gardner inspected his fingernails. "I don't know, McGriff. A lot of guys need medicine. I ain't in a position to just give it away."

"Not even for an Albuquerque boy?"

Gardner shrugged. "Go back and scrounge up whatever you can. Anything of value. If you bring me something, I might be able to part with a pill. It ain't much, but it might keep a guy alive another day."

Jake walked back to his bunk cursing Gardner's name the whole way. Leo was sleeping when he returned. Beads of sweat covered his face. Jake remembered what the captain had told him about keeping his friend awake. "Wake up, you son of a bitch!" he shouted. He slapped Leo's cheek. "Wake up!"

Leo opened his eyes with a start. "Why are you yelling at me, Jake?"

"Because you're a goddamn fool, that's why! Have you got anything left we can trade, or did you let everyone plumb rob you blind?"

Leo paused before he responded. "I had a Bible."

"That's long gone. That buddy of yours has smoked it through Corinthians by now. You have nothing."

Jake scoured his brain for what he might pawn and realized he didn't have anything either—except the photograph of Angelina. He had kept it tucked under the waistband of his underwear and it pulled the skin when he removed it. When he unfolded it, a wave of emotion passed through him. The image was creased but still clear. A pretty face might fetch something. It was all he had.

Moe Gardner was lounging in the shade of the barrack, another cigarette hanging from his rubbery lips. "Back so soon, McGriff?"

Jake instinctively made a fist. He tried to sound light and breezy. "I found something I thought you might like, Moe. A photograph of a lovely young thing. A real looker."

"She naked?"

"No, she ain't *naked*," Jake said. "But she's pretty." He unfolded the photograph and offered it to Gardner, who inspected it up close, then at a distance. He frowned. "What am I supposed to do with this? She's female, but so what? She's a little funny looking, if you ask me."

"Maybe she'll give some guy some hope, you know?" Jake said. He shrugged. "It's all I have."

Gardner sighed and gave the photograph another appraisal. "I'll give you one damn pill for this, since you're from Albuquerque. That's all I can offer. But I tell you what, I'll introduce you to my boss. Maybe he can find something for you to do." Gardner stood up and pulled out a crude wooden box from under his bunk. He fumbled around inside, then turned around to hand Jake the large pill. "You owe me, McGriff. Don't you forget it."

When Jake returned to his barracks, Leo was asleep again. Jake shook him awake. "C'mon, Leo, I have some medicine for you. Have a drink, and we'll get you fixed up." He stuck the thick, chalky pill in Leo's mouth, then handed him the canteen. Leo drank and tried to swallow, but started gagging. "Hold it down, Leo," he demanded, his voice rising. "You have to hold it down."

Leo held his hand to his throat. "Why are you doing this to me, Jake?" he asked. "Why are you being so mean?"

"Because you're my buddy, that's why," Jake said, wiping the sweat from Leo's brow. "You'll be all right. Hold it down."

The morning after the farewell party, the Jimenez family had seen the boys to the train station. Jake's encounter with Angelina had sounded a bell in his head, a deep, gong-like noise that had kept him awake the entire night. It rang so loudly between his ears, he was sure others could hear it. The din was made worse by his inability to tell anyone about it. His groin ached. He had come so close it almost made him physically ill.

The family was tired from the night before, and sad. Mr. Jimenez looked especially glum. Leo barely managed a smile. Jake shot a glance toward the benches along the wall where Angelina sat with her fiancé, who looked bloated with a vicious hangover. A breeze lifted a popcorn bag into the air at their feet. The girl wouldn't look at him.

The train steamed into the station with a roar, stirring to life those waiting on the platform. Angelina arose from the bench to join her family in the good-byes. Jake wished he could speak to her just once more, privately, but of course, that was impossible. He watched Leo whisper something in her ear that made her laugh. Leo and his father shook hands stiffly. Jake caught Angelina's eye, and she began to say something, probably something light and sarcastic like all the little comments she had whispered in his ear beside the water tank, but then she changed her mind and turned away. And already, he could barely remember what she looked like.

Jake went to see Gardner's boss the next day. His name was Ted Levin. Jake had heard about him through the grapevine. Evidently, he had spent a fair amount of time in Manila before the war, running numbers for a local family of small-time mobsters. Rumor had it he had connections on the outside. Somehow, he had managed to bribe a guard to smuggle some things in—probably by giving him a cut of the profits. Levin's barracks were on the northern edge of camp. When Jake tried to enter the place, a beefy man shoved a hand in his chest. His head was shaved on the sides like a Mohawk Indian's. "Hold it, bub."

"I'm looking for Ted Levin," Jake said.

"What's your name, kid?"

"McGriff."

"Hey, Levin," the man shouted into the building. "A kid by the name of McGriff wants to see you."

"Send him in," said a voice from inside.

The long, dim room was almost empty. As Jake got closer and his eyes adjusted to the light, he saw someone crouched in the shadows. At first he thought the man was Filipino by the way he squatted beside his bunk, but upon closer inspection he realized the man was white—and quite clean, in a spotless cotton shirt with his hair slicked back as if had just washed it. Those who had spent a few years in the Philippines before the war all sat like that. Dhobies, the men called them. Levin was the cleanest individual Jake had encountered since the war began—though his eyes were glazed, probably from a stash of morphine syrettes. At his elbow was a tin of Top's tobacco. A hefty soldier lounged on the bunk beside him. "Welcome, son," Levin said as he rolled a cigarette. "Can I get you a smoke?"

"Sure," Jake said and lit it eagerly.

The man lit his own cigarette, exhaling the smoke through his nose. "I've seen men starve themselves for tobacco."

"I need medicine for my buddy," Jake said, uninterested in small talk. "Quinine. But I don't have any money and nothing to trade. I don't suppose you take credit."

The man lounging on the bunk exploded with laughter. Most of his teeth had rotted away. "Afraid not, son," Levin said. "But we might find something for you to do. You ever catch rats?"

Jake shook his head.

"The Japs want me to help with the extermination," Levin said. "The Japs don't like the little buggers."

"Why you?"

"That's my business," Levin said calmly. "Ordinarily, I offer a couple smokes or a little food for every rat, but the payment is negotiable. Keep in mind, quinine ain't cheap." The second man barked with laughter again. "Why don't you start out with rats, and we'll go from there. Where there's a will, there's a way, ain't that right, boy?"

"Oh, I'll catch rats," Jake answered enthusiastically. "I'll be the best damn rat catcher you've ever seen."

"That's what I like to hear," Levin said and smiled.

The best place to catch rats was in the drainage ditches. The camp had a vast network of gullies, about a foot wide and two feet deep. Lush bunches of crabgrass grew along their edges. Jake began haunting these canals every day. He hunched over them for hours, a stick on his shoulder like a baseball bat. When a rat came scurrying along—whack!—down came the stick. He caught three or four a day, enough for one pill, which he dutifully brought back to Leo. In time, as his hunting skills improved, he began setting traps, which provided a greater yield. He soon assumed the mantle of the craftiest rat stalker at Cabanatuan.

After about a week of steadily taking the medicine, Leo began to show signs of recovery. He could sit up and eat. "Look at

Jiminy feeding himself, guys," Captain Dyess announced when he noticed Leo scraping his bowl. "Atta boy! The baby bull is back!" Leo looked around at his friends with an absent, faintly melancholy expression.

The general health of the camp improved as the rainy season subsided toward the end of September, though as many as three hundred prisoners continued to slip away every month. Those who remained resembled skeletons, the pale bones almost showing beneath the skin. Leo was reminded of his family's celebrations of *El Dia de los Muertos*. His parents would always build a shrine in the barn and decorate it with marigolds, dead centipedes and scorpions, and little ceramic bottles of mescal. Life was a dream. Only in dying did the soul awake. The children would suck sugar water from little wax skeletons, and chase each other, laughing, in the darkening, crisp autumn air. Now that death was real for Leo, he couldn't imagine ever laughing again.

In October, the Japanese Army called for literate laborers to volunteer to leave Cabanatuan and work elsewhere. Captain Dyess, who had been discussing escape plans for months, thought the volunteer duty might present an opportunity. He wouldn't dare try it at Cabanatuan. The Japanese had instituted a ten-to-one rule, meaning they would execute ten men for every one who attempted flight. American officers had taken to guarding the perimeters themselves after three men had been caught outside the fences. The attempted escape had led to several swift executions and a tortuous drawn-out affair for the three fugitives, who were tied to posts for days without food or water, before a guard hacked off their heads with a dull blade.

A trip to another island, however, might provide an opening. Dyess dealt himself two poker hands, one for his men to stay, another to go. He drew a diamond flush for the latter, which decided it. The men cheered when they saw the hand. Nobody wanted to stay at Cabanatuan. As they all filed out to volunteer, Dyess noticed Jake reclining on his bunk. "Aren't you coming?" he asked him.

Jake frowned. "I don't think Leo's ready."

Dyess smiled. "Sometimes we choose our missions, sometimes our missions choose us, right?"

"I guess," Jake said, bowing his head.

The volunteers left a week later. Dyess and a handful of others from the barracks arose before dawn and gathered their possessions. A rumor circulated that they were headed for Mindanao. Many of the men did not go, including Sgt. Whitaker and Larsen, because they had failed the medical exam required to make the trip. Leo was sleeping, but Jake followed the volunteers out into the misty morning air. He stood with them as they milled about in the courtyard, speaking in hushed tones. "You coming with us, McGriff?" they kept asking him.

"Nah," he said. "I've taken a liking to this place."

"See you back in the States, kid," Dyess said.

Jake nodded. He merely waved as he watched his comrades march into the low-lying fog.

* * *

One afternoon, the guards herded a large number of prisoners into the courtyard. Trucks idled outside the gates, in the same spot where Dyess and the other volunteers had departed a month before. "I guess we're finally getting out of here," Whitaker said. The tough little man had weathered into a scrap of cowhide. His beady eyes darted back and forth between the trucks and the growing throng of prisoners. "They'll probably take us up to Japan, where they can squeeze a little more out of us."

"Anywhere but here," Larsen said vacantly.

The guards loaded the men into the trucks and drove them south to Manila. They arrived just as the sun was turning the city pink, and they spent the night in an old stone prison called Bilibid, erected during the Spanish occupation. The guards pushed them all into the large open courtyard and fed them rice and fish heads.

In the morning, they filed down to the waterfront. As they walked, their eyes devoured the sights of the city, the liquor and cigarette billboards, the horse-drawn *calesas*. It had been so long since any of them had seen a building made of stone and mortar. The people came out of their storefronts to watch the procession. One civilian lit a cigarette with his lighter wedged between his first and second fingers, secretly flashing V for victory. The women tossed candy when the guards looked the other way.

The prisoners marched down to a pier where a freighter sat. The line of men waiting to board the ship ran nearly a mile long. They stood on the cobblestone sidewalk under tall palm trees. "We're going on a cruise, boys!" Jake announced to anyone who was listening. "Who's up for some shuffleboard?"

The ship was called the *Tottori Maru*. With the war going badly in the Philippines in 1943, the Japanese were loading scores of such barges with prisoners to be conveyed to more safely held territories where they would continue to serve as slave laborers. Many of the ships were unmarked as prison ships; fifty-nine of the crafts sank under enemy fire.

The prisoners walked up a gangplank, then across the steel deck and into a hatch leading to the freighter's hold. Jake took one last look at the sun, high in the sky, before he descended a narrow stairway into the black, airless cargo space below. As he stepped down, he heard the groans of men emanating from the dark. The heat—and the smell—met his nostrils like steam from a bath of sewer water. Down he went, step by step. He felt Leo's hand on his shoulder. When he alighted on the final stair, the floor below felt soft. "Get off me, jerk!" someone yelled. Jake stopped, but the line behind him kept moving, pushing him forward. He groped at the darkness and found only sweaty flesh.

As Jake's eyes adjusted, he realized the hold was packed with bodies. They were tangled on the floor and piling up along the sides of the walls like crickets crammed into a bait can. The heat was unbearable. Leo clutched at his shirt as the two climbed over the men, aiming for the back of the hold. When Jake looked around, he saw more prisoners descending.

The chorus of wailing voices began to rise. Miraculously, Jake and Leo found a small space along the wall. The metal was searing hot to the touch. The ship's engines began to rumble. The shouts grew louder. Thousands of men were shoved into a blistering metal box with no ventilation. The ship started to move. In the faint light, Jake recognized that the man next to him was an officer. "Somebody has to take charge here, sir, or we won't make it to morning," he yelled over the din.

The officer grinned at him. His eyes were eerily vacant. He offered Jake a small, hexagonal pill. "You want to get out of here, take one of these, soldier."

"What the hell is it?"

"It's Blue Heaven, my good friend," the officer said through a smile that seemed to be frozen on his lips. "The medics gave them to us." He giggled like a girl. "You must try one. They are simply delicious."

Jake put the pill in his pocket. Through the rising steam, he could see the soldiers wrestling in panic on the floor of the hold. They were out of their minds. One man emerged from the crush and ran screaming over the bodies, rising and falling as if he were wading through ocean waves. Another followed him. Jake wondered at the condition of the prisoners below their feet. "Shut up, people, and stay put!" hollered a broad-shouldered man who hung from a bracket on the wall. "The next guy who runs across dies!"

The threat accomplished nothing except to churn the boiling sea of bodies. Another man howled and began bounding over the tangled mass. The human sea swelled and took him under. *Conk, conk, conk*. They pummeled the man's head with empty canteens. Another soldier dove into the melee. *Conk, conk, conk*.

A voice rose above the clamor, someone singing softly at first, then more loudly, "The Battle Hymn of the Republic": "Mine eyes have seen the glory of the coming of the Lord. He is trampling out the vintage where the grapes of wrath are stored." The singer was standing on the stairs, high enough above the floor for everyone to see him. A pale shaft of light washed his head from above. Jake recognized him as a chaplain from Cabanatuan. "He hath loosed the fateful lightning of His terrible swift sword, His truth is marching on."

"Shut the fuck up, asshole!" someone hollered.

The man continued. "Glory! Glory! Hallelujah!"

"We don't want to hear it!" shouted someone else.

The crowd began to boo, their baritones reverberating off the walls. They refused to be moved by the song, but in their refusal they formed a loose consensus. The frenzied panic slowly dissipated. The water rocked below them, and the foul emissions of the sick began to slosh along the bottom of the hold. Finally, it grew quiet as many of the men fell asleep.

Within a few hours, the Japanese allowed two officers to go topside and send down a bucket on a rope to use as a toilet. It filled up in a matter of minutes. Many of the prisoners continued to suffer from amoebic dysentery and could not wait their turn.

"Pass the bucket," the men said, over and over again. The rope that held the pail looped through a rusty pulley. "Pass the bucket," someone else would say, and the pulley would screech and squeal as it was raised, dripping, over the hold. The mantra never stopped.

* * *

Chapter 6

Pusan, Korea

July 1943

After thirty days of rumbling over the waves, the freighter finally came to rest in Korea. The light blinded the prisoners, who had become accustomed to a world of darkness. They found themselves standing barefoot on the pier, their feet buried in three inches of snow. Shivering in the icy air, Leo watched the seagulls fighting over a string of fish guts. The bigger one pecked at the other's eye until he skittered away, only to come back with a piping *scree, scree, scree*. Leo had seen the same skirmish below deck when the Japanese crewmen sent down buckets of rice balls: the strong came away, their fingers grimy with grain, while the weak went hungry.

A truck backed onto the pier and opened its doors, revealing piles of gray uniforms. Before the men put them on, they were treated to a blast from a fire hose, ridding them of the muck that covered their skinny bodies. The guards enjoyed pushing them across the ice-covered planks with the water jet. The men emerged looking like drenched monkeys—so cold they didn't mind the abrasive feel of their new woolen shirts, trousers, and overcoats. Everyone received a fresh pair of socks and boots as well. Leo's pants were a little long and Jake's sleeves came short of his wrists, but they were glad to be rid of their filthy fatigues.

Still shaking from the cold, they marched three miles to the railroad station through yet another plundered town and conquered people. The Koreans went about their daily business with blank, dejected expressions. They were paler than the Filipinos, and took less interest in the Americans being paraded through their city. They were familiar enough with captivity; the Japanese had already occupied their country for decades.

The trains were magnificent, powerful, and spacious. Everyone got a seat and a little box of dried cod, rice, and pickled vegetables. Their tongues burned for hours from the salt. Jake and Leo sat together on a polished wooden bench facing the aisle. The Japanese had covered the windows with black cloth to prevent anyone from looking out, but Leo discovered a tiny opening where he could watch the country roll by. The landscape alternated between wide, flat fields of snow and bursts of industrial activity: huge, open-pit coal mines where steam-powered shovels plunged into the earth; shale oil plants with their smokestacks shrouded in black plumes. All day they traveled, deep into China, their final destination, Japanese-held Manchuria. The sun seemed far away, almost frozen in a slow, muted drift behind the clouds.

Whitaker sat on the same bench as Jake and Leo. Jake and he studied a page ripped from a Japanese newspaper they had found on the floor of the railcar. A photograph of a Japanese officer with a thickly cut mustache played prominently in the upper left corner of the page. They scrutinized the scrap of paper as if they might divine something about the war from the illegible characters.

On the bench across the aisle, Larsen was studying a Japanese phrasebook that a guard had handed him. At Cabanatuan, he had buckled under a two-pronged assault of dysentery and malaria. Yet, like everyone else on the train, he had endured. As the train rumbled along, he practiced his pronunciation in a low voice.

"What the hell do you think you're doing, Larsen?" Whitaker asked him from across the aisle.

"I'm learning something, and that's more than I can say for you," he replied.

"You turning yellow on us?"

"A guy should have enough sense to come in out of the rain," Larsen said. "We get beat and beat some more because we don't understand the suckers. So I figure, if I learn a few words, maybe I'll save myself a few bruises."

"Why don't you learn German while you're at it?" Whitaker jeered.

"Stuff it," Larsen snapped back.

Jake was snoring loudly, his head on Leo's shoulder. Leo's neck was tired, but he didn't want to wake his friend. Outside, snow covered the ground as far as he could see.

* * *

After three days in the relative comfort of the train, the men walked the last mile over an icy road to the Mukden prison camp. A dark wall, trimmed with barbwire, surrounded the low-slung barracks sitting in frozen muck.

The guards distributed six thin blankets to every prisoner, which seemed generous until the temperature dropped. The room rattled with the sound of chattering teeth. Dried mud filled the cracks in the walls. Small, coal-burning stoves, called *pechkas*, provided the only heat. Many of the men wrapped themselves completely in the pale blue wool, covering their faces like mummies, until nothing remained in view except their clunky boots. The blankets were filled with lice that immediately began burrowing into their clothes.

Jake was alert enough to grab a bunk closest to the squat pechka in the middle of the long ward. An orange glow emanated through tiny air holes in the chrome surface. The men closest to the stoves stuck their boots straight on the metal until the scent of burning leather filled the room.

For some still ailing from dysentery and fevers, warmth was simply unattainable. "I don't think Marshall's going to make it," Whitaker whispered, nodding in the direction of a young man shivering on a nearby bunk. After fighting three bouts of dengue fever at Cabanatuan, he'd been done in by the sea voyage. He was curled in a fetal position with his blankets clutched tightly around his shoulders.

"Somebody should get a doctor," Larsen said.

"Doc Hallinan is in the next shed," Jake offered.

The wind wailed outside. Nobody moved. The lights suddenly went out, leaving only the gentle glow of the pechka. On the verge of freezing, many of the men gathered together in the bunks for warmth. Jake ended up next to Marshall, who sucked in air with jagged breaths. Jake was still awake in the middle of the night when the breathing stopped. Unable to sleep, he could feel the body growing cold over the next few hours, and a ticklish influx of migrating lice seeking warmth.

* * *

The men received a breakfast of corn mush. The stuff tasted like rancid birdseed, but at least it was hot. A wheat bun the size of a baseball came with the porridge. It was the biggest meal they had eaten in some time, and a welcome change of pace from rice balls and *lugao*, watery rice soup. After the meal, the guards, dressed in thick winter coats and hats, led the able-bodied prisoners down the road. The biting wind slipped down the backs of their collars. Snow and ice covered everything except the occasional mud hole, which oozed from the earth like a primordial secretion.

Up ahead, a large, brick factory dominated the plain. The building had high ceilings, with lamps that hung from long wires like upside-down lily pads. Hulking steel machines crowded the room. The factory manufactured machine parts. Soon the men were lined up and told to demonstrate their skills. Many, including Jake and Whitaker, displayed ease with the equipment. Leo was not so lucky. When it came his turn at the band saw, he spent a few minutes trying to find the power switch before someone told him the machine was already on.

A guard escorted the clumsier prisoners, about two dozen in all, back to camp. As Leo was leaving, he saw Jake and the others donning white coveralls and goggles with smiles on their faces, excited by a new challenge. He leaned into the wind, cursing his clumsiness. Larsen, another reject, practiced his Japanese the entire way home. "*Sumimasen,*" he said slowly.

"What's that?" Leo asked him.

"Did you hear that Jap back there? He was saying *sumimasen,* while he was bowing to his boss. That must mean something like 'yes, sir,' or 'sorry' or something. It might come in handy."

Leo repeated the words to himself.

Back at the camp, a big, jowly guard barked at the men, apparently for their poor showing at the factory. "Stupid," he kept saying in English. He paused to remember another phrase. "Good for nothing," he added. He pointed to the barracks with a withering look, assigning the men to another guard who would entrust them with domestic details.

As the prisoners dispersed, Larsen trotted by the guard, bowing respectfully as he went. "*Sumimasen,*" he said. "*Sumimasen.*"

Leo followed his lead. "*Sumimasen, sumimasen.*"

The big guard grabbed Larsen's arm and spoke to him in Japanese. The mess sergeant responded with a few words, which made the guard smile. "You speak no good, but I have job for you," he said.

"What about for my friend?"

The guard frowned at Leo. He spoke quickly in a flurry of Japanese.

"*Sumimasen,*" Leo responded. "*Sumimasen.*"

Grumbling, the guard escorted them both toward a building in the corner of the walled compound. It was the camp infirmary, a long, narrow ward a little larger than the barracks, with beds lining each side of the room. It had two fat pechkas burning in the center aisle. A milky white light filtered down from slim windows cut high in the walls.

A doctor circulated among the beds. The guard caught his attention and pointed to Larsen, speaking enthusiastically. He then pointed to Leo with a frown and brushed his palm in a sweeping gesture. The two men laughed.

"Translator," the doctor said sternly to Larsen. "Fire," he said to Leo and indicated the pechkas. Leo hurried over to the first pechka to stoke the coals. When he opened the hatch, however, he discovered the embers had died. Relighting the thing was not easy. No matter how much kindling he used, the little black chips would not ignite. Nothing ever came easy. As he labored at his task, he watched the doctor make his rounds through the dim ward, trailed by Larsen, pushing a cart of medical instruments.

"*Do shimashita ka?*" the doctor asked each patient gruffly. The English-speaking prisoners could not respond, but that did not seem to matter. "*Doko ga itai desu ka?*" he barked at a prisoner with a huge pustule on his neck. When he did not receive an answer, he jabbed the lump with his finger. The patient screamed in pain. The doctor picked through his instruments and found what looked like a knitting needle. He dipped it in a jar of clear liquid then returned his attention to the prisoner, who tried, unsuccessfully, to fend off the tool.

The doctor advanced to the next patient. "*Do shimashita ka?*" he asked.

"I think he's asking what's wrong," Larsen offered.

The patient cowered beneath his blankets and shook his head. "Nothing. Nothing's the matter."

The answer angered the doctor even more than silence. He caught hold of the prisoner's wrist and yanked him from the bed. The man, naked below the waist, scrabbled on the floor like a crab. "*Atchi!*" the doctor shouted as he kicked the man down the aisle and out the door where the wind blew cold. "*Atchi!*" The doctor looked up fiercely and saw Leo watching him. Leo lowered his head and began blowing into the pechka.

* * *

Once the prisoners became used to the chill, the camp proved to be more bearable than Cabanatuan. The food came regularly, though it rarely varied: corn mush in the morning, soybean and onion soup for dinner. The soybeans, plain as they were, provided a wealth of protein and many of the men grew stronger. But the cold still took its toll on the weakest: more than twenty had died the first night, and many others followed in the weeks to come.

The more robust prisoners found some satisfaction working at the tool factory. Back home, metal shop had been one of Jake's favorite classes, and he had spent hours reassembling motors. The cavernous factory was stocked entirely with American-made machines: Milwaukee table drills and Cleveland shapers. American engineers had designed the workshop before the war, when the two countries were still trade partners.

An engineer by the name of Yoshio Kai, an American-born Japanese, ran the plant with a gentle hand. He gave the workers a little more food when they arrived each morning and sometimes threw a potato or carrot into the lunchtime soup. Jake looked for ways to take advantage of his situation. When the boss wasn't looking, he tinkered with the sheet metal scraps that gathered around the lathe. He cut himself a fork and knife to replace the ones he had left behind in the tropics. A spoon was all he really needed for the gruel the Japanese were dishing, but he wanted the extra utensils, if only to sneak something by his captors.

He also sabotaged whatever he could, cutting the steel crookedly or welding a weak joint. Once, when the guards instructed them to build a new floor, the men actually buried one of the lathes in the wet cement. The Japanese might never have caught on if it weren't for a British tattletale. A few of the guys suffered severe beatings for their subversion, and the rift deepened between the Americans and their English allies.

Occasionally, Jake passed Chinese villagers on the road-side as he walked to work. They always looked at the prisoners curiously but without much sympathy. One day an old Mongolian man watched them as they passed. He stood stock still, his expressionless face staring into the distance. He was there again that evening, kneeling on the ground. Jake realized he was dying, but there was nothing he could do. The next morning, the man lay completely flat in the snow. No one appeared to be the least bit interested in burying him or even dragging the body away. The next morning his shoes were missing. The following day an arm was missing, then a leg. Dogs had been gnawing on the frozen body. Soon the entire corpse was gone, leaving nothing but an impression in the snow.

* * *

Larsen continued to study Japanese. He tried to learn ten words a day—terms for the anatomy and for the complaints of the prisoners. "*Geri o shite imasu*," he told the doctor frequently, indicating that the patient had diarrhea, or "*benpi desu*" for constipation. Leo, who had always had an ear for language, learned a fair amount just hanging around the former mess sergeant.

Kawajima was the name of the house doctor, but the prisoners called him the Black Bastard for his jet-black hair and sadistic streak. Leo was no doctor, but he recognized that the man was butchering even the simplest operations. It got to the point that the prisoners preferred to suffer through almost any condition rather than submit their bodies to the Black Bastard's knife.

Leo saw the damage firsthand. In addition to stoking the coals, he was responsible for transporting the dead from the infirmary to the morgue. The ground was rock hard, far too firm to dig graves. The Japanese instructed Leo to stack the corpses like cordwood in a shed along the northern wall of the camp. The bodies piled up quickly. The first week there were nearly fifty frozen corpses in the hut; by the month's end, the number exceeded one hundred. Many died from the lack of bedpans. Prisoners with dysentery were forced to use the frigid outhouses, and many caught pneumonia.

Then a new doctor appeared in camp—a dapper gentleman who introduced himself as Dr. Naito. The simple fact that he offered his name set him apart from the Black Bastard or any other guard. When he appeared in the infirmary on his first day, in civilian clothes rather than a white coat like Kawajima, he produced vials of much-needed penicillin from his trouser pockets. He also brought big sacks of Korean oranges and tangerines, which he distributed to the patients, cheerfully whistling as he wandered between the beds. It took a moment for Leo to recognize the tune as "I Don't Want to Set the World on Fire," an American song.

Larsen would not stop talking about the new doctor that night as the men sat around the pechka. "He's just got a way about him," he told the others. "Leo, you understand, don't you?"

Leo shrugged.

"He speaks to you like you're a human being," he went on. Larsen had gained back some of the weight he had lost, and resembled the doughy figure they used to know. "When was the last time a Jap talked to any of you like a person?"

The men nodded vaguely.

"The guy brought bedpans, for Chrissakes! That alone should earn him a medal."

"That's enough, Larsen!" Whitaker blurted out. He spat on the pechka and the moisture sizzled.

"Yeah, listen to yourself," Jake added. "Are you sucking this guy's dick or what?"

The men laughed.

"I'm just trying to make the best of this," Larsen said in a chastened tone.

The next morning the guards instructed the prisoners to wait outside the infirmary rather than go to the factory. Everyone had to get in line, even the invalids. Word came down that the doctors wanted to conduct a full physical of each Caucasian there. The men shifted their weight from foot to foot as they stood in the cold.

The Black Bastard measured each prisoner's head with calipers, and then proceeded to record the length of the arm and leg and the width between the shoulders. Everyone received a number, written on a wooden tag to be worn around the neck. A guard with a camera photographed each man with his tag. The process was maddeningly slow, especially for those waiting outside the infirmary.

The line advanced to Dr. Naito, who asked each prisoner to walk toward him along a set of footprints painted on the floor. He asked them their nationality. If anyone claimed to be British, the doctor wanted to know if he was English, Scot, Welsh, or Irish. Afterward, he directed the prisoners to form two lines, even numbers on the left side of the room, odds on the right. One by one, the prisoners received a shot in the buttocks with a long needle.

* * *

Just as at Cabanatuan, the dozen or so officers at Mukden claimed their own quarters away from the enlisted soldiers. As far as they were concerned, imprisonment should still maintain the distinctions of military rank. Their sense of entitlement did not go over well with Jake, who, aside from Captain Dyess, had seldom met an officer he respected. He objected to them receiving any privileges, particularly since they no longer commanded their own men.

Yet the officers pulled it off, largely with the help of the Japanese, who honored the class system. During the long march, many of them had ridden in trucks while weaker men died on foot. On the work details at Cabanatuan, they had stood around aimlessly. Now at Mukden, they were excused from working at the factory, and Jake wanted to know why. "Are they too good to press a table drill? Do they even know how to press a table drill?" he asked Whitaker as they plodded down the road to work.

"Give it a rest, McGriff."

"Well, why aren't you pissed off about it? You're a noncom, but you march to the factory six days a week."

"Ah, but I'm not commissioned," Whitaker answered. "That's the difference. If you're commissioned, no one can touch you."

"So, what you're telling me is that you have no problem with them having the run of the camp all day, so they can go through our shit when we're working our asses off. I left a bun on my shelf yesterday, and when I came back it was gone."

"Your little buddy Leo probably ate it."

"Leo? Nah. He wouldn't take my bun. And it ain't the guards. They have all the buns they need. I'm telling you, it's got to be an officer. Don't get me started, Whitaker, you're pissing me off."

* * *

By January, Larsen had learned enough Japanese to become the official interpreter at the camp infirmary. Anyone who came for treatment checked in with him first. He took their temperatures with a scratched-up thermometer and made notes about their physical conditions. When Dr. Naito arrived, Larsen made sure all the men waiting to see him stood up and bowed. Then one by one, he led them to the far end of the dimly lit ward and reported their disorders in the best Japanese he could muster.

Leo was more cunning, for the physical examinations had aroused his suspicions. Why had the doctors suddenly taken such an interest in the welfare of the prisoners? It didn't make sense to give inoculations based on a distinction of race. To observe more closely, he intentionally made himself invisible, blending in with his surroundings. He never looked a doctor in the eye. He watched and listened as he swept the tile floor, whisking his broom over the same spot for as long as fifteen minutes at a time.

One evening Leo dumped a scuttle of coal chips into the potbellied stove and blew. The cinders flared red, then faded. The wind moaning down the chimney would spur them to flame.

The front door opened with a bang, sending a flurry of snow and grit skittering across the infirmary floor. Leo ducked out of sight beneath a gurney. None of the patients awoke; the doctors had given them little green sleeping pills again. It was rare to see guards in the medical ward, but he recognized their heavy boots laden with slushy remnants of snow. They stopped at a bed just a few feet away. Leo held his breath. They whispered something in Japanese and pointed to the wooden tag tied to the footboard. One of them raised the sheet and slapped the sole of the patient's foot, which prompted him to stir for a moment.

From the corner, they rolled out the portable surgical screens to shield the bed from view. Leo scurried to a better position behind the stove, where he could see the patient between the thin curtains, at least parts of him: thin ankles, gnarled, blackened fingertips in repose at his side, a bristly chin, forehead gleaming beneath the white lights. What was the man's name? Walker, Leo thought. No, Sloan.

Dr. Kawajima, a hulking man with a round, fleshy face entered the room, followed by the diminutive Dr. Naito, pushing a cart of medical instruments and whistling that same song, as if the record never stopped spinning in his head. Donning facemasks, the physicians spoke to one another in hushed voices, as they always did when the men were sleeping. Naito took up a scalpel, Kawajima, a pair of oversized tweezers.

When the guards strapped down the soldier's wrists and ankles, he rolled his head to the side and groaned as if he was suffering a bad dream. The doctors leaned over the body. Suddenly something caused the soldier to lurch from the table. He arched his back, the muscles in his neck taut as the string of a violin bow. A line of blood streaked across the curtain. "No!" he shouted, his voice rupturing the quiet of the room. "Please! No!"

He began bucking with the violence of an epileptic seizure. In his convulsions, he strained against the straps. His chin thrust toward the ceiling as he screamed in a keening voice that echoed off the walls. Even after Dr. Naito smothered his mouth with a cloth, he continued to emit a muffled wail. More blood stained the curtain.

A moment later, he fell quiet, and the doctors continued their labors. Leo heard a whirring sound, perhaps a surgical saw, and then smelled the scent of burning hair. Dr. Kawajima grunted, his brow furrowed in concentration. He seemed to pry something loose from the torso. Blood began to run off the bed where the soldier lay, still now, and silent.

Sloan. Leo was sure of the soldier's name. He pressed his tongue against the roof of his mouth to keep from vomiting. Dr. Naito placed a mirror beneath Sloan's nostrils. Dr. Kawajima grunted again and Dr. Naito shook his head. They packed up their tools. The ward was so quiet, Leo could hear the ice tinkling down the chimney of the stove. He turned his head to see the rows of men in their bunks. How he wished he could join their slumber. Watching had made him feel party to the murder, and he was ashamed. So he told no one what he had witnessed.

* * *

Following the operation, Leo understood that what he had seen was no mere bungled operation. There was a cold malice to the procedure, a willful taking of life, but Leo had to keep his worries to himself or risk arousing the ill will of Larsen, who clearly relished his newfound authority. Larsen would leap from the floor when responding to orders. "*Hai!*" he would shout. "*Hai! Hai! Hai!*" Or he would question the patients with a hint of skepticism, a tone he had picked up from the Japanese doctors, as if he believed the prisoners were freeloaders looking to get out of work. In addition to his duties as interpreter, Larsen was responsible for distributing the citrus fruit every morning. The even numbers received oranges, the odd tangerines.

The fruit was a Naito-inspired practice, and as far as Larsen was concerned, another reason to revere the man. The doctor, indeed, appeared genuinely concerned with the health of the prisoners, which complicated matters for Leo, who felt himself, at times, pulled in by Naito's charm as well. When the doctor would enter the ward, always dressed in a clean suit, he would address Leo by name, and shortly following the fatal surgical procedure, he assigned Leo the guardhouse in the afternoons, to tend the pechka there. There was nothing to read, but Leo could warm himself by the stove, alone with his thoughts. He kept a diary, just a few sheets of paper folded into quarters, with brief notations:

"*30 Jan 43* Everyone received a 5 cc typhoid-paratyphoid A inoculation.

7 Feb 43 Vaccination for smallpox, British only.

19 Feb 43 Several officers have been questioned about dysentery and diarrhea."

When he was away, Leo stashed the journal beneath a pile of coal in the corner of the shed. His fingers left blackened prints on the pages. The little room was dim, lit only by the pale light from the windows. His breath billowed from his lips, but the stove was warm when he sat close to it. In such moments of quiet, he pondered the medical staff's strange behavior.

It seemed they were conducting some sort of study, but he had no way of grasping the full picture, that the prisoners were subjects of a grand experiment. That Naito was taking orders from a sprawling research compound only ninety miles north of the prison camp. Leo knew only that his thoughts put him in peril, so much so that he was reluctant to share them with anyone. In time, however, he relented, warning Jake to avoid anything Naito offered—fruit, pills, examinations. Such a tall order would require guile, of course, and the utmost care to maintain appearances, especially in front of Larsen, whom Leo was convinced was dangerous.

"I think you've been spending too much time in the wood-shed," Jake said with a laugh when they spoke.

"I saw them kill someone," Leo whispered. "They cut up Sloan right before my eyes. Just be careful, and promise me you won't say anything."

Jake shrugged, twisting a piece of metal he had stolen from the factory. Imprisonment had blunted his senses, shortened his attention span. It was harder to talk to him. They had all changed. And one night, when they were sitting around the stove, he drew Larsen's ire.

"You're not supposed to like it," Larsen was telling Whitaker, referring to the repeated calls for rectal smears. "You never liked the medicine your mother gave you when you were a kid, did you?"

"My mother wasn't sticking a glass rod up my ass," Whitaker said.

"Larsen's mother used a broom handle," Jake cracked. "So now he thinks he has it good."

"The doctor does it because he cares," Larsen insisted. "Someday, when we're all out of here, we'll be thankful this man looked after us."

"Yeah, well maybe he's trying to kill us all," Jake said jokingly, but Larsen narrowed his eyes when he heard it.

"All you see is the negative," Larsen said. "Things are hard enough around here without you always dragging everybody down. Just keep talking, pal."

"What does that mean?" Jake asked.

"Nothing," Larsen said as he lay back on his bunk. "Go to sleep, Jake."

* * *

The next day, Jake's daily allotment of fruit was changed, without explanation, from an orange to a tangerine. By the end of the week, he couldn't get out of bed, weak from loss of fluid. He knew he might face a beating if a guard checked the barracks, but he was willing to risk it. Besides, he wasn't about to go to the infirmary and allow Dr. Naito to probe him with a glass rod. Leo brought him a bowl of mush and a wheat bun, but Jake could not bring himself to eat. He fell asleep with the food sitting at the foot of the bed when the others left for work.

He had been sleeping for hours—he didn't know how many—when he heard someone at the end of the barracks. He quickly rumpled up the blankets and buried himself beneath them, hoping he was sufficiently covered. The steps came closer, clunking on the wood floor. Jake tried to breathe as quietly as he could. They were careful steps, slower than the typical guard. They stopped near his bunk. He held his breath. He heard a shuffle of clothing, then the *click* of a Zippo lighter. Miraculously, the person proceeded down to the end of the barracks.

When he pulled back his covers to breathe the cool air, however, he noticed that the wheat bun at the foot of his bed was missing. The bowl of cold mush was there, but the bun was gone. He bolted to the door and saw a man about fifty feet away, walking toward the officers quarters. Jake ignored his shaky bowels and ran after him. "Did you take my food?" he asked when he caught up to the officer.

The man appeared startled. He wore the stripes of a major and was smoking a cigarette through a makeshift holder.

His ruddy cheeks glowed pink in the cold. "I don't know what you're talking about," he said.

Jake looked him over and noticed the bulge in his trouser pocket. "Then what the hell is that?"

"Watch your language, soldier."

Jake grabbed the officer's collar. "Give me my goddamn bun!"

"Get the hell off me, soldier!"

Jake felt dizzy. He clutched the man's shirt with both hands to stay on his feet. "I want my bun," he whispered. The ruckus drew the attention of the men in the infirmary. A few prisoners came out to see what was going on, followed by a pair of guards. The officer kneed Jake in the groin, sending him to the ground.

"This soldier attacked me," he said to the guards. Larsen arrived a few moments later with Leo in tow.

Jake writhed with his hands between his legs. The guards pulled him to his feet and jabbered at him. "He stole my bun," Jake gasped and pointed to the bulge in the officer's pocket.

Larsen said something to the guards, who responded with surprise, then jabbered something more. One of them thrust his hand into the major's pocket and removed a golden wheat biscuit. "That's mine," the officer said. "I saved it from break-fast."

The guards conferred. "They say it's the officer's word against yours," Larsen said to Jake. "And they want to know why you're not working."

Now it was Jake's turn to scramble for an answer. "I was too sick to work, so the factory manager sent me back to check into the hospital. On the way, I stopped by the barracks to get the bun I had saved from breakfast. That's when I found this guy taking off with it."

"You dirty liar," the officer shouted. "You were in bed all morning!"

"How would you know?" Jake asked.

The guards consulted each other again. One of them pointed toward the officers quarters and barked angrily. "He says go back to your barracks and stay there until further notice," Larsen told the major. "Jake, he wants you to check into the infirmary."

"Yes, sir," Jake said, unsure whether he was being rewarded or punished. He trotted toward the hospital.

* * *

Though Jake's illness grew worse in the hospital, he soon wanted to get out of the place. The sounds unnerved him: the low groan of the patients, Dr. Naito's constant whistling, a familiar tune, yet one that Jake couldn't quite identify. The song would echo off the walls, ebbing and flowing with the wind. Every day, Jake awoke hoping for the strength to walk out, but the illness was debilitating. To the enlisted men, he was a hero. After his altercation with the major, the Japanese guards enacted a rule prohibiting the officers from leaving their quarters during the day. They could not step foot outside until the workers had come home from the factory.

Many of the men in the infirmary, sick as they were, passed along their congratulations to Jake through Leo. They dared not make too much of a show, lest a guard take note. But from what Leo said, the legend grew in the telling as it circulated through the barracks. At first, the story went that Jake had tackled the officer and knocked him down. Then it blossomed to the point where Jake had beaten the major to a pulp; others reported that the officer had actually knelt on bended knee and apologized. Jake was given the title "Defender of the Bun." One day, in a gesture of gratitude, all the men in Jake's barracks sent him their morning biscuits. Leo piled them at Jake's feet so that he would find them when he awoke. Unfortunately, he had too little appetite to eat even one. His digestive troubles seemed to be getting worse. He simply could not keep food in his stomach.

Half the prisoners were suffering from diarrhea. To quiet them, the doctors often dispensed sleeping pills. There wasn't much in the way of medicine, but they had an abundance of sedatives. The patients gobbled them up like candy, anything to escape the dreariness of the ward. Since he had become sick, Jake tried to heed Leo's advice and avoid anything else pressed on him by the doctors. One day he cheeked his pill and fooled the Black Bastard into thinking he had swallowed it. He closed his eyes and listened to the ward settle to a hush. Soon only the wind battering the windows and the occasional click of footsteps broke the silence. The doctor was whistling a song, something familiar. Then he heard a little hiss. It sounded like the quick release of air from a tire.

Through squinted eyes, he could see Dr. Naito making his rounds wearing a face mask. He seemed to be inspecting the patients closely. *Pssst*. Jake heard it again. The doctor had what looked like a Flit gun. He was spraying something up their noses. Suddenly Leo appeared at the far door and dumped a load of coal on the floor. The doctor quickly stashed the device in his coat pocket and began writing something on his clipboard. Jake did not hear the sound again that afternoon.

* * *

Larsen continued to distribute oranges and tangerines to the prisoners. "This'll give you a boost," he said as he tossed a tangerine to Jake.

"How am I supposed to eat this when I can't even stomach a goddamn bun?"

"Just eat it, McGriff. Doctor's orders."

"Some doctor."

"What'd you say?" Larsen asked sharply.

"Nothing, Larsen. Nothing."

As Jake contemplated how he might make the fruit disappear without having to put it in his stomach, he noticed that the vast majority of those suffering from stomach ailments had tangerines as well. Then he noticed that the prisoner lying next to him—one of the few who could actually eat—was peeling what appeared to be the only orange in the infirmary. The man's leg, entombed in a cast, hung from a sling at the foot of his bed. "Hey, buddy, do you want to trade?" Jake asked.

"Sure," the man said. "I'm sick of oranges."

Jake stumbled out of his bunk and handed over his tangerine just as Dr. Naito was walking by. The doctor noticed what they were doing and jabbered at them. He took the tangerine back and returned it to Jake. He chattered some more as he waved his finger in Jake's face. Jake tried to hand the fruit to the doctor. "I can't eat it," he said.

Suddenly Dr. Naito exploded with anger and shoved the tangerine into Jake's chest. Jake begrudgingly began to peel it. Unable to hold the fruit in his stomach, however, he almost immediately vomited it into his bedpan. When the doctors passed out the sleeping pills that afternoon, Jake slipped the pill into his pocket. Once the ward quieted, Jake heard the sound of the Flit gun coming down the aisle. It was louder this time, maybe two or three beds away. He closed his eyes in case the doctors saw him. *Pssst*, he heard it again, then suddenly they were upon him. When he felt a hand on his cheek, he flinched and jerked his head away. "Don't!" he said.

Dr. Naito gave a little cry of alarm.

"What are you doing?" Jake shouted. "Let go of me! Let go!"

Jake twisted away for a moment and looked wildly around the hall for help. Leo was nowhere to be seen. The doctor pushed him back down, long enough to spray his face.

* * *

Although Jake suffered from blazing fever over the next few weeks, he was removed on doctor's orders from the infirmary. His friends gave him a hero's welcome when he returned to his barrack. "Bun Man!" they hollered as he staggered in the door. They grabbed him by the shoulders and shook his hand. "Defender of the Bun!"

"Get off me, guys," Jake said. "I'm about to shit my pants!"

The room quieted as the men realized that Jake was serious. Larsen tried to help him to his bed, but Jake pulled away. "Don't come near me," he said icily.

"We don't want you here, Larsen," Whitaker snapped. "Go bunk with the Japs."

The Swede's ruddy cheeks flushed. He looked hurt. "How can you say that? Whit, you know me. I may have this job, but I'm still on your side."

"I don't know anymore," Whitaker said.

The next morning, Jake went to the door to watch his friends leave for work. As they filed out, he noticed, to his surprise, a Red Cross truck in the walled compound. It was bringing medicine or perhaps mail. The international aid service had made sporadic appearances at other prison camps, but never Mukden. Sure enough, that evening a man stood at the back of the truck with the doors open, tossing bundles into a large crowd of prisoners. Hundreds had collected in the yard. Though Jake felt rotten, he wandered out full of hope, as the man called out names. The sky was streaked with crimson, one of the first cloudless sunsets he had seen since they had come north. "Erwin Johnson!" the man called. "Gregory Rodriquez!" At the sound of their names, the men made beelines for the truck. "Leo Jimenez!"

"Leo! Hey, Leo, there's something for you," somebody shouted. Leo battled his way to the front and collected an envelope.

"Eddy Laursen! Mark Herbst! Sam Whitaker!" As the sky grew dark, the mailman lit a kerosene lantern to read the names. He continued his roll call deep into the night. Jake's teeth began to chatter and he hugged himself for warmth.

For once, nobody minded missing dinner. Most bolted as soon as they had collected their bundles to read the dispatches in private. Finally the names stopped. About one hundred men were left standing around the truck, including Jake. "Sorry, guys," the man said. "Maybe next time."

Jake wobbled back feeling utterly alone. On the way, he picked up an opened envelope with a folded sheet of stationary inside. It was blank. Scraps of paper were strewn across his path, and he took it upon himself to gather them. He was in no hurry to return to the barracks, where he could hear excited chatter. He was embarrassed for his failure to receive a letter, as if it were evidence of a personal defect. Still, he wore a brave smile as he approached his bed. Leo was sitting cross-legged on his bunk, hunched over his letter. He looked up when Jake flopped down beside him. "Did you get anything?" he asked hopefully.

Jake flashed the open envelope. "Something from my ma." He waited patiently for his friend to finish. Finally, Leo put the letter aside.

"Well?" Jake asked.

"My parents send their regards."

"Is that it?" Jake asked. "C'mon, tell me everything it says."

Leo fell back on his bunk with a dreamy expression. "Angelina married Johnny, I guess before he left for Europe," he said. "She's going to have a baby. Or maybe she's already had it."

"Good for her," Jake said quickly and meant it. It had been ages since he had thought of the girl, and now that he was reminded of her, to his surprise, he felt nothing. The war not only had burned off any extra weight, but the soft stuff of ball games and adolescent crushes. He was stronger now, a survivor, and tough.

* * *

The snow melted in May. When the sun finally began to show its face, a group of curious visitors descended upon the camp. They came in green Dodge trucks with the windows painted shut. As they got out of the vehicles, a sudden sandstorm blasted through the yard, sending their olive-green caps cartwheeling to the outer walls, where they stuck like glue. Dr. Naito quickly ushered the visitors inside. One stood out from the others, a taller man with a thickly cut moustache. Ishii, they called him. Leo tried to look busy stoking the coals.

After a quick lunch, Naito led the group on a tour of the infirmary. The men had changed into white lab coats and donned protective face masks and rubber gloves. Leo watched them from behind a gurney. The doctor introduced them to Larsen, who had been cleaning bedpans in the back washroom. Larsen bowed deeply and rattled off a phrase in Japanese. The men applauded in appreciation. The sand scratched against the high windows on the western wall, where tarnished sunlight flickered in the storm.

The next day, when Leo reported to work, Larsen sent him to the shed where the bodies were stacked. "It's time to bury the men," he said grimly. "The ground's starting to thaw."

Leo nodded. He noticed Larsen had taken to wearing a medical coat similar to the ones the visitors were wearing. His face was drawn. "The doctors asked to see a few of them before we send them off," he added. "Naito gave me the numbers of the ones he wants." He handed Leo a sheet of paper with five Japanese figures scrawled across the top.

Larsen's lower lip began to tremble before his face cracked with a hard sob. "Whitaker died last night." He paused to compose himself, then spoke in a whisper. "It was a bacteria of some kind. Anthrax, they called it. Something left over from when they used to keep cattle here. But you better go get those bodies before they catch us talking."

Leo wandered over to the shed in shock. Whitaker had spent the previous few days in the infirmary with an infection, but no one had considered it serious. Just the day before, the sergeant had ribbed him for pushing the broom too slowly. Now he was a body among all the others. The stacks nearly reached the low ceiling. The cold had kept them perfectly preserved. So many arms and legs. So many frozen faces. They all had wooden number tags tied to their toes.

He searched for Whitaker's number, keeping his eyes on the tags as he poked about. He found him in the back, looking as if he were merely sleeping, his tight features pinched into that familiar scowl. A lesion marked his cheek. When Leo lifted the body gently from the pile, he marveled at how light it was, as insubstantial as a child.

The entrance to the infirmary was roped off with a sign that said "Keep Out." Larsen grimaced when he saw the body. He had pulled himself together and now wouldn't look at Leo.

"I'll miss him," Leo said sadly.

Larsen shrugged. "Get back to work. These guys mean business."

Leo brought the rest of the bodies as quickly as he could. The doctors had cordoned off a corner of the ward with portable screens. All the patients were asleep.

The doctors were too engrossed in what they were doing to notice Leo. The bodies he had collected were laid out naked on five tables. Beneath the surgical lamps, they seemed to thaw a little, their limbs turning limp. One of the visitors peered through a movie camera, filming the operation. Larsen was fussing with them, tying knots around their penises, and stuffing cotton into their butts and mouths. The tall gentleman with the moustache was giving a lecture of some sort, referring to various aspects of the corpses. The men in white coats nodded repeatedly, the bright light gleaming on their foreheads. When Larsen finished his task, then they began cutting into the bodies.

Leo was close enough to see the important doctor working on Whitaker. He opened his chest with a surgical saw and was just removing the heart when he saw Leo. He shouted something and pointed to the door. He yelled again.

"Get out of here, Leo," said Larsen. "You're not supposed to be in here."

* * *

Chapter 7

Frederick, Maryland

April 1945

Murray and Molly were eating dinner when the phone rang. He was beginning to dread phone calls at odd hours. Molly was nine months pregnant, nearly immobile. "Don't answer it," she said on the third ring, just as her husband stood up.

"I have to," he said and hurried into the kitchen. He spoke for a few minutes, then emerged, a look of alarm on his face. "I have to pack a bag, love."

"Don't be silly."

"It's a matter of national security. I've been called across the country."

Molly covered her mouth. "What happened?"

"Something has landed in Montana. They want me to check it out. I don't know anything more."

"But what if I go into labor?"

"Your due date is more than two weeks away," he said, surprised that she would question his call to duty. "I'll be back long before then."

Murray boarded a plane to Butte, Montana, the next day with a few members of his staff from Camp Detrick. He squinted at the incident report on the way over—he had forgotten his reading glasses. Evidently, a balloon, thirty feet in diameter had landed in an empty field. No one was hurt.

Murray's team drove from the airport through fields of birch and oak, far into the Montana wilderness. In a pasture, they found the balloon, black with a white stripe, deflated on a patch of wild flowers. The team stood around the flattened mass, shifting their weight from foot to foot. None of them dared touch it. A technical crew came in and carefully removed the balloon for Murray's men to inspect in a local laboratory. By the time they had completed the packaging, however, Murray received notice of another balloon landing in Spokane. He stowed the evidence in the trunk of a car to take with him and then drove with his team to Washington State. There they found the same scene, except the deflated balloon, entangled in a tree, carried what appeared to be an incendiary device, attached to a string.

The balloon's skin was almost as thin as cigarette paper, four or five sections glued together with rubber cement. An ingenious modulating device made sure the craft maintained altitude: if the balloon flew too high, the modulator released a little helium; if it sank too low, the modulator discarded a sandbag to lift the craft. The incendiary device carried a sealed capsule filled with powdered magnesium. The capsule had a fuse attached to the ballast mechanism so that the balloon would ignite upon landing, but somehow the trigger had failed to function.

The inspectors combed every inch of both the inflatables. On the one from Montana, they discovered a row of Japanese characters scrawled faintly in ink at the base, but they found no evidence of bacteriological tampering on either. Murray was relieved. For the moment, his job was done. He spent a day quickly writing up his report, hoping to get home before the big day.

Given the markings and materials, it was almost certain they had been launched by the Japanese. As the war was winding down in Europe, American B-29s were heavily bombing Tokyo, and the Japanese were fighting back with the ferocity of a trapped wild animal. Kamikaze pilots smashed their planes into aircraft carriers, and ordered their own country's citizens on Okinawa to commit mass suicides instead of being captured. The Americans decided the appearance of the balloons signaled a new wave of even more desperate attacks.

Yet the balloons had come up clean. So why would the Japanese bother to send them? Had the balloons carried packets of Japanese encephalitis, a virus that had never previously surfaced in the United States, mosquitoes could quickly have spread the disease to epidemic proportions. But apparently the enemy wasn't ready to transport germs just yet. On the other hand, if these first balloons had started forest fires, Japanese intelligence would pick up on the news reports and know where they had landed. The next ones might bring freeze-dried encephalitis—or anthrax, enough to wipe out vast numbers of livestock, not to mention entire towns.

The phone in Murray's room rang. It was Ira Baldwin from Camp Detrick. The Canadian government was reporting more balloon landings. He would have to go check them out. Murray sighed. His wife was expecting him home, he said. Could someone else go? No chance, Baldwin told him. Murray stood up from his typewriter. Outside, the wind was battering the green branches of the trees. He allowed his nose to touch the cold glass. There would be miserable weather in Ottawa, no doubt. The phone rang again. Balloons had landed in White Horse, Alaska, and were raining on Grand Rapids, Michigan. More had landed as far east as the St. Lawrence River in Quebec. The army was moving to implement a secret battle plan, "Lightning Strike," to guard against a domestic biological attack.

Murray called his wife from Fairbanks, Alaska, where it was still so cold, he thought his lips might stick to the phone. Her due date had come and gone and still no baby. Frozen inside, he was numb to her jagged words. He would be home in time to pass out cigars, he told her, when the operator cut in to say his time was up. He had become the balloon hunter, scouring the tundra in the glass belly of a bomber. One of the balloons had exploded and killed a woman in Helena, Montana; another had caught fire and fried a fishing party in Oregon. Still, none had shown any evidence of bacterial substances.

The military made sure the public never heard about the hundreds of balloons landing across North America. The press never got a whiff of it, or if they did, they kept quiet in the interests of national security. Reports would cause widespread panic; they would also convey to Japanese intelligence that the balloons had successfully reached American soil. For another week, Murray searched the beaches of San Diego, then Hawaii, while Molly's voice grew increasingly strained on the other end of the telephone line. "Don't they know that your wife is a week late?" she asked, almost frantic. "The doctor told me he would have to perform a cesarean if the baby doesn't come by Friday."

"I'll be back by then," Murray assured her.

"I want you back now."

Murray caught himself before launching into all the reasons he had to finish his assignment. His explanation wouldn't matter to her, and when he thought about it, it didn't matter to him either. "I'll tell Baldwin I simply can't do it. I'll catch a red-eye and be home before you wake in the morning."

But she was crying again. "This work has changed you, Murray."

* * *

Chapter 8

Harbin, Manchuria

April 1945

Ishii Shiro plucked a slice of mackerel sashimi from the black lacquered tray. His chef had prepared an ornate spread of the finest cuts of fish: sweet shrimp and yellowtail, fatty tuna belly, and bonito. Laid beside little plates of potato, spinach, and rice, the morsels gleamed under the harsh light. Once sumptuous, the dining room now smelled of mildew, the result of a leaky ceiling during the family's three-year absence from Manchukuo. The precious red carpets held so much water they almost squished under foot. The velvet patterns on the walls were blotched with mold.

Still, Ishii was entertaining at his lavish Manchurian mansion again, though on a smaller scale than the early days when the high, mahogany ceilings echoed with cackling laughter and there seemed to be no end to the money. He could afford to have sushi flown in from the Home Islands, even after many of the country's military planes had been grounded, lacking fuel and spare parts. His daughter Harumi and his dinner guest, Mitsuichi Kuritsu, a wealthy businessman, sat with him at the far end of a long walnut table. "It was a mess, I tell you," Ishii told his guest. "And it was all your fault." The general's cheeks were flush with sake. He was joking with his friend, but there was a bitter edge to his jibe.

"I believe you played a small part in the affair," Kuritsu said. He had a compact build, a square jaw, and close-cropped hair.

They were discussing how Ishii had been exiled when the Japanese government discovered his kickback scheme with Kuritsu's medical supply company. He had, over the years, collected vast amounts of money under the names of phony investors. Eventually the deal had resulted in charges of graft and bribery. Such an indictment might have ended the career of an officer of lesser stature. But the government was so afraid of Ishii it actually promoted him to general, an unprecedented honor for a member of the Medical Corps. Nonetheless, to quiet any controversy, Ishii had been transferred to Nanking.

As the Allied forces were beginning to reclaim territory, the situation in Nanking had become too dangerous for the family, so Ishii's wife had taken their six children back to Chiba. Ishii had stayed, establishing an Anti-Epidemic Water Unit in the war-torn city. Here, as at Ping Fan, the facilities had been designated a water purification center, while behind closed doors the scientists studied the effects of biological experiments on human subjects.

Now, with the enemy pounding the Home Islands, Ishii was needed back in Manchukuo. When he had returned a few months before, he didn't bother sending for Kiyoko, his wife, who had grown old and ugly to him. In her place, Ishii had brought his eldest daughter, Harumi, to keep him company and watch over the house. The sixteen-year-old girl knew nothing of the true nature of her father's work. As far as she was concerned, Ping Fan was a world-renowned microbiological research facility. Because of her, at dinner, the gentlemen spoke of their troubles with the government in oblique terms and couched their discussion within the context of the war. "One decisive victory is all we need." Ishii struck the table with his fist. "I'll give the white devils something to think about yet."

Kuritsu glanced at Harumi, who was nibbling her fish quietly with downcast eyes. The girl had pulled back her thick black hair into a knot, revealing a graceful neck. "Your daughter has grown into a lovely young woman, Ishii," he said. Harumi blushed and stared at the bits of bright green wasabi littering her plate. Kuritsu's attention bothered her, but as her father's colleague, he could say such things without fear of reprisal. He was as brash as Ishii and just as lascivious. His eyes glittered in the bright light. "Where is her mother? Where are her lovely brothers and sisters?"

"They are still in Chiba," Ishii responded, his mouth full. Harumi lifted her head to listen to her father's answer. "My wife suffers from pleurisy. The cold air up here is no good for her."

"Oh, I'm so sorry," Kuritsu said. "Chiba must be awful with the bombings. I hear half of Tokyo is on fire. Are they all right?"

Ishii nodded. "They will move here soon."

"So it is just the two of you in this big house?"

Ishii nodded and stuffed an octopus tentacle into his mouth, allowing it to protrude slightly as he chewed.

Kuritsu turned to Harumi. "And how do you like it up here in the wilds?"

Harumi blushed again, but met his gaze for the first time that evening. "I like it very much," she said. "The air is clean. And the children are strong in spirit. My friends and I want to make balloons for the war."

Ishii looked at her sternly. "It is time for you to go to bed."

Harumi immediately stood up and bowed to the men. "Good night," she said and departed without another word.

As Kuritsu turned to watch her go, his eyes fell on the barren walls, then the dark emptiness of the next room. "Where is your furniture?"

"It's all at my mother's house in Chiba," Ishii said with a sigh. "I had to move my things before the government stole them." He had shipped crates of silk kimonos, gold bullion, and whatever else he had accumulated from the Kwantung Army's plunder. He'd entrusted it with the village elders, who would take good care of it. They sent him money when he needed it. He motioned to the scraps of fish remaining on the lacquered tray. "I'm not exactly without funds."

He changed the subject. "We were this close to covering the Marianas with fleas," he said, extending his thumb and index finger to show the width of a centimeter. "I sent a team from Nanking. Seventeen of my men went armed with canisters packed with the insects."

Kuritsu poured himself another glass of sake. A perplexed look crossed his face.

"So the idea was that the fleas would hang around until the American soldiers got there?

Ishii nodded. "Millions of them."

"Then when the soldiers landed and got out of their planes, the fleas would bite and make them sick with what, the flu?"

"Plague."

"How many American soldiers would be affected?"

"Thousands," Ishii responded without hesitation. "Three, four thousand men. *That* would make the Americans think twice about landing on our territory."

Kuritsu raised his eyebrows skeptically. "What came of the mission?"

"A submarine torpedoed the ship."

"Twenty-four thousand Japanese soldiers died in defense of the Marianas," Kuritsu said somberly. "A lot of them jumped from the cliffs to avoid capture."

Ishii's eyes flashed. "Never mind. I've got big plans," he said, as excited as a schoolboy describing a new science project. "I believe these balloons my daughter referred to might turn the tide. We've been sending them out with self-detonating fire bombs, so we can track where they land in North America. Our intelligence reported fires along the western coast. In the meantime, I've developed a ceramic pod to use as a transport for plague-infected rats. I've even installed a device with oxygen to keep them alive. When the balloons land, the pods will break and the rats will be free to spread their mischief. But that's still in the future."

Kuritsu cracked a smile. "I wouldn't count on it to halt the fire-bombing of Tokyo."

"No, of course not." Ishii brushed away his objections. "This is a long-range plan. And if the balloons don't work, I've developed another strategy—for a hang glider attack."

Kuritsu nodded politely.

Harumi retired to her room on the second floor. She could hear her father and his guest's voices as they talked below. Her father sounded excited. She looked out her bedroom window at the tree behind her house. The light from the moon came through the clouds, casting a pale blue glow on the leaves. Beyond the stone wall marking the property line was the Sungari River. On the rare clear day, she could see its silver form snaking through the prairie. The old mansion creaked in the wind. The house evoked fond memories from her childhood, but its sheer size felt menacing. She did not like sleeping in a home full of empty bedrooms.

Once she had bumped into her father in the dark on her way to the bathroom. She couldn't see anything. He had grabbed her wrists to steady her. "You're all right," he said. "It's just me." His breath had smelled of alcohol. After they bid each other good night, it had taken an hour for her heart to stop racing. She shivered slightly as she recalled the incident. Before he had appeared at their home in Chiba, she had feared he might be dead. Three years had gone by without a word. He had left them some money, but necessities were scarce. Harumi, who had assumed responsibility for maintaining the house when the cough went deep into her mother's lungs, could not buy underwear or winter coats for the children. She had to stand in line for hours to purchase tofu, ramen, and miso.

No letter, no telegram. Her mother often wondered whether Chinese guerillas had killed Ishii at his house in Nanking. Time passed and the war continued. Then one day a band of soldiers had knocked on their door and handed her sick, frail mother a bamboo spear to defend the household in case of military attack. Her mother stared in astonishment at the long pole in her hands, while her three-year-old son leaped up and down, clamoring for the weapon. The next week, a group of government officials carried the temple bell from the nearby shrine where it had hung for more than one hundred years. They needed the iron.

Harumi remembered her father appearing in the doorway one evening at sundown, wearing his officer's jacket. He was taller than she had remembered. But he somehow looked thinner without his mustache, older perhaps. After speaking quietly to his wife, he had emerged from behind the *shoji* screen where she lay sick and studied Harumi with a strange look in his eye. "You have grown up," he said. Within a week she was on the train with him to Manchukuo. They spoke no more than a few words over the entire length of the journey.

In the icy chill of her bedroom, Harumi thought about her brothers and sisters. She prayed her mother's health would improve. For some reason, she felt guilty for coming with her father. She knew he kept secrets. Nevertheless, she believed he was a great man and would follow him anywhere. She climbed into bed and covered her head with the blankets. A patriotic song from school went through her head. "From now on, I'll put aside my childish thoughts and go the way of the *shishi*, men of high purpose." Those brave young samurai were willing to forego their families to further the revolution. Harumi hoped only she might live up to their example.

The wide-open prairies of Manchukuo led her to imagine that she was, indeed, a part of something grand in the making. On the train, she had seen herds of wild ponies galloping in the wind. She had seen fields of red sorghum stretching to the horizon and acres of wheat under summer clouds. The dark tufted stalks grew as tall as corn. One of the few times her father had spoken to her, he had waved his arm at the land with a flourish and told her that soon it would be home to more than five million of her countrymen.

The first day at school, Harumi had blushed when she stood and introduced herself. She had been even more embarrassed when her classmates burst into applause upon hearing her family name. She was fond of the girls in her class. Like her, they were mostly the daughters of military men, eager to contribute whatever was necessary to the war effort. Many stayed after school to sew buttons on army uniforms.

Her father treated her kindly most of the time. When they had first arrived in the lonely old house, he had asked her what she wanted to eat. In jest, she had told him pound cake, but he soon came home with butter and eggs and sugar, enough to make ten pound cakes. He bought soda and rice candy, items that had virtually disappeared from the stores in Tokyo. He claimed he could get anything, whatever her heart desired.

Harumi had always known her father commanded respect, but she was overwhelmed with pride when he received an award from the emperor for his work in Nanking. It was a breezy day with clouds hovering like cliffs against the piercing blue sky. Her father had stood stiffly on stage in the Harbin town square, the wind buckling the tails of his coat. The emissaries sent by the emperor had traveled hundreds of miles to honor him, and their regal bearing left no doubt to anyone in attendance that the war would be won. Harumi treasured the name of his award: the Third Order of the Golden Kite and the Middle Cord of the Rising Sun. She imagined a kite streaking high enough to touch the sun where it would burn in a flash of light.

* * *

Ishii had made an appearance at Ping Fan on his first day back in Manchukuo. It had felt like a homecoming, complete with a standing ovation when staff had spotted him in his old wood-paneled office overlooking the main laboratory. He had bowed graciously from behind the glass window, then slid it open and clapped his hands. "No time for salutations," he announced. "Just take heart that I have returned. Now get back to work. We have a war to win." He pumped his fist in the air. Masaji Kitano, Ishii's replacement while he was in Nanking, applauded respectfully but wore a bland expression on his face.

Ishii had never liked Kitano, who before taking over the operations at Ping Fan had managed the biological weapons program in Mukden, though he never operated on the prisoners. The scientist lacked Ishii's flair for politics, but he was considered the better researcher. During his tenure at the Army College in Hoten, Kitano had published several well-regarded reports on the effects of anthrax and dysentery on Caucasians. The doctor certainly had his followers, and Ishii had always suspected that it was Kitano who informed the government of his financial indiscretions.

As one of the first orders of business, Ishii reassigned Kitano to work in the rat house—not to manage it, but to work under Ishii's brother, Takeo, who had lost his hand from an infected rat bite. Though Kitano had expanded Ping Fan's human research branch and even wangled new, innovative equipment from the Home Islands, Ishii declared the facility a mess. When his assistants showed him the new chemical precision gauge, an instrument so sensitive it could register the atmospheric pressure of a mosquito's flight across a room, Ishii dismissed it with a wave of his hand. "I ordered that thing months before I left," he said.

He toured the massive compound, taking careful notes. He surveyed the bacteria plant, with its noxious scent of boiling pig fat. He inspected the animal cages and checked the prisoners through a slot in their cell doors. In one cell, a man lay on a bench, having lost both legs to amputations. Open sores covered his face and arms. "Smallpox," Ishii said to himself as he examined the chart. "Are you giving these things enough to eat?" he asked an assistant. "We don't want them dying of starvation."

Within a week, he gathered the factory's upper ranks in his office to discuss a plan of attack. His brothers Takeo and Mitsuo slumped at the table with identical expressions of gloom. Most of the other officers and managers in the room appeared equally despondent. Kitano, however, wore an enigmatic smile as he sat in the corner, away from Ishii's inner circle. "Come now, gentlemen, why the long faces?" Ishii asked with gusto.

"In case you hadn't heard, our country is at war," Takeo said bitterly. "And we appear to be losing."

"Tell me, brother, whatever gave you such a ludicrous idea?" Ishii turned to him with surprise. He paced around the table, occasionally pausing at the window to watch the bacteria-manufacturing machines below. His eyes danced, as he glanced from face to face. Though he had lost weight, his large head still lent him an imposing physical presence.

"The Anglos have retaken Burma…Manila. Without Germany, we fight alone," Takeo said resignedly as he caressed the stump where his hand once was.

"And Russia's rescinded its neutrality pact," added Mitsuo. "It's only a matter of time before the troops come knocking at our door."

"Is that all?" Ishii asked. "Have you little girls finished crying?"

Takeo slapped the table. "You asked us—"

Ishii cut him off. "I asked if you were finished. Now it's my turn." Ishii loftily raised his chin. "Gentlemen, we don't have time to sit around whimpering about what's gone wrong. You seem to have forgotten that we have at our fingertips the most powerful weapon known to man. And I assure you, we will use it to smite the white race before this war is over." A dried grain of rice from lunch clung to Ishii's cheek, but no one at the table dared point it out. He shot a glance at Kitano, who continued to display a bemused expression. "We are not bureaucrats filling our journals with research that no one will read. No, we are soldiers! Willing to die, willing to kill!"

He pointed to Mitsuo. "Brother, you mentioned Russia. I want you to send a team to plant rats along the border. When the Russian troops arrive, I want my lovelies to be waiting. I want them in Voroshilov, in Chita Blagoveshchensk, and in Khabarovsk. Especially in Khabarovsk. I despise that vile city."

He turned to his other brother. "Takeo, we need rats. I want you to contact headquarters and request that every brigade set traps. Figure out how much food it takes to feed three million of them. I want you all to begin breeding animals—rabbits and gerbils, anything that carries fleas."

He was rolling now, striding around the room with authority. "Gentlemen, we need fleas. How many are we producing right now, Tanaka?" The man was caught by surprise and paused to do the addition. "Come now, we don't have all day," Ishii barked at him.

"We're breeding about seventy-five million fleas a week," Tanaka said as he counted off his fingers. "That's with approximately four thousand breeding machines."

"What if I got you a thousand more machines and another fifty staff?"

Tanaka struggled to keep up. "Then I suppose we might reach one hundred million insects a week, maybe every few days."

"I want three hundred kilograms of fleas by September," Ishii commanded. "That's approximately one billion fleas, is it not, Major?"

"Yes, sir."

Ishii pivoted to address the group as a whole. The grain of rice had fallen off his cheek. "I expect our opportunity to present itself by the end of the summer, assuming the Americans ever land in our beloved country. We have six months to prepare for my grand plan."

He paused for effect. "I call it Cherry Blossoms at Night. We will send a team of kamikaze pilots in a submarine to the west coast of America. From their planes, carried on board, the pilots will release a massive cloud of fleas over a large city called San Diego." He looked around the room with confidence.

The men sat silently. "The planes will travel by submarine?" Mitsuo asked timorously.

"Yes," Ishii answered. "I've seen the designs. The wings enfold like a baby bird."

The room fell silent again, until a peal of laughter came from the corner. "Cherry Blossoms at Night?" Kitano asked when he caught his breath. "That's so poetic."

Ishii grabbed the handle of the sword on his belt, ready to cut off Kitano's head. Before he lunged, however, he remembered that killing him would likely bring swift retribution from the officer's allies. Brute justice was the rule in the northern hinterlands. He yanked the stubby man to his feet by the collar. "Do you have a question about my plan, General?"

Kitano tilted his bullet-shaped head back to meet Ishii's gaze. "Why would the Japanese Navy waste its precious submarines on such a scheme when the craft are desperately needed to defend the Home Islands?"

"The submarines would be back before they were needed," Ishii responded, then stopped himself from engaging any further in an argument. "Get out!" he shouted and shoved Kitano toward the door. Kitano laughed again as he made his way down the hall. Ishii, his face flushed, turned back to the men. "Now, where was I? Ah yes, San Diego," he said as if Kitano's insurrection had been a negligible interruption that he'd already forgotten. "San Diego is a major metropolitan city, a center of industry, an ideal target."

* * *

Harumi had wanted desperately to volunteer for the paper balloon project. The work was done in an abandoned school on the edge of Harbin, which was quite a distance to travel on foot, but she didn't mind. With her father's permission, she went there with two friends after classes one day, marching in formation, which made them laugh. Harumi was a head taller than the other girls. She had found a razor in her big empty house and convinced her friends to cut their fingers and scrawl "shishi" in blood on white headbands, which they now wore self-consciously.

The brisk afternoon wind blowing in their faces smelled of fresh grass. Tiny green leaves were unfolding, wrinkled and moist, from a long hibernation. Winter held on so long in Manchukuo, the first taste of spring tasted like sugar on the tongue. As they walked, the girls giggled for no apparent reason—everything seemed funny.

Leaving the familiar neighborhood, crossing the viaduct, and strolling through the Russian-styled shopping area, with its bright signs emblazoned in Cyrillic characters, they beheld a section of the city they had never seen before: an area on the outskirts, filled with cardboard huts and broken-down shacks. The paved road dissolved into a muddy wallow. Naked toddlers stared at the girls as they passed. Brown little creatures with light freckles and shaggy hair. Harumi and her friends lowered their voices to a whisper.

"Don't speak to them," said Tetsuko, whose father had made millions as a military supplier. "You can't trust the coolies. They hate us."

A dog ran by with a ragged stuffed doll in its mouth.

"They're related to monkeys, my father told me," added Yoshie. She lived with her mother in a modest home near the Chinese quarter of Harbin. The two had subsisted on a military pension ever since the girl's father had fallen into the blades of an airplane propeller.

The balloon factory came as a welcome sight. The workers had spread wooden platforms across the yard to serve as drying boards. Old women were gluing sheets of rice paper together with a light blue paste. A handsome man in a black jumpsuit appeared and showed the girls how to fold and glue the thin parchment. "The paste comes from potato plant, but don't eat it," he warned. They giggled at the suggestion. He checked their hands, then their ankles. "Where are your socks?" he asked Yoshie.

"I don't wear them," she said haughtily. The girl was particular about her appearance.

"You must always wear socks," the man said. "We don't want the hair on your legs puncturing our balloons."

The girls stole sidelong glances at each other and tittered in embarrassment. They could not believe the man was speaking so openly about Yoshie's legs.

"No hairpins or jewelry either," he said as he counted off the rules on his fingers, "and don't forget to keep your nails short." He led them across the playground. A tall ginkgo tree dominated the yard. Its triangular leaves fluttered in the wind. They entered the school's dark, yawning auditorium.

A machine blasted steam in a regular cadence, sprinkling water droplets on the girls' faces. "This is where we make sure the balloons are airtight," the man said with a flourish of his arm. In the dim light, Harumi made out the dark shape of a balloon bobbing against the high ceiling. The sight astounded her. It was amazing to see something so massive, yet so light. She was thrilled to be part of it all.

* * *

In late spring, Ishii flew to Hsingking, the capital of Manchukuo, to enjoy a taste of female companionship. He took the plane reserved for medical emergencies; the red cross on the side of the fuselage prevented an attack. The general knew how to fly, but he was no fighter pilot. Above the rippling clouds, the general often found moments of peace, but today, the echoes of Kitano's laughter rang in his head. He wished the plane were equipped with machine guns just so he could pull the trigger and feel the power of bullets spraying the air.

Ishii kept a limousine parked outside the airport in Hsingking, and retained cars in all the cities where he had set up satellite water purification units: Canton, Saigon, Rangoon, Mandalay, Bangkok, and Bandung. He had spent hundreds of thousands of yen on the vehicles, taking them as write-offs in the expansion of his operation, but they actually served as transportation to the local brothels. He knew all the madams by name, having met many of them when they were still virgins, for that was still the only class of woman he would accept as a playmate in bed. Ishii was willing to pay huge sums for such girls, more than the entire house might earn in a year. Most of the money went to the madam, but he always made sure to take care of the girl as well. If he liked her, he sometimes tipped enough for her to start her own shop, where someday in the future he could purchase another fresh young girl. It was an investment of sorts. "Bring me a child of beauty," he would call to the madam as he entered the bar. "No need for a granny."

The younger the better, but only up to a point; they had to have hair on their genitals, for the delta was a deep obsession of his. He loved to run his fingers through a girl's black patch, which he would nuzzle, excited by the suggestion of the crevice it protected. Of all the houses in China, he liked the one in Hsingking the best. It did not look like much from the outside—a shabby little storefront nestled in a cluster of print shops and laundries. Curtains covered the windows, and there was no name on the door. But the façade belied the sumptuous luxury of the interior. Pink Italian granite covered the floors; gold embroidered silk lined the walls. Ishii's largesse, at the expense of the Japanese government, had funded a secret palace in the burgeoning city.

"Commander Ishii," said a young woman with long dark hair, high cheekbones, and a delicate complexion. She had only just turned twenty-one, but for Ishii she was ruined. "You should have called. I don't believe I have anyone in the house right now to suit your tastes."

"I suggest you find someone," the general said as he sank into a velvet-cushioned chair. "In the meantime, bring me some brandy." The woman brought him a tray with a bottle and a small stack of dried fish cakes. "These smell familiar," he said and winked at the woman. He poured himself a shot and tossed it back. The liquid burned his tongue. He was still smarting from Kitano's derision.

From behind a satin curtain, the madam emerged with a very young girl on her arm. "Commander," she said, and guided the adolescent into the officer's line of sight. "You are in luck. This apple blossom just arrived yesterday from a village in the mountains. I believe she will be to your liking."

The madam led them to a large room with a window overlooking a bamboo grove filled with chirping blackbirds. "Be gentle," she told Ishii as she slipped out the door.

Ishii sat in the frame of the open window. A warm breeze filled the room with the scent of gardenias. "Remove your clothes," Ishii told the girl kindly.

She did not speak Japanese and appeared confused by Ishii's request. He beckoned her with his hand, and with a lightning-quick motion, he ripped open her robe. The girl burst into tears as she tried to cover herself with her hands. Without a moment's hesitation, Ishii stuck his fingers inside her, searching for her hymen. Finding nothing, he slapped the girl in the face, and roared for the madam, who came quickly. Ishii held the girl by the arm as he might handle a plucked squab. "This is no virgin," he said. "The gate to heaven has already been breached. I felt it with my own fingers."

"She is a farm girl, Commander," the madam pleaded. "She has performed physical labor, but, I assure you, she has never known a man." Ishii sighed as he appraised the girl again. "She is all we have," said the madam.

"I won't give you more than one hundred yen for her."

"She is yours, Commander, at no cost," the madam said with an ingratiating smile. She pinched the girl's cheek. "Isn't she pretty? Now be nice."

Ishii fell back on the bed in a huff. Slowly, the girl began to drop the clothes still hanging from her body. At least she was young, fourteen, maybe fifteen years old. Younger even than Harumi. She was shy. Ishii liked that. Her breasts were tiny and pale, with little pink buds for nipples. And that lovely cleft. The hair stood on end as if an electric current ran through her veins. Ishii shut the blinds, then pulled the girl to the bed. He knelt over her pelvis and lightly caressed the follicles with his cheek. His breathing grew labored. Then quickly, he pinched a tuft of the hair between his thumb and finger and plucked it from her flesh. The girl shrieked in pain. In an instant it was over. Swollen drops of sweat fell from the general's brow onto the girl's naked belly. Outside, the birds chattered and trilled in the bamboo grove.

* * *

During the long summer months, when the light lingered on the horizon past midnight and the iridescent colors of the northern lights crackled across the sky, Harumi spent many hours alone. Her father had suddenly changed his mind and now forbade her to work on the balloon project, saying that she needed to work at Ping Fan. At his request, she helped take care of the staff's children living at the complex and tended to the rabbits raised by the hundreds in cages behind the chapel. As the general's daughter, others always treated her with the utmost respect, but for some reason her position never won her entrance into the research area.

When she was not at Ping Fan, she whiled away the time at home, often listening to the radio for news about the war.

The reports of gallant victories on land and sea always lifted her spirits, and she wondered when the Americans would finally surrender.

Harumi spent time outdoors, too, basking in the sun. The garden was lush with wild vines tumbling over the crumbled stonework like an invading army. She sat there reading a book she found on her father's shelves called *The Heart of Things*.

Written just after Emperor Meiji died in 1912, the novel was a tribute to an era when men, like the suicide pilots of this war, held the sanctity of the imperial throne above all else. One of the anecdotes concerned General Nogi, a majestic war hero who killed himself as the imperial cannon announced the death of the emperor. As a young officer, many years earlier, Nogi had lost his company's flag to the enemy, but he did not commit suicide then. He waited thirty-five years before performing the sacred ritual of *junshi*, and then followed his lord to the grave. The sacrifice inspired Harumi. She believed she knew a bit about guilt and secrets, and following a heroic figure to the end.

Her father was hardly ever at home; sometimes he was gone for days at a time. Harumi never knew where he went, and when she asked for him at the compound, the staff was equally at a loss. He was a very busy man. On rare occasions, she accompanied him on balloon launchings. The men would release four or five at a time from beneath a wide net. The inflatables always floated quickly into the air, heading east. Harumi tried to keep her eyes on them for as long as she could, until they became tiny dots in the sky. One evening, she asked her father what purpose they served.

"For now, we use them to chart the winds of the Pacific, but soon they will drop deadly weapons on America," he said. "In due time, our country will discover that they represent the key to victory in this war."

"How?"

"Because they don't require pilots," he scoffed, as if the answer were obvious. "No need for sacrifice."

"But isn't that the point? Dying to bring honor to our country? I can't imagine anything more beautiful."

Her father looked at her strangely, as if he were noticing his daughter for the first time. A serious expression crossed his face. "Don't talk like that."

"But wouldn't you be proud if I were to join the pilots of the Divine Wind?"

"No, I would not," he said quickly.

His answer surprised her. "But General Nogi—"

"Oh, forget General Nogi!" He was angry now. "General Nogi is a fairy tale."

"I don't understand," she said. A brisk wind had kicked up. In the distance, the sun was setting below a mass of clouds as dark as a battleship. The balloon crew was walking back toward the base.

"I would much rather you live a long and prosperous life than diving into a destroyer," he snapped.

Her father's words frightened her. They contradicted everything she had learned in school. "I'm confused," she said.

His face glowed in the light of the setting sun. "I suppose these are things for a father to understand."

* * *

Chapter 9

Harbin, Manchuria

August 1945

Harumi first sensed something was amiss when she noticed the servants conferring in the kitchen. The moment she entered, they scattered like rabbits. She turned on the radio to listen for breaking news, but all she found was classical music. Then she retired to the covered porch just outside the kitchen door, where she could hear the music and read. The August morning was warm. The potato vines, washing over the trellis, were in bloom with their intense yellow centers and explosion of white petals. She flipped open a book her civics teacher had suggested she read over the summer called *An Outline for the Reconstruction of Japan*, but she found the language dry and dated. A discussion of economic reforms was the last thing she wanted to read on a balmy summer day.

She closed her eyes, but just as she was dozing off, a message interrupted the broadcast. "Hiroshima suffered considerable damage as the result of an attack by a lone B-29. It is believed that a new type of bomb was involved. The details are being investigated." The newscast went on to say that a massive force of Soviet troops had gathered at the northern border of Manchukuo and that Japanese civilians should evacuate immediately.

Harumi jumped to her feet. Of all the times for her father to disappear! She knew there was no way to reach him, wherever he was. She paced about the kitchen. Suddenly, it became very important for her to make sure her friends at the balloon factory were safe. She needed to talk to someone. As she trotted down the street lined with majestic brick houses, she saw families loading their cars with personal belongings. "Go home, little girl," a man shouted at her. "The streets are not safe."

Harumi continued her journey despite the warning. The shops downtown bustled with activity: customers carrying large boxes of supplies, Chinese merchants nailing boards across their windows. On the outer edge of the retail district, however, where the shantytown began, the streets grew quiet again. The Mongolians lounged in the sun or poked at the garbage in their yards with sticks. Here no one seemed to be going anywhere.

The balloon factory also appeared unaffected by the news. The old women were still pasting sheets of paper outside in the playground. They were thin and haggard, their faces smeared with dried goop. Harumi noticed one woman scooping a dollop of paste into her mouth. Her smock hung loosely from her shoulders. Someone had cut down the mighty ginkgo tree that had adorned the courtyard.

The auditorium was dark when she poked her head inside the wide door. She could see faint silhouettes running back and forth like crabs. The blasts of the steam machine were deafening. Drops of water fell from the ceiling, creating a slippery surface on the floor. As she tiptoed farther inside, Harumi called for her friends. "Yoshie?" she cried. "Tetsuko?"

"Harumi?" someone called. "Is that you?" Someone approached from the shadows. It was Michiko. Harumi recognized her from school. "Do you have anything to eat?" the girl asked. She clutched Harumi's sleeve.

"Where are Yoshie and Tetsuko?"

"They are here somewhere," Michiko said. "I will find them for you." Soon Michiko returned with the girls and they cried in each other's arms.

"Take us with you," Yoshie pleaded. "We're starving and they won't let us sleep."

"There's no more paste," added Tetsuko. "The girls have eaten it all."

Harumi felt a rough hand on her back. "Get back to work," a man's voice said. "If you don't make your quota, you won't eat."

"The Russians are coming," Harumi told him. "They said we must leave."

"Oh, no you don't," the man said. "Get back to work!"

Harumi bolted for the door. The three girls shrieked and followed her. The foreman did not chase them. As they ran home, Harumi's friends squinted in the light. They were covered with dried paste. It was in their hair and smeared across their faces. Their ribs showed through their blouses. Their bare feet were caked with mud. "What happened to you?" Harumi asked.

Yoshie and Tetsuko were having so much difficulty walking—between the blinding light and their raw feet and the panic of escape—they could hardly speak. "It was awful," said Yoshie, whose pretty cheeks were hollowed thin. "They were so mean."

"They gave us pills to make us work longer," Tetsuko said.

The peasants, loitering in the doors of their hovels, watched the three pass.

"Who made you stay?" Harumi asked.

"The foreman," they answered in unison.

"My parents came to take me home, but the foreman sent them away," Michiko said between sobs. "He told them he was acting on orders from the army."

"It was your father," Tetsuko said accusingly to Harumi. "The orders came from him. I heard the man say so. He said we had to stay upon the orders of Lieutenant General Ishii Shiro. I heard it with my own ears."

Though the accusations were painful to hear, Harumi believed every word. It was becoming increasingly clear that her father was not the honorable man she had believed him to be.

* * *

Ishii received word of the bomb just after he returned to Ping Fan from his three-day bender in Hsingking. The radio announced that more than a million and a half Soviet troops were pouring into northern Manchukuo, armed with nearly six thousand tanks and five thousand airplanes. It was only a matter of days before they would reach Harbin. Ishii listened to the news with an aching head. He knew it was time to pack up and go, but for the moment, his hangover rendered him immobile. Through his office window overlooking the factory floor, he watched the scientists scurrying like ants sprayed with vinegar. He was utterly depressed. There was no choice but to begin the destruction of his magnificent compound.

He told his top commander to exterminate the prisoners at the compound. His brothers appeared in his office ten minutes later with sweaty, panic-stricken faces. Ishii told Mitsuo to start packing the laboratory's research material; Takeo should release the rats into the wild.

"Are you crazy? What if someone gets bitten?"

"Just do it!" Ishii hollered with a dazed look. "When you're finished, collect all the dynamite you can find."

Takeo bowed and left the room. Ishii staggered down to the prison where the prisoners were kept. The guards had thrown flasks full of toxic chemicals into the cells. The sound of machine gun fire stuttered through the labyrinthine halls. "The guards are finishing them off," an officer explained.

"Burn them," Ishii instructed. "I want no trace left when you're finished." His head thumped painfully when he walked. His penis felt raw, chafed from its long hours of hard work. He suddenly remembered Harumi. He would have to return home immediately to make sure she was safe.

The lights were ablaze in all the rooms of the house. His daughter was packing her things. Tears welled in her eyes when she saw him.

"I came to tell you we have to leave, but I see you've anticipated that," Ishii said. "Tomorrow a train will take the staff and the families home. They'll take care of you." He reached to touch the back of his daughter's neck, but she recoiled as if his hand were an eel.

* * *

At Ping Fan, Ishii's top officer was unable to burn the prisoners' bodies completely, even after they had been doused with gasoline. The bones and iron manacles resisted the flames. The collection of organ samples, soaked with formaldehyde, had proven difficult to destroy as well. In the end, the staff had dumped organs, bones, manacles, and ashes in the Sungari River.

Ishii nodded in approval.

Ping Fan itself proved almost indestructible. Almost three days of repeated detonations were required to demolish the main buildings. Finally, the men loaded the fleet of Dodge trucks with fifty-kilogram bombs and sent them into the concrete blocks with bricks bearing down on the gas pedals. As night fell, Ishii gathered his inner circle around a campfire off the base. His face was blackened from the dirty work. A second bomb had fallen on the Home Island, he told them, this time on Nagasaki. He dispensed potassium cyanide pills in case the Soviets captured anyone. Together the scientists and army officers sang the Kwantung Army song as the fire crackled and spat sparks into the night.

"I want to thank every one of you for the work you've done," Ishii said. "As some of you will remember, I, myself, built this facility nearly ten years ago. And I have no regrets. We did great things here—" As he spoke, a thunderclap resounded behind him, and a large section of the laboratory crumbled to the ground. The general looked back for a moment, then solemnly turned to face his men. "As your commander, I want you to make a solemn oath. Upon your return, you will forever live a life in the shadows, and never utter word about your time here."

* * *

Harumi boarded the freight train with her friend Yoshie and the girl's mother. Yoshie was doubled over in pain with a sharp ache in her belly. No matter how her mother tried to console her, she would not stop whimpering. They were lucky to find seats on the floor of the boxcar. Most of the women and children fleeing Manchukuo had to stand. Many of the men, desperate to escape, clung to the exterior.

As the train rattled down the track, Harumi held her friend, who kept vomiting. The ride through China took days. The train made few stops. When they passed through villages, the peasants spat into the open cars. Some threw rocks, which clanged against the cars.

In Korea, the train paused to refuel, and villagers approached, offering jugs of water. The Japanese passengers refused them, believing they might be poisoned. Yoshie fled to a ditch running parallel to the tracks. She came back moaning and holding her stomach, looking as weathered as an old woman. "I lost it," she whispered to Harumi as she returned to her place on board. "I lost it."

"You lost what?"

Yoshie broke into tears again. "I was pregnant."

"Where did it come from?" Harumi asked.

"The man," Yoshie said quietly as she struggled to catch her breath. "The man at the factory raped me."

* * *

A broad military transport ship slipped through the fog shrouding Yokohama Bay early one morning in mid-August. It was an unscheduled berth, which drew the attention of the customs officer on duty. When the inspector approached the ship to inquire about its cargo, a crew member threw down a solid gold ingot and told him to go away. The piece of metal felt heavy in his hand, heavy enough for him to oblige. What did he care anyway? The war was over and they were all going to hell.

Ishii smiled as he watched the officer return to his little shack on the pier. He ordered his brothers to lower the ship's motorboat and load it with three crates of documents—his entire life's work. He instructed the crew to convey the rest of his belongings to the train station and told them he would meet them at the Kanazawa shrine.

The three brothers piloted the little boat into the foggy bay, turning north to follow the rocky shore. A thick forest of black pines drenched the hills in a deep shade of green. Dozens of wrecked ships crowded the bay. The brothers had to pay close attention to avoid becoming entangled with the twisted metal. They docked in a grotto marked by a mighty pine, and carefully hoisted the crates onto the rocks. Ishii surveyed the cliffs riddled with caves.

"It hasn't changed a bit," he said as he strode toward a deep cavity in the rock. The family had often spent time on this shore when the boys were children. "Let's try this one." The cave was dark inside. The walls whispered with the gentle sound of the surf. They hiked until they could go no farther and the white circle of the entrance was no longer visible. "Leave the crates here," Ishii said. "Off the floor if you can. We don't want them getting wet."

When they made their way to the shrine that afternoon, they found all but two members of the crew snoring on the floor. The two who were awake were listening intently to a squeaky voice reading a speech on the radio:

"Despite the best that has been done by everyone—the gallant fighting of military and naval forces, the diligence and assiduity of our servants of the State, and the devoted service of our one hundred million people, the war has developed not necessarily to Japan's advantage."

"Who is this idiot?" asked Ishii angrily.

His men shushed him with round eyes. "It's the emperor."

Ishii felt the hair on his arms stand on end.

"Should we continue to fight, it would not only result in the ultimate collapse and obliteration of the Japanese nation, but also it would lead to the total extinction of human civilization."

"This is a hoax," blurted Ishii. "It has to be a joke."

"Shhh," the men hissed.

"We are keenly aware of the inmost feelings of all our subjects. However, it is according to the dictate of time and fate that we have resolved to pave the way for a grand peace for the generations to come by enduring the unendurable and suffering what is insufferable."

Ishii sputtered in disbelief. "I'm calling the War Ministry before I believe a word of it."

No one else spoke. Takeo and Mitsuo curled up on the floor and went to sleep. It was the first time most of the men had heard the emperor's voice—this was his first public speech. The country had surrendered.

* * *

Chapter 10

Mukden Prison Camp

August 1945

The sound, a deep rumbling above the clouds, made Jake shudder. The last time he had heard it, all hell had broken loose. An armada of bombers, airplanes larger than he had ever seen, had pounded the factory and prison complex with devastating loads. Evidently, the pilots were unaware that their own men worked inside the building below. The raid had killed nineteen prisoners and bloodied another fifty. Guards and prisoners had jumped into the trenches together, companions for a terrifying hour.

Jake was pretty sure the sound indicated only one plane now, but Jake moved toward the shelter of the factory, just to be safe. A few other men huddled along the wall, pointing at the horizon. Klute, a gunner from Santa Fe who had claimed Whitaker's bunk was there, sitting with Conrad and Sproul, two pilots Jake didn't know very well. "Ain't they pretty," he heard Klute say.

"Look for a white one," said Conrad, an old veteran of the air corps. "The colored ones carry supplies, the whites are for personnel." That's when Jake noticed two parachutes, one red, one orange, descending slowly, stark against the slate-gray sky. Then, sure enough, a white one popped open, then another and another, until five came falling like popcorn kernels on the wind. "What'd I tell you?" Conrad said. "Hot damn."

They watched in awe, and not a little hope, as the aerials dropped out of sight far beyond the wall. "Maybe the Russians are finally making a move," Klute offered.

But Conrad had changed his mind. "Naw, I bet it ain't nothing but Jap maneuvers."

"Maybe they're our own," Jake said optimistically. "Come to spring us loose."

The others vetoed the idea as they returned to work, afraid to allow themselves to entertain the notion. They had spent three years here in Hoten, as prisoners at the machine factory, and for all they knew, they might work another three before the war ended. Jake had spent a year of that time in bed with dysentery. The Black Bastard would test the prisoners' health by making them run a lap around the yard. If they made it without messing their pants, he deemed them healthy enough to work. It was only in the last few months that Jake could successfully meet the challenge, and even now, he often felt weak. He would have died without the help of Leo, who had sprinkled a pinch of ground chalk, dug from the foundation of the barracks, into his corn soup every day. The dust helped soak up the liquid from the bowels. Naito and the other doctors in the infirmary had given up on him, though they continued to take stool samples.

He didn't trust the doctors, but he could thank the guards for allowing him to recover in peace. Recently some had become rough again. The war was turning against them, judging by the Japanese newspapers discarded at the factory, which Yoshio Kai, the factory foreman, amiably agreed to translate. The papers always reported tremendous naval victories, but the battles were drawing closer: first Guadalcanal, then the Philippines, then Formosa.

Rumors about the parachutes circulated through the barracks that night. Then reveille came as early as usual the next morning, but the guards did not show up to lead everyone to the factory. The men gathered around, awaiting news. If something didn't happen soon, they felt they would either explode or die of broken hearts. No one could sit still. Jake was one of the first to spot a small party of men in clean green uniforms approaching the office of the commandant. A redheaded lieutenant and another man went in, while a couple of others waited. When one of them lit a cigarette, Jake howled with delight. Smoking in front of the camp headquarters—or anywhere—without an ashtray was punishable by ten days in solitary confinement. Yet here were these guys puffing away with impunity. Jake whooped again, setting off a chorus of hoots and whistles throughout the barracks. Soon the redheaded officer strode from the office into the yard, where he shouted to the prisoners. "Hey, fellas, the war's over. You're free!"

A hush fell over the camp. The men now hovered near the doors of the barracks like wild animals, sniffing the air for danger. Silently, they assembled in the yard, until they surrounded the redheaded man. Finally, someone spoke up. "Say, who won the World Series in forty-two?" and with that, bedlam reigned.

With a wide smile, Leo watched the men crowd around the two officers. Crouched on the barracks steps, he basked in the sun, warming his cheeks and forehead. Freedom. The word soothed him, and he could feel something loosening inside. It dawned on him that he might never have to eat corn soup again—that he might actually see his family and begin his life anew. More than anything, he looked forward to making peace with his father. He imagined coming home lean in body and spirit, his own man.

Joy rang out all that morning. After raiding the commandant's quarters, Red Cross food packages and mail were distributed. Leo received another batch of letters, which he immediately tucked under his arm and took to his bunk. While many of the others went wild, gorging themselves on the foodstuffs they'd found, he spent most of the day reading. Papa had purchased a large swath of land to the north; Mama had fought a long bout with pneumonia; Angelina and her husband had moved to their own house with the new baby—the details fairly glowed on the page.

A steady stream of food began to descend on the camp over the next few days. Supply planes came flying overhead at low altitudes, and fifty-five-gallon drums began to fall from the sky. One broke an officer's leg. A big double-barreled load crashed through the roof of one of the barracks and burst on impact, sending thousands of sticks of spearmint gum across the floor on a tide of orange marmalade. The men lapped it all up like puppy dogs.

Though Leo ate ravenously—Spam, corned beef, fruit cocktail—he couldn't consume much at one sitting. Lack of food had shrunk his stomach. Some of the men, having served themselves too much chow, sat before their plates for hours, waiting until they were hungry enough to eat more. No one wanted to waste anything. At one of these meals, Larsen unexpectedly joined Leo for dinner. The mess sergeant ordinarily ate alone—few of the men spoke to him anymore—but he had shared the work at the infirmary with Leo, which apparently gave him license to share a table. Leo was too softhearted to reject the overture, despite his hatred for the man. "I can't wait to get out of this shit hole," Larsen said. He moodily looked around the mess hall, then began shoveling into a half-eaten bowl of custard.

"I heard Naito slipped away yesterday," Leo offered guardedly, though he no longer had anything to fear. The rescuers had rounded up the guards and doctors in a barracks hall to be turned over to authorities. "Someone said he's on the lam."

Larsen brooded over his bowl. "He can go to hell for all I care."

A record player was discovered and someone hooked it up to a loudspeaker for everyone to hear "Sentimental Journey" over and over again. That night, beneath a bright gibbous moon, Jake and Leo climbed on the roof of the barracks. From their perch, they could see the Manchurian plain stretching for miles to the dark, low-slung mountains, not unlike the Sandias in their heft and build. "I told you we'd make it," Jake said and blew the foam from a freshly opened beer.

"Yeah, well, I still don't know if I believe you," Leo said, only half joking. Something prevented him from being as excited as the others, from completely allowing himself to enjoy the moment. He wouldn't fully exhale until he stepped on American soil.

"What the hell's the matter? You've been about as cheerful as a wet smack since they let us go."

"I'm happy," Leo protested, then sighed. "I'd just like to think we'll return better than we were before. That somehow we learned something from this experience. No regrets, right? Isn't that how it's supposed to be? But then I see in the mirror and laugh. I mean look at us, Jake. We're a mess. And I can just hear my father now, saying he told me so."

"Fuck him," Jake said. "You've survived a trip through hell—are you really worried about what your father thinks?"

Leo chuckled, embarrassed and a little relieved. "I won't take any guff, that's for sure. I don't see myself staying in Albuquerque any longer than it takes to get into college anyway."

Jake furrowed his brow, surprised. "Where the hell are you going?"

Leo shrugged. "As far away as possible."

"Ah, now you're talking nonsense," Jake said, waving him off. "You and I are sticking together."

Leo watched the stars, searching out the constellations for the first time in ages. He wanted to start fresh, to be free of the prison camp and the shame and guilt he felt for the awful things he had seen. But he sensed the entanglements of friendship and family wouldn't make it easy, and this ambivalence evoked a different kind of guilt. "No point in making plans until we get out of here."

* * *

One morning, after a night of carousing in Mukden, a group of the men came back riding on the back of a huge bull. The animal belonged to a villager who had used it every summer to cart away the human waste accumulated in the pit below the latrines. The men had run into the owner in town and either bought the beast or simply taken it. Even the weakest prisoners came out to see the grand homecoming, the men riding high on the bull's mighty shoulders. The thing could have pulled an oak from the ground.

A crate of Jack Daniels had found its way into camp, a gift from the skies, and Jake was swigging from his own personal bottle. The liquor burned his insides, yet he continued to drink, as if the alcohol would wash out the filthy taste in his mouth. He too wanted to forget it all and start anew. His legs felt heavy as he followed the crowd into the yard.

No one knew how to kill the bull. They tried hammering the animal over the head with a two-by-four, but the beast merely groaned and remained standing. The lowing attracted an even larger crowd. They tried shooting it, but the bullets bounced off the skull. Finally, someone retrieved a carving knife from the kitchen, and slit the thick veins of the neck. Everyone watched the bull bleed to death on its knees. Then they took to it with hatchets until large hunks of flesh lay strewn about and the earth was soaked with blood. They roasted the pieces all day, laying the meat straight on a pit of smoldering wood chips.

By dinner, the whiskey was nearly gone. Many of the men went bare-chested in the warm evening air, soot smeared across their sweaty faces. The talk had turned mean in the yard. A fight broke out over some trivial matter. It began when a hearty punch to the arm was returned with an alarming blow to the head. The two men rolled around in the dirt for a while before they gave up, exhausted. A man lay near the barbecue pit, passed out. No one dragged him back to the infirmary, even though everyone knew he was still suffering from dysentery. It served him right, they figured. Shouldn't have been drinking in the first place. Drunk and hungry, the men ripped at the grisly bull flesh with their hands. The meat, still red in the middle, tasted like burned rubber bands, but nobody cared. Once the beef was gone, they piled tables and benches, even mattresses, into the pit to fuel a bonfire.

"Hey, the Japs have got to eat, don't they?" Klute hollered.

"Let's feed them corn mush," Jake said with a loud laugh. He took another pull from the bottle, and felt the urge to vomit. He'd already puked once, into the coals.

"I got a better idea," Klute said. He tied a large hook, taken from the factory, to a rope cut down from the flagpole. He tossed the rigging over a horizontal bar extending from the roof of one of the barracks. "Bring me one of them legs," he said. Someone dragged over a massive haunch, still sputtering from the embers. "Now go get them Japs," he said.

Soon a handful of Japanese came stumbling into the firelight, their hands cuffed behind their backs. They were terrified. Many looked as if they had been severely beaten. Klute pulled on the rope so that the meat dangled just over their heads. A huge group had gathered for the spectacle, even Larsen, whom Jake saw hovering at the edges, a nervous smile on his lips. The mere sight of the man was sickening. Jake hated him more than the Japanese. "Now, go on, eat!" Klute shouted at the prisoners cowering within the circle, but they still didn't know what was expected of them.

Klute lowered the meat to eye level, and someone shoved it in a prisoner's face. "Go on, take a bite!" the guy said. Craning his neck, the Japanese man tried nibbling at the hunk of blackened flesh. Soon the others followed his lead. It wasn't easy, especially without the use of their hands. Klute yanked up on the rope, and everyone roared, then dropped it down again, allowing it to bounce this way and that among the captives, who tore at the meat as if their lives depended upon it. Grease covered their faces.

As the novelty of the game was beginning to fade, Jake snuck behind Larsen and pushed him into the circle. "I know you're hungry, Larsen. You always are. So eat!"

Larsen laughed, embarrassed, and tried to slip back into the crowd, but the men wouldn't let him escape so easily. "Go on, join your friends!"

Jostled by the Japanese prisoners in the ring, Larsen recoiled, then appealed to comrades. "C'mon, guys," he said. "Enough already."

The circle opened slightly, but Jake collared him and shoved him back. "Take a bite, Larsen. You ain't getting out of there until you do."

Larsen searched in vain for an ally in the crowd. Someone swung the slab at him, nearly bowling him over. Angrily, he grabbed the mass and held on as it rose, lifting him off his feet.

* * *

A couple of days later, the men finally gathered the few things they had and boarded a train bound for the port city of

Dairen, about two hundred miles south of Mukden. Jake took nothing but the clothes on his back. Leo, on the other hand, packed a bounty of a souvenirs: silk kimonos discovered in the guardhouse, a stethoscope from the infirmary, a Japanese teakettle.

After debriefing, Leo received approval to continue the journey home, but Jake failed his physical and was transferred for treatment at a hospital in Osaka, where there was nothing to do except fill out mountains of forms. Among the papers was an order forbidding him, under threat of court martial, to discuss his experiences as a prisoner of war.

"What the hell is this?" Jake asked the doctor.

"It's routine," said the doctor, who had obviously never seen a day of combat. "The army wants to make sure you go through the proper channels before you divulge classified information."

"Classified? What part of my experience as a prisoner of war is classified?"

"That's for the army to decide, now isn't it?" the doctor said. He had a trim goatee and a habit of rattling his pen between his teeth.

"You mean the fact that we were stuck on Bataan for three months eating monkey guts to survive? Is that what you consider classified? Or that MacArthur abandoned us there to die?" Jake tried to tell him about the prison camp, but the doctor cut him short. "I'm not interested in your war stories, son. You and I both know a man can't survive working twelve hours a day on nothing but a bowl of soup."

"I don't want to hear any war stories either," Jake said angrily. "I have my own. But you'd better watch what you say, calling guys like me liars. I've survived three years scratching in the dirt for a bite to eat. Call me a liar again, and I'll shove that pencil down your throat."

The doctor opened his mouth, aghast. "I could have you court-martialed for speaking that way to an officer."

Jake cackled bitterly. "How could you possibly make me suffer any worse than I already have?"

He signed the waiver form, crumpled it into a ball, and bounced it off the doctor's chest. Dissent would only prolong his seemingly interminable incarceration. He knew the game—he had learned it as a kid. It was better to move on. Let go. He was so tired of fighting.

* * *

Jake yawned and stretched as he stepped off the bus at the Albuquerque station. Every muscle in his body ached. He had spent the entire ride drinking sour coffee mixed with brandy until he thought his bladder might burst. Anything to stay awake. He'd started having nightmares, always back in the hole with the two Japanese soldiers.

Rather than putting him on a train with the returning veterans, the military had stuck the former prisoners on an old Greyhound with the windows blacked out. As soon as Jake saw the bus, a ramshackle relic from the Hoover administration, he finally admitted the unspeakable truth: the army was ashamed of him. Hence the request to sign the disclosure form, and now the shades over the windows, preventing him from even enjoying the view of the passing countryside upon his return home. Evidently, the army deemed them unfit for public consumption, with their pencil necks and hollowed cheeks. It would only spoil the victory party.

But no one was going to cry for Jake's misfortunes. He reminded himself that he had once been considered a likable guy. He hadn't forgotten how to turn on the charm, especially with a few drinks under his belt. It would take awhile to get himself back in shape, but as the misery faded from memory, his life would return to normal.

The sand hissing down the sidewalk cast wan halos around the streetlamps. The flying grit obliterated the stars. From the bus station, it was a short walk to North Third Street, where he planned to stop at the first bar he saw. The lights were on at the White Elephant. A banner, clinging to the building by a single cord, flapped in the wind. Jake could make out the word "Welcome" and another word, "heroes" maybe, he couldn't be sure. A lean man with thinning hair and a bushy beard stood behind the bar. "Come on in, soldier," the bartender said with a wave. "First drink is on the house."

"Whiskey," Jake shouted jovially, loud enough to hear his voice echo from the walls. He dropped his duffel bag on the floor.

The bartender poured a shot from a bottle without a label. "You look like you've been run over by a train, boy."

"I've lost a few pounds," Jake said and looked around for company. The place was almost empty save a few farmers talking quietly in the corner. His eyes returned to the shot glass on the bar, one moment brimming with amber liquid, the next moment empty. "Another."

The bartender poured until the whiskey sloshed over the rim. "Did you grow up around here? I recognized some of the boys when they came home a few months ago, but you don't look familiar. Of course, the shape you're in, your own mother might not recognize you. You're nothing but skin and bones."

"Rice diet, ever hear of it?" Jake asked with an uneasy laugh. "Actually, I pitched for Albuquerque High, a few years back. The name's Jake McGriff. Took 'em to the state championship. Threw a no-hitter once." He stood up and assumed his pitching stance. "I had a knuckler, if you remember."

The bartender shook his head. "Don't follow sports."

Jake knocked back the shot and slammed the glass on the wood. "Give me the bottle," he said, and called the farmers to join him. The paunchy men ambled over reluctantly. It had been a long day and they would have to get up early the next morning. The eldest in a white, hard-shelled cowboy hat looked Jake up and down. "You're coming back awful late, soldier. Where were you stationed?"

Jake took another shot. The mix of coffee and whiskey burned like battery acid in his stomach. "I'm buying the drinks, what does it matter?"

"Just asking."

"The Philippines."

The men grunted and cleared their throats, as if the answer held significance. "Were you one of those guys stuck on Bataan?"

Jake nodded.

"So you surrendered?" asked the eldest.

Jake scowled. "General King surrendered. Look, I don't want to talk about it."

"So you had it easy then."

Jake slammed the bottle on the bar, unintentionally breaking it. "I said I didn't want to talk about it," he said, almost pleading.

"I didn't mean anything by it," the farmer said. "Hey, Charlie! Looks like the kid's empty. Get him a drink on me."

The bartender tossed a wet towel. "Mop it up, soldier."

Swallowing his pride, Jake smiled, the born charmer. From his pocket he removed a wad of cash. "Another bottle, senor, for my new friends."

* * *

Unable to look at his father, Leo stared out the window of the old pickup on the way home from the train station, bewildered by the streets teeming with activity. Albuquerque seemed to have doubled in size. He had forgotten how stately the buildings were downtown: the Hotel Franciscan, the Little Chief Diner, the Kimo Theatre with its ornate Navajo touches. Everything looked familiar yet different somehow.

His father drove in silence. The first person Leo had seen on the platform was his mother, wrapped in the black shawl she wore to funerals. She hadn't recognized him—none of them had—even when he had walked right up to her. His voice broke the spell. "Mama," he had said quietly and watched her face register a look of horror before tears welled in her eyes. Immediately, the women encircled him, smothering him with hugs and kisses. "Oh, my baby, look at you," his mother cried. "You're so thin!" His sisters pulled at his clothes, nearly dragging him to his knees. If Leo could have had one wish, he would have chosen to spend the entire evening floating within their warm embrace.

His father had offered a hand, then clutched his son close in an awkward grip. Though the creases in his face had deepened, Juan Jimenez still seemed to exude a crackling, almost frightening vitality. "We'll get you back into the swing of things in no time," he had said. "Harvest is just around the corner."

"*Dejalo tranquilo*," his mother had said. "Leave him alone. The boy is tired. Look at him." They all studied him for a moment with looks of sympathy.

His father took him in the truck, while the women went home in a separate car. Once settled, Leo found the courage to turn his head and peer at his father's stiff profile as he drove down Fourth Street. He wanted to say something, anything to start the relationship on the right foot, but the words wouldn't come. After all these years, he was still terrified of the man. "Did you kill anyone over there?" the rancher finally asked.

"No," Leo whispered, awed by the swirling flow of traffic around the car. The neon lights of restaurants and taverns slid across his vision.

His father laughed. "Not even one?"

Leo shook his head.

His father parked downtown, across the street from the Lobo Theater, and they entered a dimly lit tavern. It was a fancy place, with thick carpets and a majestic, mahogany bar. "What will you have?" his father asked.

Leo stared blankly at the luminescent bottles lining the wall, the greens and reds. "I'll have a Coke," he said, realizing after the words left his lips that his father would disapprove.

"A Coca-Cola?" His father opened his eyes wide. "You spend three years in a prison camp and the first drink you order is a soda pop?"

"I'll take a Budweiser then," he told the bartender, though alcohol made him sick. He wasn't going to let his father push him around.

"One drink will not hurt," his father said and ordered them both tequilas over ice. Now Leo had two drinks to finish. When they arrived, his father lifted his shot glass with a look of pride. "I can't tell you how happy I am that you returned home alive." Leo nodded and took a small sip of the molten liquid. "All of it," his father said. "That's good medicine."

Leo ignored the command, and took a sip of the beer, recognizing the opportunity to stand up for himself. "I know how to drink, Papa," he said. "It was tough what I went through, but I learned a lot. We have some catching up to do."

"All in good time," his father said distractedly, apparently preoccupied with a group of important-looking men at the end of the bar. For a moment, it seemed he was about to introduce him but then must have thought better of it. He turned his back on them and looked at his son with a puzzled expression. "So in all that time, you did not kill even one?"

* * *

Jake fell with a crash into the dim, dusty hole. Dirt and pebbles showered his head. It was hard to breathe, there was so much dust. They came at him with shovels. He heard the clang of metal on his helmet, then a shout: Banzai! A soldier emerged from the shadows wielding a shovel aimed at his gut. Banzai! He tried to lift his arms to defend himself, but the narrow hole prevented him from maneuvering. The man came at him.

He awoke with a start. A shaft of sunlight blinded him. Sitting up, he found himself in a dingy room with Lucy Ramirez, naked at his side. When they met at the bar, he had remembered her from high school, a fleshy girl who liked to laugh. The light from the window illuminated her bare buttocks. Outside, the putter of an idling diesel truck told him the workday was well underway. Lucy pulled the covers up over her back. In need of a drink, Jake limped out of bed on shaky legs. All he had was his grimy khakis to put on. Though he knew he was broke, he checked his wallet. Sure enough, after a week on North Third Street, his money had run dry.

The pipes groaned in the walls as he shaved and combed what the army barber had left of his hair. He squared his bare shoulders in front of the mirror. A scar flared across his scalp where a Japanese guard had pounded him with a bamboo cane. His nose, crooked from various blows, was red and chapped.

"You look swell," Lucy said from the edge of the bed. She was sitting with her arms folded around her breasts. Her hair was a tangled nest. A cigarette hung from her lips. In the smoky light, the blue circles under her eyes gave her a sickly appearance. "Don't forget to give me my money."

"I gave you twenty dollars last night."

"The hell you did," she growled, still drunk.

"Do you have any perfume?" he asked. He was badly in need of a shower. She rummaged through her purse, then threw a bottle that hit him in the back. "Watch it!" he said. The perfume stung when he slapped it on his raw face. He had made friends during the week, bought more drinks than he could count. When he drank, he was strong. His true self, laughing and heroic, emerged. Lucy had looked good in the dim light with her long, black eyelashes and round caboose. She had laughed at his jokes and let him talk. She hadn't commented on his naked, skinny body in the darkness of their room. She made him feel like a treasure, and he loved her for it. But this morning she looked like a pudgy raccoon. He tossed his bag over his shoulder and moved toward the door.

"Where the hell do you think you're going?" she asked.

"Home."

"I got news for you, Jake," she said, exhaling a cloud of smoke. "You *are* home."

* * *

Chapter 11

Tokyo

August 1945

Murray Sanders leaned over the port side rail of the *SS Sturgis,* eager for a glimpse of the rocky shores of Japan. As the ship steamed into Sagami Bay, his eyes trawled the rugged, blue hills and cultivated terraces in search of something that might reveal a hint of the country's character. A week before, atomic bombs had been dropped on Hiroshima and Nagasaki. Murray had been preparing for months to join the scientific investigative team once the war came to a close, but he had never imagined it would end so quickly—before the arrival of troops, even before the arrival of General MacArthur.

The ship threaded its way through a narrow channel between the minefields laid as a final defense of the island. A thick cloud mass hung low in the sky. From a distance, Yokohama appeared relatively intact, considering the incredible number of bombing raids reported in the newspapers. When the ship drew closer, however, Murray saw that the buildings were nothing more than broken shells.

Of all the scientists in the country, he had been picked by MacArthur to join the country's leading intelligence personnel in preparation for a formal occupation of Japan. In his letter, the general had personally called him America's top man in biological warfare. "We need you badly," the letter had read. They needed him. Yet Molly had objected, claiming he should spend more time with his newborn son. She had relented, of course, and even packed his suitcase, enclosing a note assuring him that she would always love him dearly. He whispered a little prayer to himself when he found it, vowing to make things right with her upon his return.

His orders had changed at the last minute. Burma had been his original destination, but when the war ended so suddenly, his superiors decided to send him straight to Tokyo. There was grumbling, he knew, over the politics. Beneath the tinkling of glasses at his farewell party, he had caught murmurs about his father-in-law steering the plum assignment his way. He didn't care if his colleagues called him an opportunist. He'd send them all postcards from Japan.

He took the photograph of the Japanese gentleman from his briefcase again. Ryoichi Naito. The name was the same as that of the man who had tried years before to get his hands on the yellow fever virus from the Rockefeller Institute. But surely it could not be the same fellow. Or could it? Murray's superiors at G-2 had assigned Naito to serve as point man to the country's scientific establishment. Perhaps the doctor had informed for the Americans during the war. Murray would ask, once he figured out how to find him.

Murray studied everything G-2 had given him. The prime target was Shiro Ishii, the mastermind behind Japan's germ warfare operation. Murray had seen his name in many reports at Detrick. Ishii had engaged in biological research under the guise of operating water purification units stretching from Manchuria down to the Philippines. He was suspected of having been behind the toxic air raids reported in China, and may have even conducted experiments on living human beings, though this information was of questionable reliability. Murray snapped the briefcase shut.

The ship was packed with specialists and investigators of every stripe, mostly civilian anthropologists and sociologists, recruited to assist with intelligence gathering. Murray would serve under Karl Compton, a major figure in the science world, though how much he knew about germ warfare was open to question. Compton had been a consultant on the Manhattan Project, and his field was particle collision. He was technically a civilian, but as chief of Scientific Intelligence, he wore the oak leaves of a lieutenant colonel. Before the trip, Murray had earned a promotion to lieutenant colonel as well. Despite their rank, he and Compton were really professionals serving the war effort. Once this assignment was over, Murray hoped that he could win a tenure-track position at MIT. And why not? As the general had said, he was America's foremost expert in the field of germ weaponry and the only one in Japan. Life was sweet.

The passengers lined up in a seemingly endless queue to disembark. Murray scanned the pier for a bathroom as he waited. When he stepped off the gangplank, a Japanese man approached him, no doubt looking for money. He had heard that thousands of beggars were roaming the streets of Tokyo. But this man was well dressed, wearing an elegantly cut brown suit and a chocolate-brown fedora. "Sir, may I have a word with you?" the man asked in perfect English.

"Not now," Murray said and stiff-armed his way into the throng of confused Americans milling about the promenade.

"But sir—"

"I'm sorry, I'm in a hurry."

"Murray Sanders?" the man asked.

Murray wheeled around in surprise. "How do you know my name?"

"I am Naito." He bowed formally.

Murray opened his mouth in astonishment. "But how—"

Naito revealed a photograph of his own, a snapshot of Murray at Camp Detrick.

* * *

MacArthur arrived in Tokyo a week later, leading a full motorcade through the heart of Tokyo to the Daiichi Insurance building, headquarters of the Supreme Commander of the Allied Powers, dubbed SCAP for short. The acronym came to refer to the general as well as the entire occupation machine. A long line of black limousines rolled through the streets under a sky darkened with humming fighters and bombers. Murray rode three cars behind the general in the parade. Karl Compton sat across from him, legs crossed. He and Murray stared out the window, marveling at the raw devastation of the landscape. Almost nothing remained—here and there a broken wall or a lone chimney, a rusty safe embedded in the earth, a row of corrugated steel shacks, then twenty blocks might go by, a wasteland of craters and piles of shattered brick.

"I hear LeMay's pilots dropped about seventeen hundred tons of incendiary bombs here," Compton said. "Can you imagine? Seventeen hundred tons!"

"Obviously, nothing less would have forced the emperor to come to his senses," Murray said.

"The two big ones probably helped," Compton replied.

Though Compton was a generation older than Sanders, the two men looked as if they might be brothers. They had similar features, the same square jaw. Compton's crystal blue eyes darted back and forth behind wire-rim glasses as he scanned the desolate pulverized streets. "You don't see anyone out there, but you know they're watching us."

The motorcade came to a halt in front of the Daiichi building, across from the algae-covered moat encircling the emperor's palace. As MacArthur stepped out of the car, a flurry of flashbulbs popped, bathing him in light. He paused, allowing the photographers to get their shots. Ever the showman, the general would wait for the cameramen to set up before wading ashore—sometimes repeatedly on the same beach—as he reclaimed the Philippines.

Murray soon made himself comfortable in a cozy little office one floor below the general's. The investigation got off to a rough start. On the first day, Naito had brought him the bad news that Shiro Ishii was dead. Prodded further, he said the scientist had been shot, but he wasn't entirely sure of the circumstances. He was equally uncertain about the fate of Ishii's headquarters in Manchuria. He assured Murray that he knew all the principal players in Japan's scientific community, but

became vague when asked about his own background and
qualifications. Apparently, he had studied at the University of
Pennsylvania and, as Murray had suspected, turned against his
colleagues after losing an internecine fight for government
funding. When the subject of his defection came up, he claimed
he had to rush off to an appointment. In subsequent meetings,
he always found ways to change the subject. There was something strange about Naito, and Murray intended to take it up
with MacArthur at their first meeting, which he hoped would
come soon.

The general called Murray upstairs soon after he had
settled into headquarters. Dressed in baggy khakis, the commander was taller than Murray had imagined. He slouched like
other men his size. The general's skin, he noticed, was smooth,
almost translucent, and his slacks revealed a crease midway
up the thigh where they must have hung on the hanger. "Welcome, sir," the general said and motioned to a divan flanked by
two worn leather chairs. "May I offer you a cigarette?"

Murray accepted, though he didn't smoke. He sat down
on the edge of one of the chairs. When the general tossed him
a box of matches, he lurched for them. He would have been
devastated had he let them fall. His hand shook as he lifted the
match to his lips. To his surprise, the commander had chosen
an office without a window, though it was by no means shabby.
Portraits of Abraham Lincoln and George Washington looked
down from walnut-paneled walls. An onyx clock sat on the
bookcase. MacArthur fell into the other easy chair and casually
crooked his leg over one of the arms. He paused to light his
pipe, then met Murray's gaze. "So you're Hallstrom's boy."

Murray cleared his throat. "Son-in-law."

"Good man," the general said ambiguously. He paused to relight his pipe. "How goes it, Saunders? Have you caught up with this Ishii character yet?"

Murray coughed. He chose to ignore the general's mispronunciation of his name. "Not exactly, sir," he said, reluctant to begin with bad news. "But I have met with my contact who has promised me an introduction to all the major players. Which reminds me, about this man Naito—"

"We want everything," MacArthur interjected. "Everything we can lay our hands on. Offensive, defensive, we want it all. Have they developed a crystalline bacterial toxin, for instance? What about their photographic techniques in the study of airborne microorganisms? Everything."

Murray was impressed by the general's grasp of the details. MacArthur read everything—scientists at Camp Detrick had been struggling with the very same issues. "With my background, I don't believe it should be very difficult, but as for my contact—"

"Don't underestimate them, Saunders." MacArthur stood up and began to pace the floor. "They are not a God-fearing people."

"I only meant to say—"

"We are here to break their idols of ritualism," MacArthur raised his voice as if he were addressing a crowd. The curl of his lip hinted at a smile, but it appeared that he was serious. "We are here to teach them the maturity of enlightened knowledge and truth."

Murray wanted to get back to his questions, not only regarding Naito but also the news about Ishii. The general was on a roll now, though, his voice high and dramatic as he stabbed the air with his finger for emphasis. "This is an opportunity without counterpart for the spread of Christianity among the people of the Far East," he declared. "If not Christianity, it's going to be Communism." Murray stubbed out his cigarette and listened patiently.

* * *

A gritty wind blew through Imperial Plaza as Murray skirted its borders in search of Naito. Though the sun was bright and warm, the insistent breeze nagged at him, engulfing him at times in thick clouds of brownish brick dust. A loose piece of iron banged against the skeleton of a toppled building nearby. Milling crowds rotated around the square like fish in a tank. Many gathered around a bulletin board posted with long vertical notices, put up by families in search of loved ones lost in the war.

A group of poorly dressed, middle-aged men were standing by a platform for what seemed to be a minor communist rally. Murray recognized the *Red Flag* newspapers tucked under their arms. The man on stage, clad in a homemade sweater, was railing against something or other, probably the widespread shortages. Murray had heard that oranges were selling for as high as ten yen, most men's hourly pay. Even matches were in short supply; businessmen were leaning out their office windows with magnifying glasses to light their cigarettes. No question, there was plenty to complain about.

Naito had promised to introduce Murray to an important scientist, someone who had worked closely with Ishii in Manchuria. This lead sounded promising, more so, at least, than the last person Naito had taken him to meet, supposedly a confidant of Ishii's from the university. The old man had been holed up in a bombed-out office, no glass on the windows, papers scattered across the floor. It took nearly an hour before Murray learned that the professor had lost touch with Ishii nearly a decade before.

Murray noticed a fellow American standing next to him, smoking a cheroot as he watched the firebrand on stage. "Do you have any idea what he's saying?" Murray asked him.

"Ain't it obvious?" the man said gruffly. He wore round glasses and a porkpie hat. "You don't have to know the language to see that he's fed up. His country's finished, and now he's got the white devils bossing him around like their shit don't stink."

"Is that really what he's saying?"

The man grinned, his cigar jutting from the corner of his mouth like a rusty drainpipe. "How the hell should I know?"

Murray nodded. Beyond the circle of listeners, ragpickers thronged the square. The plaza had once served as the parade grounds for military displays. Some among the crowd appeared completely oblivious to their surroundings, as if the American bombings had crushed their spirits along with the landscape. Near the bulletin board, two American officers were speaking to a man in a light green three-piece suit. The flying grit was so thick, it took a moment before Murray realized it was Naito. He quickly waded through the crowd to catch him. But the listless bodies impeded his progress; when he tried to push past them, many awakened and gave him their elbows. Naito was alone when he reached him. "I've been waiting for twenty minutes," Murray said. "Where have you been?"

"Right here," Naito said.

"Who were you speaking to?"

"No one," the doctor said with an enigmatic grin. "I have been reading the notices, waiting for you."

"But I saw you—"

Naito tugged at his elbow. "Our man from Manchuria had a previous engagement, but come with me to dinner tonight. I have someone else I want you to meet."

They met that evening at a bustling Japanese restaurant near the embassy. Americans in uniform packed the low tables. "The man joining us tonight owns the company that manufactured Ishii's water filter," Naito said. "He knew the scientist well. I'm sure he can provide some assistance in your investigation."

"I've heard that before," Murray said. "We've met three times already, and I don't know much more than when I started."

"Patience, my friend," Naito said with his usual impenetrable smile. "The country is in disarray. The people have scattered like seeds in the wind..." The doctor ordered a round of Suntory whiskeys from the waitress. Looking around, Murray lost himself for a moment in the chatter of the dimly lit room. The man he had spoken to earlier in the square was sitting in the corner, a press pass now tucked in the band of his hat. He sat hunched aggressively over the table as he listened to a Japanese man sitting across from him. Murray wondered what newspaper he worked for—probably one of the Communist rags. The air was thick with the scent of cologne and cooking oil.

A man in a blue blazer approached the table and bowed curtly. He was trim, with a long face. Naito and Murray stood up to greet him. He appeared at ease, a person accustomed to making other people wait for him. He looked to be about forty—a few years Murray's senior. "Mr. Sanders, may I introduce Mitsuichi Kuritsu, esteemed owner of the Nihon Tokushu Kogyo," Naito said proudly. "In America, you might compare his company to General Electric or the Ford Motor Company."

Murray lifted his eyebrows in admiration. Naito turned to his friend. "Mr. Sanders is looking into our country's scientific approach to war."

"How so?" Kuritsu asked.

"Chemical and biological weapons," Murray replied. He had finished his drink and motioned to the waitress for another. "I'd hoped to meet a man named Shiro Ishii."

"Ishii?" Kuritsu asked. "I haven't seen him for quite some time."

"He's dead," Naito said quickly. "The doctor was shot in the face."

"Oh?" the man asked with concern. "I did not know."

"I went to his funeral in Chiba," Naito said.

"I'm surprised you hadn't heard," Murray said, sensing a crack in the story.

"In these confusing times, I never know who is alive, who dead," the man said cheerfully. "Even some who are alive will hang from the gallows soon enough."

"May I ask how you knew him?"

"Ishii? Oh, we were old friends," Kuritsu said and caught Naito's eye. They both laughed. "My company made the water filter he designed. We make a variety of medical instruments. Cardiology machines. Respiratory pumps. We manufacture most of the hospital equipment in Japan."

"I see," Murray said. The restaurant seemed to be getting louder, too noisy to speak comfortably. While the two men exchanged some words in Japanese, the waitress brought a tray of tempura and sukiyaki.

"Dr. Naito says that you come from a research background," Kuritsu offered.

Murray nodded.

"We could use a man like you," Kuritsu said warmly. "And we pay very well."

Murray grinned, delighting in the attention. "How much are we talking here?"

"Five thousand a week."

"What's that in American dollars?" Murray asked, astounded by the figure.

"I was referring, of course, to dollars. The yen is worth nothing."

Murray chuckled, imagining all the things he could buy for Molly at such a salary. It would make it all worth while. But a moment later he came to his senses. He couldn't accept a bribe. "I like my job just fine, thanks," he said.

"Has Mr. Kuritsu offended you, Mr. Sanders?" Naito asked with concern. "He meant no harm."

"No, no," Murray said lightly. "I'm flattered."

"It was a serious offer," Kuritsu said, holding his gaze.

Suddenly the room felt close. Murray stood up, his head spinning from the whiskey and close quarters. He didn't know who might be listening. "I'll think about it," he said. "But for now, I'll have to say good night."

"What about dinner?" Naito asked.

"Another time," Murray said, already a few steps from the table. On his way out, he noticed Compton dining with a group of Japanese businessmen. Murray turned away, hoping his boss would not notice him.

Outside, a brilliant full moon hovered just above the gap-toothed skyline. The streets were still busy. Couples walked arm in arm along the sidewalks, illuminated occasionally by paper lanterns dangling overhead. Murray ducked into an unfamiliar bar. It was a tiny place, just three tables and a jukebox playing American standards. Though he knew he would pay for it later with a splitting headache, he ordered another whiskey. As it arrived, the reporter sat down next to him at the bar. "So what did they offer you?"

Murray gasped. "Who the hell are you anyway?"

"I asked you a question," the man insisted in a deep, raspy voice. "I know Kuritsu tried to stick some money in your pocket. Fess up." He scrutinized Murray's face.

Murray sipped his drink. "I get the sense you're following me."

"I'm interested in germs, just like you," the reporter said and thrust out his hand. "John Powell, *China Weekly Review*."

"So you're sniffing around for a story."

"Something like that. Actually, I'm curious to see if someone in your position has the balls to tell the truth. See, I know you've been assigned to look for biological weapons. I just don't think the old man's interested in finding any."

"That's ridiculous," Murray said. Now he knew the man was a loon.

Powell went on as if Murray hadn't said a word. "The war's over. Now Macky's here to make friends. We need the Japs more than they need us. Mark my words, the emperor will get to keep his job. The instigator behind Pearl Harbor and all the rest, and I bet the fucker gets off scot-free."

"Why would we need the Japanese?"

The reporter chuckled. "You ever hear of Communism? It's us against the Soviets now, and there's nothing between the two countries but this island."

Murray took a sip of his drink. There was no arguing with a true believer. He couldn't see the emperor remaining in power, but truthfully, he didn't care one way or another. "Well, then maybe we *should* be handling the occupation with caution."

Powell flashed a look of disgust. "You government types are all alike. Real stand-up guys." He finished his drink, ice and all, and motioned to the bartender for another. "So, did you find Ishii yet?"

"Ishii? He's dead," Murray said quickly, glad to get one up on his drinking partner. "I confirmed it tonight."

"Au contraire, my friend," Powell said, wagging his finger. "Word on the street says he's alive. I went to the funeral up in Chiba. A big affair with all the local dignitaries, but they never showed his face. He's gone underground somewhere. Find him and you've got dynamite."

"If you know so much, why don't you write about it?"

"I would if your boss MacArthur would let me," Powell said. "Believe me, I've got a shitload to write, but if I were to publish now, I'd be kicked out of Japan before the real story came out. That's why I need you."

"My investigation is confidential," Murray said, annoyed. "So I wouldn't hold your breath."

"Oh, don't worry, I ain't expecting much," Powell said with a chuckle. "But you never know. Maybe we can help each other. Even a blind squirrel finds a nut once in a while."

* * *

Someone knocked on his door late the next morning. Murray stayed in bed, hoping whoever it was would go away. The knock came again, pulling him to his feet. Through the peephole, he spied Naito in a wine-colored suit with a matching bowler. Murray opened the door and sat on the bed. "Where have you been?" the doctor asked with concern. "I came three or four times looking for you."

"Late night," Murray grumbled, pressing his thumbs into his forehead to dispel the pain.

From behind his back, the doctor held out his palm upon which sat a large pearl, dark gray, almost black and brain like. "A gift from Kuritsu, who sends his regrets that you could not stay for dinner last night."

"He's generous, your friend," Murray said. "But I'm afraid I can't accept it."

"It's nothing," Naito said, and quickly tucked it in Murray's pajama pocket. "A gumball to bring home to your son."

"How did you know I have a son?" Murray asked, too tired to argue anymore about the jewel. He leaned forward, resting his elbows on his knees. A pang of guilt pulled at his insides like a bout of indigestion. He hated Naito for making him feel this way.

His guide remained standing with his hands behind his back. "I'm going to meet a friend for dinner tonight," he said. "A doctor by the name of Masaji Kitano. He worked in Manchuria. I thought you might join us."

Murray chuckled. "You will have to go ahead without me. I'm afraid I've failed miserably as an investigator."

"But you have hardly begun—"

"I know enough to realize I'm not cut out for it. I'm a scientist. Besides, the Russians are coming soon to do their own investigation. They can finish what I began and do a far more thorough job than I've done."

Naito sat down beside him. "The Russians. I have heard nothing."

In truth, Murray had no plans to resign. He was merely feeling mean and wanted to needle his unctuous host. The Japanese were terrified of their neighbors to the north. "So when do you leave?" Naito asked.

Murray shrugged. Naito suddenly rose. "I must be going," he said. Murray raised his hand to bid the man good-bye, but the doctor left without saying another word.

* * *

Naito appeared at Murray's door again the following morning. Though he was dressed in his usual finery, he looked a bit disheveled. His tie was crooked and there was a trace of stubble on his chin. He immediately lit a cigarette. From his coat pocket, he produced a thick document, which he handed to Murray. The two sat down at the foot of the bed while Murray read the document, scrawled in a clumsy hand:

"There occurred a big consternation in the circle of higher officers of Japanese Head Quarter when your inquire about biological weapon began. A long time disputation was done, whether they should answer to you with the true or not. The chief of Bureau of War Affairs has the fear that the fact that Japan had some laboratories for active biology research will bring a big misfortune to the Emperor."

"Who wrote this?"

"I did," Naito said, his face pale. Beneath his polished accent, it appeared his understanding of the language was severely flawed. Murray wondered how he kept up. The document went on to break down the chain of command of those involved in biological weapons research. At the top of the list was the emperor, though the letter made it clear that Hirohito was not directly involved in research. Next came the War Ministry and the Bureau of Medicine. The document claimed the bulk of the research was done at Harbin, under the command of Shiro Ishii and Masaji Kitano between the years 1936 and 1945. It went on to lay out the organization of the water purification units that acted as fronts and the source of their funds. It detailed the pathogens studied including cholera and dysentery, salmonella and anthrax, and outlined the modes of delivery through bombs and artillery shells. Finally, it ended with a plea: "I ask you to understand that I am staking my life doing this Information; I shall be killed if anyone knows that I have done it. My only hope is to rescue this poor, defeated nation. − Ryoichi Naito"

Murray paused to reread the last line, then turned to Naito, who was looking out the window, where light filtered through the white paper shade. He avoided Murray's gaze. "This is interesting," Murray said calmly, hiding his excitement. It was the Rosetta stone he been looking for. His offhanded bluff about the Russians had frightened Naito into action. "I will have to show this to General MacArthur immediately. But I have one question for you. Did the army ever use human beings as the subjects of its experiments in Mukden or anywhere else?"

"No!" Naito whispered. He had lit another cigarette and looked straight into Murray's eyes. "Never."

Murray nodded. "You will have to excuse me now," he said as he stood up to get dressed. "I'd like your help arranging interviews with the men included on this list."

At the door, the doctor turned to Murray. He appeared genuinely frightened. "Please don't tell anyone I gave you this," he said. "My life is in danger."

Murray met with MacArthur that afternoon. Compton was there, as well as Charles Willoughby, chief of intelligence. The steely man with the thick Austrian accent was known to intimidate even the hardened veterans of MacArthur's inner circle, but Murray had always found him extraordinarily friendly. While the three read mimeographed copies of the letter, Murray's mind kicked forward in leaps and cartwheels, imagining how he would advance the investigation. At last, he might earn a measure of respect.

"The man could use a few lessons in grammar," MacArthur said after breezing through the communication. He picked up the first page and glanced over it again, while the others finished reading. "It seems we're getting somewhere though. What do you think, Compton?"

The older gentleman furrowed his brow. "We need details. We have to speak to the scientists themselves. The ones who were actually running the operation."

"Yes, but will they talk?" MacArthur asked.

"They won't say a word," Willoughby cut in. "They won't dare risk exposure to war crimes prosecution."

The general chewed on his pipe contemplatively. "Well, we are not given to torture," he said quietly. "If necessary, offer them immunity, Sanders. Tell them you have a promise from MacArthur himself. But get the data. We want the data or no deal."

Murray nodded.

"And what about this fellow Ishii?" the general asked as an afterthought. "It says here he ran the program for years."

"I'm glad you asked about that, sir—"

"My men tell me he was shot," Willoughby said gravely.

"Shot? What, dead?" MacArthur appeared shocked. "Did you know about this, Sanders?"

"I'm not so sure, sir," Murray said quickly to avoid another interruption. Willoughby shot him an icy glance.

"A reporter told me Ishii is actually still alive."

"Who?"

Murray was tripped up by the question. What did it matter? He had drunk too much whiskey to remember names. "Powell, I believe."

"John Powell's a known Communist," Willoughby said. "Don't believe a word he says." He slapped a large hand on Murray's shoulder and smiled. "You've really found something here with this document. Stick with what you have, and don't

bother listening to reporters. They'll tell you all kinds of nonsense."

"Get on it, son," MacArthur said. "Get your facts straight
and move, move, move."

"Yes, sir," Murray said, as he stood up to leave the room.
Willoughby was still smiling at him confidently. Murray wondered how he had gained such a mean reputation.

* * *

Once he delivered MacArthur's pledge of immunity, the
Japanese scientists emerged like carp from the depths of a
pond. Every day, Naito would visit the Daiichi building with
another doctor in tow. Each repeated the same general story:
offensive weapons were developed on a large scale, including
canisters containing contaminated fleas, *Uji* bombs. Vast quantities of plague, cholera, anthrax, and glanders were produced,
yet at no time had the Japanese used these hazardous materials
on the battlefield, nor were they ever applied to anything but
rats and monkeys.

Having worked as a section chief at Camp Detrick, Murray
found it hard to believe that the Japanese would go so far as to
drop more than two thousand *Uji* bombs in field trials without
ever detonating one experimentally in combat—especially in
light of the intelligence reports he had read regarding suspicious air attacks on Chinese villages like Changteh. Yet the
scientists adamantly denied employing such tactics. Murray
decided to humor them with the hope that someone would
eventually divulge the true facts.

His suspicions were further piqued when Powell invited him for drinks one evening to meet a former engineer from the Japanese Medical Corps. They met at the same bar, only this time, they sat at a back table, which afforded them more privacy. When Murray arrived, Powell was already seated across from a gangly Japanese man in a black beret. "So, Murray, old pal, how goes the investigation?" Powell asked.

"Terrific, actually," Murray replied. He was debating whether to share his breakthrough with his new acquaintance. He liked the fellow, but didn't trust him, not after what Willoughby said. He suddenly wondered if he should even be speaking to Powell, and a twinge of fear came over him at the thought that he might be seen in the wrong company. Science was so much more clear cut than this business of intrigue. He wondered if he was the only investigator who felt unmoored.

Powell introduced his companion as a Mr. Ishikawa who served in Manchuria during the war. "I am engineer who work in Unit 731," the man said. "I come with information, top secret." From a cloth satchel, he removed a tube of paper and unrolled it on the table. It was a diagram of a bomb. "They call this *Uji*. Outside made of porcelain. Flea in chamber."

"Wow. I haven't seen this before," Murray said as he leaned eagerly over the picture.

"I thought you might be interested," Powell said.

"Did it work?" Murray asked.

"No," the man said and frowned. "Bomb break. Flea die from fire."

"That's what I've heard."

"But it kill some prisoner," he added. "Some die."

"You're saying they used prisoners to test the bomb's effectiveness?"

The man nodded.

"Were these people alive?" This was something new—and frightening. "Were they infected?"

The man stood up, clearly discomforted by the conversation. "Top secret. I go. If Ishii know, I die."

"Ishii? So is he alive?"

"He alive," the man said and walked quickly out of the bar.

"What did I tell you?" Powell said smugly.

Murray shrugged. "How do I know he isn't one of your Commie friends?"

"Oh, so now I'm a Communist."

"Admit it," Murray shot back.

"Let me get something through your head, Murray," Powell said. "Ishii was a very bad man. He infected innocent women and children with diseases. I saw it with my own eyes. He experimented on living human beings, including our own men. He did stuff that would make you throw up right here on your shoes. And if you don't get your facts straight, these Japanese fuckers are going to get away with it. Mark my words."

"You've got your story and I've got mine," Murray said.

* * *

Powell's father, the legendary founder of the *China Weekly Review*, had been labeled a communist as well—by the Japanese, when he had been the only one bold enough to criticize the imperial government's occupation of Shanghai during the 1930s. The truth was that both men prided themselves on their freedom from ideology.

The newspaper had taken a strong editorial stance against Japanese imperialism throughout the region, whether it was the takeover of Manchuria or the pillage of Nanjing. John's father's standing allowed him to describe politics "as he saw it," which often differed from the official positions reported in other newspapers. And at times, he was guilty of embellishment to make a point. It was this aggressiveness, and the discrepancies, which cost him dearly in the end.

The day after Pearl Harbor, the Japanese took full military possession of Shanghai, and almost immediately, imprisoned the old man as a spy. John miraculously escaped aboard a Panamanian freighter, one of the last ships to safely leave the harbor. Two years later, his father was returned to the United States in a prisoner exchange program. John personally carried him off the ship, for he had lost his feet to gangrene in a Japanese prison cell.

In the final years of the war, the younger Powell had returned to Asia, reporting for the U.S. Office of Information in China. He saw awful things: beheadings, a woman raped in the plain light of day, a village torched to rid itself of plague germs, a nine year-old girl orphaned, whispering to her dead sister. John had made a name for himself writing these stories, and like his father, made a few enemies for reporting something different than his competitors. But unlike the old man, he wouldn't stray over the line of factual accuracy. There was a comfort in playing by such rules, but in his heart, he sometimes wondered if cowardice was at the root of his fastidiousness, and if somehow, he was failing his father.

* * *

Murray reported to a meeting with MacArthur and Willoughby the next day. Proud of his progress, he came armed with a file full of interviews, all corroborating the basic premise that Japanese scientists had indeed developed biological weapons for defensive purposes. Establishing the existence of the program was a victory in itself. It was what he had come to do. While his superiors leafed through the affidavits, he mentioned the curious anecdote of his meeting with Powell and the Japanese engineer the evening before. Of course, he found the corpsman's claims of interest, and not a little disturbing, even if they were unreliable.

Willoughby dismissed the story with a brush of his hand. "Not even worth discussing."

Murray continued, however, believing himself on safe enough ground that he could at least express his passing doubts. He had never been able to officially confirm Ishii's death, after all. And Ishikawa's finely drawn diagram of the flea bomb certainly looked authentic, lending credence to his allegations. He was only thinking aloud when he said tentatively, "I wonder now, sir, if the offer to grant immunity might have been premature. If the Japanese did, in fact, experiment on prisoners, that would constitute a serious violation of international law."

"No need to inform me of the law, Sanders," the general said, leaning back in his chair. He puffed on his pipe in contemplation. He turned to Willoughby, who sat with his hands folded in his lap. "What do you think, Charles?"

Willoughby looked up from his reading and fixed Murray with an icy stare. "As I've said, I find the entire line of thought preposterous."

MacArthur nodded. "It sounds like you're making this more complicated than need be, old boy," he said. "You've done great work getting your man to spring this confession. Don't unravel on us now."

Murray was surprised by the lack of concern. "All I'm saying, General, is that we now have more questions than answers since we offered immunity. I don't believe it's too late to rescind it."

MacArthur had pulled out a nail file and now appeared deeply troubled by the cuticle on his middle finger. He did not look up from his task. "Charles?"

"Have you ever conducted an investigation, Mr. Sanders?" Willoughby asked, his hushed voice rising to a shout that filled the room. "Because I've never heard such nonsense in my life!"

Murray's stomach dropped in fright.

The officer's face was red and twisted into a monstrous expression. "You're an investigator, sir, here to explore the extent of this country's weaponry program, yet you occupy yourself with hearsay and innuendo."

Desperately, Murray turned to MacArthur, still casually filing his nails. But Willoughby wasn't through: "So I would advise you listen to your commander, sir, and come back to us with a report."

MacArthur looked up. "Charles is right," he said coolly. "I would suggest you concentrate on the facts at hand."

Murray quickly collected his papers. Willoughby chuckled as he escorted him to the door, his anger vanished. He had made his point. "I've met investigators like you, clinging to your conspiracy theories, always looking for that pearl of great price." He looked at Murray intently. "Don't muck this up by asking a lot of unnecessary questions, lad. Just do your job and you'll save us all a great deal of trouble."

* * *

Murray spent the following evening trying to write his report, but nothing came out the way he wanted to say it. His black mood prevented him from even finishing a thought. The onset of a head cold made it worse. Occupation personnel were coming down with all kinds of serious illnesses, contracted, no doubt, from the malnourished Japanese people. Two officers had already been sent home with advanced cases of tuberculosis. It seemed the entire country was sick with something.

Fishing around in his desk drawer for an eraser, he found the black pearl. He tossed it in the air and felt its heft as it landed in his palm. He'd sell it when he returned home and buy a pretty dress for Molly. It occurred to him that Willoughby had said something about a pearl. It sounded like a threat. Might he actually know about the gift—and use it against Murray if crossed?

The spy chief had definitely humiliated him. In private, the dressing down would have been bad enough, but he had screamed at him in front of MacArthur, whose recommendation held the key to Murray's future. It was his own fault. He had dug his own grave. Why on earth had he prattled on like that? Lesson learned; he would keep his emotions in check when it came to his final report. Whether Ishii was dead or alive no longer mattered. The question of human experiments remained unanswered and, therefore, irrelevant. Murray would stick to what he could document: while the Japanese had approached their germ warfare program with enthusiasm, they lacked the imagination and technical sophistication necessary to employ it on the battlefield. Murray made no mention of human experiments. He wasn't here to save the world.

He stayed at the office late that Friday night, making the final changes. When he was finished, he handed the document to MacArthur's secretary and asked her to mimeograph thirty copies. "Take good care of it," he told her. "The general will want to see it." Despite his misgivings, he was pleased with his work. He had his family to think about. If he played his cards right, he might just get that appointment to MIT. He was glad the hotel was only two blocks away. He was so tired, he collapsed on his bed and fell asleep in his clothes.

* * *

Sometime later in the night, he was awoken from a fevered sleep. He heard a knock at his door. The lights were still on in his room. "Who's there?" he called weakly.

"It's me, Powell," a booming voice said.

As he rose, bouncing spots of color momentarily blinded him. His back ached. The pudgy American stood in the door, chomping on the ravaged stump of a cigar. He shoved a stack of papers in Murray's face. "What the hell is this?"

"Where did you get that?" Murray asked, realizing it was his freshly minted report.

"There's a stack of them sitting outside the office of the C-in-C," Powell said. "They're marked 'restricted,' so they're open to the press."

"They should be marked 'top secret,'" Murray said and tried to snatch the papers from Powell's hand, but the reporter dodged him.

"I've read it, so there's not much you can do about it now."

Murray pushed past the reporter. "I have to make sure no one else gets it."

"Why bother?" Powell asked. "It's a piece of shit anyway."

Murray sighed. Even coming from a lousy reporter, the comment felt like another slap in the face. "We have different jobs, Powell. I have to rely on facts."

"This has nothing to do with the facts, and you know it, Murray," the reporter replied with more disappointment than anger. He tossed the report on the floor as if it were diseased. "This is you bowing to pressure."

Murray collected the document and tucked it under his arm. "You don't know what you're talking about."

"The hell I don't," the reporter said. "I can't believe you'd put your name on this."

"The Communists have an agenda too, you know," Murray protested. "There's no proof. And if you really believed what you claim, you'd write about it, MacArthur be damned."

"That's my own failing," Powell said gravely. "This is yours. You'll live with this for the rest of your life."

"Shut up!" Murray shouted. He could hardly remain standing he was so tired. He realized he must be coming down with something. But he had to return to GHQ to find the rest of the reports. "You have no idea," he said as he staggered back from the door.

There was anguish in Powell's voice as he called after him. "How could you do it, Murray?"

Outside the general's door, Murray found the stack, just as Powell had said. He counted twenty-nine and exhaled a sigh of relief; it spared him the humiliation of having to report a security breach. MacArthur's office appeared dark through the glazed window of the door, but Murray saw some flashes of light. He knocked timidly. Someone yelled for him to come in. As he entered, he heard the whirr of a movie projector. The general, along with a few guests, were watching a Western. He recognized Compton sitting on the couch alongside Willoughby, who glanced up with a broad smile. And there beside them was Naito, looking just as pleased. "You look ill, Mr. Sanders," he said.

The light flashed intermittently across their faces. "Sanders!" MacArthur called, noticing him for the first time. "Have a seat. We're watching the *Bells of Rosarita*. How's that for the comforts of home?"

When Murray turned toward the voice, the projector blinded him. He felt faint.

"Have some popcorn," MacArthur said. "We just finished perusing your top-notch report."

Murray found his way to a chair next to Willoughby, who smiled broadly at him with an almost paternal look of kindness. "I...I would like to have it back," Murray managed to say. Perhaps it wasn't too late to do a more thorough investigation. "I need more time."

Roy Rogers was riding Trigger across a desert plain. The beautiful Dale Evans had inherited a circus, and it was up to

Roy to save it from thieves. "More time?" said the general. "Nonsense."

"They used humans," Murray said, pointing at Naito. The screen flickered before his eyes. Trigger's whinny pierced his eardrum. "They killed people."

"What on earth are you talking about?" asked Compton.

"Guinea pigs—"

Willoughby cracked his knuckles.

"You've done enough here, Sanders," MacArthur said. "It's time for you to go home."

* * *

Chapter 12

Tokyo

May 1946

Shiro Ishii's back and knees hurt from crouching on the floor like an animal, but he was determined to prove to his daughter that her monkey had fleas. Vile creatures, monkeys. Granted, they were not known to carry fleas, but Ishii had seen this one picking through its mangy fur. They were everywhere, razor thin creatures with legs so powerful they could leap distances two hundred times their body length, with an acceleration of two hundred gravities.

He had once adored fleas. He still kept a photograph of his favorite species, Pulex irritans, nailed to the wall. Yet the insects had turned on him. They bit his wrists and shins, sending him into paroxysms of scratching. He feared a diseased strain might have returned with him from Manchukuo. Who knew better than he that there were more than one hundred species around the world carrying the plague bacillus. Others, like

Xenopsylla cheopis, carried murine typhus, a rickettsial disease. Some bore tularemia and Russian spring-summer encephalitis.

Ishii was already suffering from a debilitating case of chole-cystitis, a result of gallstones, which made him terribly flatu-lent. As he crawled across the floor of his apartment, he almost wept in pain. Suddenly, he saw a black spot leap from a crack between the dark brown floorboards and fly a foot in the air with terrific forward propulsion. Ishii caught the flea in his fist when it leapt again and clenched it tightly. Slowly, he opened his hand enough to pinch the little creature between his fingers until he heard a deeply satisfying pop.

Though it was almost noon, the lieutenant general still wore his sleeping kimono. Sometimes he spent the entire day in his gown—even a few days, if he could get away without washing and changing. As far as he was concerned, he had retired. Why not dress comfortably? Why not eat cake with rice wine for breakfast? Harumi worried too much. She had a lot to learn about the ways of the world. Yet he loved her dearly. He only wished she would get rid of that vile monkey.

Moshi was the thing's name. It was always screeching and making a mess, throwing objects or tearing out the pages of Ishii's books. For some reason, it held a particular disdain for him. Whenever he entered the same room, the monkey be-came agitated and hurled food. Still on his hands and knees, Ishii looked up and spied the animal in the kitchen sink, no doubt picking out scraps from the drain.

He had objected to returning to Tokyo. The city of ashes, he called it. When the Americans had discovered him living at his mother's home in Chiba six months after the end of the war, he told them that his wife and mother were gravely ill and needed his medical attention. The officers had treated him with the respect befitting a gentleman of his position. They had not arrested him, but had simply requested his presence in Tokyo. In response to their humility, he had complied. He brought Harumi with him to care for the house. He had come to depend on her.

The village elders had done their best to hide him. Before the destruction of Ping Fan, he had paid them handsomely in real estate holdings and with a vast cache of loot taken from military stockpiles in Manchuria: pig iron, rubber tires, *tatami* straw matting, steel pipes, cement. To ship the goods alone had consumed the last of his savings. In light of the country's grave shortages, the materials had become incredibly valuable, and the elders had repaid him. Not only had they agreed to make a formal announcement of his death, they had actually staged an elaborate funeral in his behalf and later provided henchmen for his protection.

While in hiding, he had kept an eye on MacArthur's investigation. Leave it to his old friend Naito, who sent the officer scurrying this way and that without giving a hint of anything that could prove damning. Naito, that oily rascal, was a perfect decoy, with his cosmopolitan wardrobe and polished English. Ishii had met frequently with the others to coordinate their stories. Under strict orders of the occupation, he had instructed the researchers to divulge everything except *to* and *ha*, the code words for human subjects and offensive biological weapons. Naito had done well, even extracting a promise of immunity from the investigator, Sanders.

Ishii spotted another flea. He had become quite good at it. His search led him under the dining room table. They were everywhere, these fleas. The monkey screeched and threw a handful of wet rice at him. The rice splattered on the table above him. Ishii smiled. The beast had missed. Quickly, he grabbed a scrap of food he found on the floor and hurled it in the direction of the monkey.

* * *

"I want to go home, Moshi," Harumi whined to her pet. She was kneeling on the bed, brushing her long, thick hair. The monkey scrambled into her lap, where he proceeded to preen himself like a cat. Poor Moshi. The city, reduced to charred wood and rusty metal, was no place for him. It was no place for humans either. In an attempt to win back her favor, her father had purchased Moshi for the family immediately after the war. The younger children loved the animal. They had put it on a leash and watched it tiptoe over the wet paths of the garden after a winter rain. The monkey had even made their mother, Kiyoko, laugh when he leapt atop her bed and pranced like a little soldier. It was wonderful to hear her laugh.

The moment did not last long, however. Her father had burst into the room and demanded they remove Moshi, claiming its fleas might endanger their mother's precarious health. Harumi knew from her science classes that monkeys do not carry fleas, but what did that matter? Her father was stubborn and crazy. The gift of a pet monkey would not change her anger at him for having ordered her friends to work twelve-hour shifts, six days a week, at the balloon factory. And nothing could silence the swirling rumors that he had poisoned people in secret experiments.

She had been home in Chiba a few months when the American agents came knocking. She had tried to lie about her father, as instructed, but the agents had refused to leave. Soon she was on another train with her father, this time to Tokyo—with Moshi, of course. She had insisted on bringing him. When they returned to the ravaged city, she shuddered to think that her father had allowed his family to endure such brutal devastation. The closer they drew to the center, the worse the damage appeared, until they saw whole neighborhoods flattened into a pale dust resembling rice flour. The rains eventually washed away the powder, but they could not cleanse the streets of begging children or war veterans, dressed in white, pleading for a few coins.

Harumi heard her father in the other room. He was always crawling around in search of fleas, which she knew were imaginary. She had almost forgiven him until she happened upon an article in one of the American newspapers and learned what was behind the whispers: "Lieutenant General Shiro Ishii, said to have directed 'human guinea pig' tests on American and Chinese prisoners of war in Manchuria, was ordered arrested for questioning today by American counterintelligence authorities."

The more she thought about it, the more the story made sense. That was why he had never allowed her to enter the research facilities at Ping Fan. That was why the wives would never discuss their husbands' work. Just a few weeks earlier, a photograph on the front page of the *Asahi Graph* had caught her eye. Above the image of a mushroom cloud was the simple phrase, recycled from the heights of wartime sloganeering: "Truth that emerged out of lies."

She no longer knew what to believe. She put down the hairbrush and caressed the monkey's head. Across the room hung a silver-framed mirror, another gift from her father. She gazed at her reflection, then allowed her hair to fall across her face.

* * *

The stocky American had obviously tried to acquaint himself with Japanese culture before his arrival and had failed miserably. He was too forward with his ingratiating smile and awkward bows. The Americans were even more stupid than Ishii had imagined. Ishii observed the man from behind the shoji screen that separated his room from the front of the small apartment. Harumi had explained that her father was bedridden and unable to answer questions except in the comfort of his home. The agent had been happy to oblige.

The American lingered in the anteroom, exchanging pleasantries with Harumi, who spoke exquisite English. Ishii did not like the way the man looked at her so boldly. She was not for sale like the vulgar *panpans* lurking outside Ueno Station. The man introduced himself as an emissary from the American President Harry Truman.

Ishii had heard about how Naito had taken the first investigator to meet poor, old Dr. Yonetsugi Miyagawa in his bombed-out office at Tokyo University. Ishii had not spoken to the doctor in ten years, since the old days working with Koizumi at the Tokyo University. The visit must have scared the elderly professor out of his wits. Ishii giggled to himself at the thought. Through the space between the screen and the wall, he watched as his daughter led the American toward his room.

"Charming place you have here," the man said, glancing at the paintings decorating the walls. "Much nicer than many of the others I've seen in Tokyo. Does your father collect art?"

Harumi smiled. "These pieces are ancient Chinese ink drawings, dating back to the eighth century."

"Beautiful," the man said.

Ishii's command of English fell far short of his daughter's, but he would use the weakness to his advantage and feign ignorance when it suited him. He sat up in bed as the two approached. In preparation for the interview, he had gone to the trouble of washing his hair and dressing in his finest black kimono. Just before they entered, he flipped open a book and began scanning the pages. "Father, Lieutenant Colonel Arvo Thompson is here to see you," Harumi announced.

Ishii looked up. "So soon?" He put the book aside. "Forgive me, sir. Please sit down." The American leaned forward to shake Ishii's hand. "I'm sorry," Ishii said. "Where are my manners?" He extended his hand carelessly, as if his guest might kiss it. The investigator sat on the small chair beside the high bed, where Ishii could look down on him. Harumi went to make tea.

The agent was visibly nervous. "As a man of science, I am tremendously honored to meet you," Thompson said and laughed awkwardly. "I'm thrilled, actually. From everything I've heard, you are preeminent in your field."

"And what field would that be, Mr. Thompson?"

The investigator chuckled again. "Why, biological warfare, of course."

Ishii studied him coldly. "Are you referring to my study of vaccines?"

"Well, yes, and other…" He trailed off. "We know you were working on other things as well."

"Hmm." Ishii said and fell silent. Across the apartment, Harumi could be heard pouring water from the kettle.

Thompson cleared his throat. "Let me start over. What I mean to say is that we understand you possess valuable information. We hope to learn from your research."

"I see."

"Of course, I understand such information does not necessarily come free, and we can talk about that. The most important thing is that the conversation stays here, in this room. "

"Are you worried about the Russians, Mr. Thompson?"

The agent laughed loudly. "Worried? No. We just don't want them mucking around in our business. I don't think there's anything wrong with saying that."

Harumi brought in the teapot with small cups and sesame cookies. "Thank you, ma'am," Thompson said. "That looks wonderful." He turned to Ishii. "Perhaps we should be alone."

"She stays here," Ishii responded.

Thompson grinned. "Fine. I just thought—"

"You thought nothing," Ishii barked.

The agent cleared his throat. "Well, shall we begin the interview?"

"Who said I would grant an interview?"

"That's why I came today. Surely you knew that?"

"Your man Sanders promised the others immunity," Ishii said flatly. "I want it in writing."

"I'll have to consult with my superiors about that," Thompson said. "I'd just like to get a sense of what kind of information you have. These are just some basic questions."

"Harumi, go and get my things to show the gentleman." The girl promptly stood up and left the room. Ishii followed her out with his eyes. She possessed such a shapely form.

When the girl returned, Ishii demonstrated his famous water filter. In the interest of decorum, he used tea rather than urine. He also proudly displayed the culture cabinet, a glorified humidor, explaining that it was used to respond to the demand for large-scale vaccination operations. He made no mention of the germs he had bred in the cabinet to use as weapons. Thompson was clearly impressed.

"Now about those questions," the investigator said, more relaxed, now that the ice had been broken.

"You may ask, but I may not answer," Ishii responded curtly. Just as he said this, he saw a flea hop along the top of his blankets. He cursed under his breath as the agent persisted in questioning him.

"Fair enough. Let us begin with plague, shall we? What field tests were made with the organism?"

"Due to the danger, there were no field experiments with that organism," Ishii lied. Suddenly he saw the flea leap again, and this time he pounced on it with his hand. "Excuse me," he said to the investigator with a false smile, and slowly rolled the flea between his fingers. "Now then. What was I saying? Oh yes, plague. There were a great many field mice in Manchuria, and it would have been too dangerous to conduct experiments. The mice could very easily have started an epidemic."

"I see," said Thompson, jotting down some notes. "We've heard from Chinese sources that plague was started in Changteh, China, in 1941, by airplanes flying over and dropping infected material. Do you know anything about this?"

"Of course not," Ishii exclaimed. He was still watching for fleas. Where there was one, there were many. "It's impossible to drop plague organisms from airplanes."

"But rats, rags, and bits of cotton infected with plague were dropped and later picked up by the Chinese. Surely that's how it must have started."

"Are you a man of science?" Ishii asked sarcastically.

Thompson nodded. "I'm a veterinarian by trade."

"Then you should know that if you drop rats from airplanes they die."

Thompson changed his tack. "What about yellow fever?"

"What about it?"

"We have evidence that Japan tried to obtain the yellow fever virus from the Rockefeller Institute."

"I don't know what you're talking about." Ishii scratched his wrist.

"Who first authorized the beginning of biological warfare research in Japan?"

"There were no orders to research biological warfare," Ishii responded, his voice rising. He scratched himself viciously beneath the blankets. "If there had been, we would have received all the money, personnel, and materials we wanted to carry it out. Since there were no orders, we conducted our experiments on a very small budget in the Water Purification

Bureau." He could tell his arm was bleeding, but he continued scratching.

"Did the emperor order the research?"

"No."

"Was the emperor informed of the research?"

"Not at all," Ishii answered angrily. "The emperor is a lover of humanity. He would never have consented to such a thing. That is all I will say. Go away and do not come back until you have your commander's guarantee on paper. Now go. I must rest."

Thompson sat back in his chair, then nodded and stood up. "We'll continue later. In the meantime, I'll speak to General MacArthur about your request."

The investigator bowed deeply. Ishii merely shooed him away. Harumi escorted him to the door. Once alone, the doctor inspected his wrists, rubbed raw.

* * *

Harumi began to take notes on the interviews between Arvo Thompson and her father. The agent had yet to deliver a written promise of immunity, but her father had yielded, given a verbal pledge. He seemed to enjoy toying with the American.

One day, her father sent her to general headquarters with a note hinting at new, tantalizing details. Crossing the Little America district, a few square miles of Tokyo spared by the air raids, Harumi saw the wives of the occupation forces coming out of the Post Exchange with fifteen-pound hunks of meat, their grocery bags overflowing, while her own countrymen searched the gutters for scraps and cigarette butts.

She hated to see her people fawn over the white strangers. They referred to General MacArthur in terms of godliness, while degrading themselves haggling over the price of a kitchen knife at the black market. *Yama-ichi* bazaars had cropped up all over the country. Former military manufacturers, many of them friends of her father's, had quickly adjusted to the postwar climate. Instead of swords, they produced kitchen utensils; in place of helmets, pots and pans, all sold at the open-sky markets. Some of the merchants were veterans, former pilots who had come home with their planes full of loot.

Gone was loyalty to country; solidarity had vanished. Men were now elbowing aside old women for a five-pound bag of rice. Gone were the sword and the jewel, replaced by Hawaiian shirts and sneakers. Harumi felt that her entire education had failed her. The hundred million fighting, bright and strong. The pilots of the Divine Wind hurling themselves at the enemy. Where were they now?

She passed people planting gardens on the plots of bombed-out buildings, on torn-up median strips. They were waiting for turnips to grow from the blackened grime so that they could feed their families. If her father were an honorable man, he would have killed himself by now, like his mentor, Chikahiko Koizumi. The great man, bald and round as a Buddha, had come to their home in Chiba to pay his respects. The occupation forces were pursuing him, he had said over dinner. He had killed himself that night atop the hill in their garden. Meanwhile, her father hid at home, crawling on the floor in search of nonexistent fleas.

* * *

The fleas were breeding in large numbers. Ishii saw them everywhere, in the floorboards and the carpets, in the creases of his silk kimonos. Though he had smeared repellant over every centimeter of his body, they had tattooed his skin with an inscrutable brail. Praying against infection, he scratched the bumps bloody. He rarely left his fumigated bed at all. Too dangerous. He could not risk exposure to parasites or other enemies lurking in the shadows.

He knew fleas had once killed millions in the Black Plague in Europe. The cat flea, the human flea, the sticktight, the chigoe. The pregnant chigoe burrowed into the flesh of the foot, where a cyst would form to protect her. Encapsulated in the pus-filled lump, her belly would swell to the size of a pea. Secondary infection could kill a man. The cat flea might attach itself to a dog or a fox, a civet, or a mongoose—or a human, if a proper feline was unavailable. An entire species of fleas preyed on chickens, another on Asian pikas. Yet the creatures supposedly avoided monkeys. Ishii pondered the theory as he watched Moshi drinking water from the toilet. He was convinced the infestation had come with the little animal with the white face and bad manners. He was sure of it.

So far, the only evidence of disease came in the form of his continual indigestion. His flatulence alone gave Harumi enough reason to avoid him. She tried to be polite, but he sensed her true feelings, simply by her increasingly frequent absence. Always running out the door in her high heels. The American midget, Mr. Thompson, harbored feelings for her. Ishii could practically smell it on the man.

Ishii never revealed the magnificent scope of Ping Fan to the American, who eventually returned to America. Yet he had other problems. Ominous letters were arriving in the mail. Just the day before, he had received one from a few of his former underlings:

> To Your Excellency Shiro Ishii
> Former Lt. Gen. Army Med. Corps.
> Dear Sir:
> You must be surprised to receive this badly scribbled, rude letter so unexpectedly. We were your subordinates at Nanking. After the termination of the war, we came back to Japan, but the defeated Japan was not very cordial. Our homes were burnt and our wives and children were dead, and though we have nothing, we did manage to rehabilitate, but the waves of inflation have finally subdued us and we are experiencing difficulties obtaining tomorrow's food. Because of our hardship, we are about to fall into committing wicked deeds, but by all means we want our thoughtful commanding officer to rescue us.
>
> While we were at Nanking, we were ordered to carry out some gruesome work, and we did perform our duties faithfully. It must have been a difficult task to bury all those materials after the war was over.
>
> Because of our current hardships, we thought of dying more than just once, but when we thought about it, we realized that if we have enough courage to die, then we certainly should be able to overcome our trials and accomplish anything.
>
> Please, we beg you, our commanding officer, that you loan us, the unfortunate ones, as our rehabilitation funds, a sum of 50,000 yen, which will be positively returned to you within two months. Please give the money to the messenger.
>
> From your former subordinates.

Ishii would not bow to the demands. These cowards did not scare him. Not with two plainclothes policemen guarding his apartment. He had notified American counterintelligence as soon as he received the letter. Within an hour, two officers from the *Kenpetai* had arrived for his protection.

As if threats of blackmail were not enough, the Russians had arrived. Some thugs had approached Harumi on the street and threatened her. Awful, ugly men. The sentries out front provided only a limited sense of security. They might be able to stop the impoverished Japanese, but Russian agents were a different breed. They were out there, somewhere. Ishii remained attentive to the dull murmur of the streets. He listened for an accent in every voice that drifted through the window. Any minute he expected the Russians to smash down his door. Whenever he closed his eyes to nap for a few minutes—he was so tired from lack of sleep—he would jolt awake from a thump or a clank or a thick Slavic growl. The Russians would not approach on bended knee like the sniveling Arvo Thompson. They would extract the information by force. The fear of torture made his belly quiver.

The Americans were frightened as well, he could see. They would surely break down in despair if he spoke to the Russians. This was his trump card and he would play it in due time. First, however, he would have to get to the root of this flea problem. Through his peephole in the shoji screen, he spied the monkey playing with a red ball in the next room. The dirty thing was infested, he knew it. No matter what the medical books claimed, that monkey had fleas.

He crouched behind the screen and clucked his tongue to call the animal. He scattered a few rice crackers on the floor. When the monkey appeared, Ishii pounced on him. The little beast was stronger than he had thought, shrieking and scratching at him. He managed to pin it to the floor long enough to inspect its fur up close. The door opened, and Harumi came into the room. "Get off him, Father," she shouted.

"He has fleas!" Ishii cried as he hunched over the creature. The monkey would not stop screeching.

* * *

Harumi was caught by surprise when an unfamiliar American appeared at the door. The large man introduced himself as Norbert Fellows. He was in the neighborhood, he explained, and thought he might drop by unannounced. He hoped he was not imposing.

Harumi shook her head as she regarded him warily. "Please, come in."

"Thank you," he said with a nod. He was a huge man, with a wide smile and a deep, smoky voice. He was handsome, like the American actor John Wayne. He sauntered into the dim foyer and looked around. "Beautiful drawings," he said, admiring a sketch of a vertical hilltop, shrouded in mist. "Eighth century, aren't they?"

"Yes," Harumi said. She could feel herself blushing.

"Where did your father get them?" the man asked.

The girl did not know what to say. Her father, scratching himself silly in the back room, was no doubt listening. "Manchuria, I believe."

Moshi chirped and jumped into the man's arms, where he curled up like a baby. Harumi had never seen him behave so affectionately with anyone but her. "Is he here?" the visitor asked.

"Who?"

"Your father."

"Oh, yes, of course," she said. Her cheeks burned as she went back to her father's quarters. She found him frantically ransacking his armoire for a fresh kimono.

"Tell him to wait," he said. He scratched the back of his thin calf. "I will see him when I am ready and not before." Despite her father's command, Harumi led the American back immediately. They entered just as Ishii was scrambling like a spider onto the bed to assume his pose as a bedridden feudal lord. He looked aghast when he saw them. "Forgive me," he said, smoothing the covers over his legs. He glared for a moment at his daughter. "I did not expect company."

"I'm sorry," Fellows said in a husky voice. "I just arrived and wanted to make the most of our time."

Ishii looked the man up and down. "That's what the Russians said," he said coyly.

"The Russians? You spoke to the Russians?"

"You might say that," Ishii said. "Or it might be more accurate to say that they spoke to me. It seems they are very interested in what I have to say."

Fellows cleared his throat. "Let's cut the bull," he said. "You haven't talked to anyone."

Ishii was shocked. No one had spoken so rudely to him in years. And in front of his daughter. "I'm not accustomed—"

"I'm not finished," the American said. "If you'd like, you can go ahead and speak to the Russians. Find out how they treat you. I don't think you'll like it." The man paused to let the words sink in. "Or you can talk to me. Now. No more bullshit. I'm not interested in war crimes. I'm interested in the technical and scientific information you have to offer."

"That's what your predecessor said, but as I told him, I want immunity in writing," Ishii demanded, though his voice quavered.

"I don't have the authority to offer anything in writing," Fellows said, "but I have a promise from the highest sources that any information obtained in this investigation will be held in intelligence channels and not used in war crimes programs. This comes straight from General MacArthur himself."

"Why should I trust you?"

"I trust him, Father," Harumi suddenly offered in their native tongue. She could see this man would bring an end to the questioning and lift the family from disgrace.

Ishii looked at his daughter, his face crimson. After taking a moment to regain his composure, he turned back to the American. "If your government were smart, it would hire me as a biological warfare expert," he suggested.

"We can talk about that," Fellows said. "But before we go any further, I need you to tell me something."

Ishii glanced at Harumi, then returned his attention. "What? What is it?"

"We are aware that Japanese scientists, captured by Soviet armed forces, have confessed to testing biological agents on living human beings. Are they speaking the truth?"

Ishii stared at his accuser, searching the man's face. A full minute passed before he finally spoke. "Yes," he whispered. "Yes."

Harumi winced when she heard her father's response. It confirmed the worst of her suspicions. Finally, she was hearing the truth.

"Good," said the investigator. "If you can provide documentation of your work, I can promise you immunity, Mr. Ishii, and possibly more."

Ishii sat up straight. "It is all hidden away—eight thousand slides from more than two hundred cases—all at my disposal. I have given a great deal of thought, you know, to the tactical problems of biological warfare. I can write volumes, including modes of strategic and tactical employment."

"Before we talk about a job," Fellows said, "we'll have to discuss what you're going to say to the Russians."

"I won't tell them anything, I swear," Ishii said. "I won't let them in my house."

Fellows lifted an eyebrow. "It may not be that easy. We have granted them an official visit."

* * *

Over the course of a few weeks, Fellows visited Ishii almost every day to gather information and instruct the doctor on what to say when the Russians came. He was not to mention human experiments or field tests. Nothing about flea production or the organizational structure of Ping Fan. Most important, he was forbidden to say he had ever been briefed by the Americans.

In turn, Ishii provided a wide selection of documents and led the investigators to key experts, all promised immunity, who compiled an in-depth report describing their experiments on humans. His inner circle prepared a memorandum on chemical and herbicide research. Ishii gave his own account of his days in Harbin, as well as slides and micrographs. He had buried some of the records under the rock garden behind his apartment in Tokyo. Most of the documents were still hidden deep in a cave off Yokohama Bay.

In Fellows' presence, Ishii tried not to scratch himself. In private, though, the fleas continued to dance like a swarm of electrons in the corner of the room. He watched them warily. He avoided the flea-ridden floorboards except to go to the bathroom. In emergencies, he would hop across the room on his toes as quickly as he could. The fleas rarely caught him that way.

* * *

Harumi wore her finest clothes in anticipation of the Russians' arrival. She was nervous. An off-handed gesture might reveal her acquaintance with the American agent. As she applied lipstick and rouge, she reassured herself that Mr. Fellows would protect her against danger. The flutter in her chest quieted whenever she heard his voice, deep as a bullfrog's.

She trusted that this man would clear her family's name. Though her father was a murderer, she believed that the force of history had played a hand in his crime. In another time, with another fate, he might have been a great statesman, or perhaps a doctor on par with the great Shibasaburo Kitasato, who invented vaccines instead of poisons. Of this, she was sure.

Harumi heard a knock at the door and ran to open it. A large group stood outside. As instructed, she did not greet Mr. Fellows or any of the other American agents she recognized. She merely bowed. They spoke to her politely.

Then Mr. Fellows formally introduced the American agents, including himself, as if they had never met. "Where is your father?" the Russian officer asked.

Mr. Fellows laughed nervously. "Dr. Smirnov is eager to meet your dad. We all are. Is he ready?" Just as he asked the question, Moshi appeared out of nowhere and jumped into his arms with familiarity.

The Russians stepped back, clearly shocked. Harumi followed their eyes as they looked at Moshi and at Mr. Fellows. "I'm so sorry, sir," she said and grabbed the monkey from the American's arms. She started down the hall and motioned for the group to follow. "My father has been waiting for you."

Her father, in fact, had spent the morning enshrouded in a mosquito net, picking at the scabs on his knees. But when the group entered his room, he was as serene as a priest. He greeted them from his bed with a gentle bow of his head. "How may I be of assistance, gentlemen?" he asked with a smile.

The discussion proceeded uneventfully. The visitors left within an hour. Fifteen minutes later, Mr. Fellows returned with a wide grin. Harumi listened to the two men laughing in the other room. They spoke quietly for a while, and then she heard her father cackle. Mr. Fellows appeared a few minutes later to say good-bye.

"So long for now, my dear," he said with a warm smile. "I'm heading back to the United States."

"I won't see you again then?" she asked sadly.

"Oh, I don't know," he said. "You'll have to ask your father about that."

Her father was still chuckling to himself when she closed the front door and went into his room. On his lap was a briefcase. He scratched his arm absently.

"What's so funny?" she asked him.

He opened the suitcase. It was packed with stacks of American dollars.

* * *

Chapter 13

Albuquerque, New Mexico

November 1946

Murray's wife brought him a bowl of chicken broth to sip in bed while he read the newspaper. After nearly six months on his back, he could get up to putter around the house, but his strength came and went. Every night he went to bed coughing. On the return flight from Japan, he had spent the final hours in the airplane's tiny bathroom spitting blood into the toilet. His doctor discovered several lesions on his lungs, indicating an advanced case of tuberculosis. Shortly thereafter, Murray and his family, at the suggestion of a TB specialist, moved to New Mexico for the sunshine and dry air.

Tommy waddled into the doorway with two fingers stuck in his mouth. "Dada, bed," he said, pointing to the place where Murray spent most of his time. He knew he wasn't supposed to enter the room.

"Dada will be better soon," Murray said, though he knew the words didn't mean a thing. He felt cheated. During the first year of his son's life, his work at Camp Detrick had consumed him. Then his assignment in Japan had taken him away. Now, he had all the time in the world, but his illness prevented him from even reading to the boy.

Molly stepped around the toddler when she came to fetch the empty bowl. "Tommy, don't bother your father."

"He's not bothering me, love," Murray said. "Let him stay. I won't let him get any closer."

"You need your rest. I heard you coughing all night."

"I'm fine, aren't I, Tommy?"

"No!" the boy said from the doorway. It was his favorite word.

"See, he agrees with me," Molly said with a smile.

Murray returned to his newspaper in search of wire stories about the occupation, hoping to find any mention of Japan's biological weapons program. He still considered it his project, though his former colleague, Arvo Thompson, had taken over the investigation. A couple of months earlier, his old friend John Powell had written an article for UPI reporting that security forces had located Ishii in Chiba and planned to interview him about allegations of war crimes in Manchuria. The item was no more than a paragraph or two buried deep in the paper, but reading it had upset Murray. So Powell had been right: the bastard was alive after all.

More than once, Murray had dreamed he was back in Japan, searching for Ishii. In one of these dreams, his superiors jabbered at him in Japanese. In another, he caught Naito injecting his pearl, which he seemed to have misplaced, with the yellow fever virus. Occasionally, just as he was drifting off, another blunder in his investigation would prick a nerve, and he would awake with a start, cursing his carelessness. He had been manipulated with incredible sophistication. A whitewash was what his superiors wanted, and ever the good soldier, he had unquestioningly met expectations.

His illness made him reflective, and in the dark hours when his coughing held him captive, he admitted to himself that he had been perfect for the role. All he had ever wanted was to get ahead, to please. Beneath the posturing and politics, he had been adrift. He had allowed himself to be coerced from the day he began working at Camp Detrick.

Now here he had done his part, and what did he have to show for it? He could forget about that coveted job, at least until he was up and walking again. No one from Detrick had even sent a letter of condolence. The only one to show any concern was John Powell of all people, who called, still fishing around for a story. Murray couldn't possibly have helped him, given his confidentiality agreement; if nothing else, he liked to believe his word was good for something. But he decided he liked Powell.

What haunted him more than anything else was the tragic fate of Arvo Thompson. An old pal from Detrick had sent Murray a copy of Arvo's final report from Japan. It, too, had failed to raise the question of human experiments. Murray could only conclude that someone, Willoughby maybe, had gotten to his friend as well. Then a week later he heard that Arvo had shot himself in the head. The implications were very disturbing. Of course, Arvo was a drinker, a heavy one at that, but he had never shown any signs of depression. What had driven him to take his own life? Was it guilt?

A local article caught his eye about a young veteran who had been dragged through the Bataan Death March and then shipped up to Korea to work as a slave laborer for the Mitsubishi company. Such stories were appearing regularly. When MacArthur had called for a few divisions to be shipped to the Philippines before the war, the troops had come, entirely by chance, from New Mexico and Texas. Albuquerque had scores of returning prisoners of war, many in need of continued medical care. Naturally, Murray wondered if any had been exposed to biological agents. When he felt a little better, he though he might ask around, informally of course, just to satisfy his curiosity.

He took a breath and felt the tickle. He tried to suppress the cough, holding his breath, but that only made it worse. The hacking came in waves, at once relieving and torturous, as if his body were rejecting something evil from deep inside.

* * *

Jake had no interest in returning to the little adobe shack where his mother lived—if she were even still there. Why bother? She hadn't written him one measly letter during the war. Hungover and weary from his weeklong binge, he hoped he might once again find a home at the Jimenez house, and he wanted to see Leo.

He hitched a ride up the hill, and then stood for a long time at the wrought iron gate, gazing at the tall Victorian house. A gentle afternoon breeze carried the scent of burning leaves. He walked slowly, dreading the inevitable questions. All he wanted was for the family to take him in as if he had never left, but he sensed it wouldn't be that easy.

Realizing he had forgotten to bring a gift, he picked a handful of daisies from the side of the road. He wished he'd had a drink before he came. On the porch, however, he banished his doubts and nausea, and forced himself to smile.

When Mama Jimenez opened the heavy oak door, a moment passed before she shrieked and covered her mouth. Quickly, she clutched him to her heavy breast, crushing the flowers. "*Oh, pobrecito, mi pobrecito.*" She beckoned him in, and told him he'd arrived at a good time. Dinner was almost ready.

Leo appeared behind her, smiling. The two embraced. "Where have you been?"

Jake shrugged. "Staying busy."

Leo sniffed the air. "I guess you've been drinking."

"Haven't had a drop today," Jake said jovially. The alcohol was coming though his pores. "Why, are you offering? I'll take anything you've got."

Leo regarded him with concern. "Are you OK?"

"I'm fine, Leo," Jake snapped. He didn't appreciate his friend's tone. "I'm dying of thirst here. Jesus, bring me a beer or something."

When he followed Leo into the house, he noticed Angelina sitting on a dark velvet couch in the parlor, and his stomach lurched. She stood when he walked into the room. "Jake," she said quietly. She had become a beautiful woman, fuller than before. Exactly as he remembered her, only more so. "How are you?"

"I'm all right," he said. He wished he had taken a shower. "I'm doing swell actually."

"It sounds like things were awful over there."

He chuckled and waved his hand dismissively. "Has your brother been telling stories?" He grinned at Leo. "It wasn't easy, but we made it, didn't we?"

"With flying colors," Leo deadpanned.

Jake laughed loudly now. "Well, sure we did, pal. What's wrong with you? We came through like champs."

"Leo's grumpy because papa's driving him crazy," Angelina said and wrapped her arm around her brother's shoulders. "He just got here, and now he says he's leaving again. We're trying change his mind."

"He'll snap out of it," Jake said, hardly hearing what she said. He couldn't get over how lovely she was.

"I'll check on dinner," Leo said, and left the two standing together.

"How about that beer?" Jake called after him, smacking his lips. He was parched.

Angelina returned to her spot on the couch, and motioned toward the other end for Jake to sit down. "Please, make yourself comfortable."

"I'd rather stand," Jake said, suddenly self-conscious of his appearance. Still clutching the flowers, he rocked back on his heels, then laughed at the awkward silence. "I probably look different than when I left."

Angelina smiled easily. "I think you look fine."

Jake nodded quickly and noticed the bouquet of daisies in his hands. "Oh, these are for you—and your mother."

"I figured," Angelina said, admiring the dusty, crumpled blooms. "I have the perfect vase for them."

Following Angelina into the dining room, Jake was surprised to see how much Leo's little sisters had grown.

They were already sitting at the table. He breathed in deeply. It was all so comforting: the smell of hot coffee, onions frying in the pan, the lamps filling the corners with amber light. Mama Jimenez smiled as she bustled through the swinging door from the kitchen.

Jake sat down in his old chair. Leo sat beside him, while Angelina took a seat across the table. Soon Jake heard the clomp of boots on the tiled floor. Mr. Jimenez appeared a moment later, tall and lean in jeans and a checkered flannel shirt. He clapped his hand on Jake's shoulder. "Welcome, son," he said, then turned his attention to the kitchen. "What's cooking, Mama?"

Her response came sharply. "*Eso no es cosa tuya!*"

"It *is* my business," the rancher said gleefully.

The food arrived soon enough, stewed chicken in a red sauce, steaming enchiladas, and tortillas wrapped in green flannel napkins. Mr. Jimenez led the table in grace. When everyone was served, he broke the silence. "Before we begin, I want to honor our guest." His eyes grew moist. "Thank you, Jake, for sticking by my son. I understand that he might not have survived without you."

"Aw, I don't know about that," Jake said awkwardly.

"Jake killed rats to get me medicine," Leo announced.

"*Eeeewww!*" the girls shrieked.

"Hush!" Mama Jimenez shook her head.

"He took good care of me," Leo said.

"But then I got sick, and it was his turn to play nurse," Jake added. "So I guess we're even."

Mr. Jimenez raised his wine glass. "Let's have a toast, shall we, to our fine heroes, Jake and Leo."

Jake felt his spirits rise with the clinking of glasses. It was the first time since the war that anyone had offered him anything more than pity. He noticed Angelina smiling at him. Everything would be OK.

"While you were away, business has been good," Mr. Jimenez said. "We bought some land from the pueblos in the foothills. It's rocky, but good grazing."

"Isn't it dangerous for the cattle?"

"We have goats now as well. This land is for them. You should try Mama's stew." He kissed his fingers. "Delicious."

"I'm supposed to watch over them," Leo said, rolling his eyes. "Now I'm a shepherd."

"Yes," the rancher said with a clap of his hands. "At least, this was the plan. Unfortunately, Leo has chosen to spend more time filling out college applications than doing honest work."

"Leave him alone," Mama Jimenez said gently.

Mr. Jimenez sniffed. "Anyway, he has a job. It will be there when he's ready." He turned to Jake. "You know, I have Angelina's husband, Johnny, working for me now." As if on cue, a young man with slick blond hair and a large hawk-like nose wandered into the dining room, wiping his hands with a towel. "Speak of the devil," Mr. Jimenez said and pounded the table. "My right-hand man. Never quits before dinner."

"Better late than never," Johnny said happily. He sat down next to Angelina and gave her a kiss on the cheek. Suddenly feeling ill, Jake gulped down his wine. His diet of pickled eggs and pork rinds didn't help a stomach that still had a hard time keeping anything down. So she had married the idiot after all.

The sound of a baby crying came from the other room. "That's Anthony," Angelina said, getting up from the table.

Soon she reappeared with a little boy in tow. He had huge green eyes and his father's nose.

Jake abruptly stood up. "Excuse me," he said and rushed to the bathroom. He felt so nauseous, he could barely splash warm water on his face. Face it, he told himself, she was never yours. You were never in her league.

* * *

After they said good-bye to the young parents, who left to take the baby home, Juan and the boys went back to his study. Leo noticed, as they ambled down the hall, that Jake stank of raw sweat and alcohol. Now that they had returned to civilization, the tics that his friend had developed in prison stood out, the hitch in his step, the nervous twitches. Jake was in need of serious medical attention, which was disconcerting, because Leo felt he couldn't afford the luxury of playing caretaker. He had to take care of himself.

A row of family photographs hung at eye-level along the corridor, images so familiar that Leo hardly bothered to look. But Jake was fascinated by them. He stopped at the last one before the door, a picture of Leo, maybe fifteen years old, posing beside a magnificent boar, strung up on a rope. Jake laughed and pointed to the photo. "Hey, Leo, you never told me you shot a pig."

"It was a good day," Mr. Jimenez said.

Leo offered a faint smile. In the quiet of the study, he sensed an opportunity to open up a little. "They did the most awful things over there, Papa." He looked at Jake for confirmation. "I can't get them out of my mind."

"Hmm," his father murmured as he sat down, a long cigar jutting from his teeth. He leaned back in his chair and put his boots up on the desk. A cloud of smoke gathered around his head. "You say they did bad things to you. Tell me."

Leo looked at his hands folded in his lap. "Well, they beat us. Every day, they knocked us around."

"It looks like Jake took a few lumps," his father said lightly.

Jake grinned, glad to be noticed. He fidgeted with his empty brandy glass, then rubbed the lump on his forehead lovingly. "Yeah, they knocked me around something terrible."

Leo found himself almost afraid to speak of the acts he had seen in the infirmary, still ashamed of his silence after the doctors killed Sloan. But he pushed himself to speak with the hope of shedding the traumatic memories. "I think they were doing experiments on the men, intentionally making them sick."

"Oh, I don't know about that," Jake said. "The jury's still out on that one."

"What are you talking about?" Leo asked, incredulous. "You almost died of dysentery after they sprayed something in your face."

"Yeah, but a lot of guys with the shits never got sprayed. I asked them. And some say the shots saved their lives. So it's a wash, as far as I'm concerned."

Leo was speechless, unsure whether his friend was in denial or had simply lost his mind.

"I think Jake's saying he's ready to put this awful experience behind him," his father said gently. "I know it's hard. This war was awful. But it's over now."

* * *

Sitting atop a wooden fence, Jake used his thumb to shove the cork into the bottle, then chugged down a couple of mouthfuls. Wine ran down his chin. He lit a cigarette and took a long drag that made the ember spark and crackle in the dark. It felt good to be home.

Leo insisted on standing, his hands in his pockets. It was late, and cold. He had tried to slip off to bed when his father had retired, but Jake wouldn't let him. They hadn't seen each other in weeks, and Jake wanted to catch up. He hadn't been sleeping well. The restless twitch in his leg kept him up nights, and the nightmares persisted, always back in the hole, fighting for his life. They both stared out over the ranch and Albuquerque twinkling beyond, all in the soft grip of early winter. The town appeared far wider than Jake remembered it. "This place has changed," he said.

"Not enough," Leo replied, kicking the dirt.

"Ah, it isn't that bad." Jake took another drink. "It ain't Mukden, that's for sure."

Leo turned to face his friend. "I'm leaving, Jake."

Jake laughed in disbelief. "When are you going?"

"As soon as I get accepted to college somewhere. The sooner the better."

"Well, shoot," Jake said, and took a drag from his cigarette. He shouldn't have been surprised by the news—Leo had said as much before—but never so plainly, as if their experience together counted for nothing. But Jake wouldn't show he was hurt. It wasn't the first time he'd been deserted. "Well, don't worry about me," he said. "I can take care of myself."

"The drink's going to kill you, Jake."

"Fuck you," Jake said angrily. "You should talk. You're the one moping around all the time." His voice turned whiny. "Oh, poor me. I hate this town. I hate my family." He snubbed out his cigarette on the top of the fence. "Hell, your father has a right to be disgusted with you." He knew the words would hurt his friend, who flinched when he said them. "Sorry," he said. "Listen, just do me a favor and stay."

"Why?"

Jake laughed, embarrassed to admit what seemed so obvious. "Jesus, doesn't friendship count for something?"

* * *

Jake landed a mechanic's job at Bert's Auto Shop the next week. "You look like shit," Bert said, pushing his glasses up the bridge of his nose with a grubby finger. "But if I see you work hard, I'll keep you on. I won't do you any favors, though, just because you're a veteran. You screw up, you're out of here."

He need not have worried. Every day, Jake tirelessly fixed stripped transmissions and leaky radiators. The boss gave him Benzedrine to help him along. The pep pills did wonders for his system. He no longer needed to eat much. All day the two drank whiskey and water and talked while they worked on the cars. Jake felt good as long as he could keep rambling about everything under the sun—except the war. Once in a while, he ran into a someone he knew. Most of them looked like him, skinny and strung out. Though he was glad to see them, he didn't like talking about old times.

He had come up with a plan to start his own shop, rebuilding cars from odds and ends from the salvage yard. All the returning GIs were starting new lives and looking for something cheap to drive. There were parts to be found all over the city: carburetors, crankshafts, exhaust pipes, entire engines that need nothing more than a little tweak and spit polish. Jake took to sleeping at the garage. The place had everything he needed: a toilet and shower, a hotplate. When the air turned frosty, he slept with Lucy down on North Third Street. She made him take a bath before he came to bed, and was always nagging him for drinking too much, but he was growing fond of her.

On the Friday before the long Christmas weekend, Jake was just closing up when a faded red coupe pulled onto the front lot, steam pouring from its hood. The bennies were wearing off, and Jake's jaw ached from grinding his teeth. He was in no mood for company. He picked up a broom to look busy. A man in a long coat stepped out of the car and immediately fell into a coughing fit. Still hacking, the man staggered into the garage. "Leave it to me to overheat a car in the dead of winter."

Jake barely glanced up from his sweeping. "You can leave your car here and we'll get to it Tuesday."

"Is there any way you can take a look at it now?" the man asked. "I'm going to need it over the holiday."

Jake sighed and let his broom bang on the floor. "If your radiator is cracked, there's nothing I can do until next week."

"That's fair."

"You got anything to drink?" Jake tried on the off chance of a hidden flask.

"I'm afraid not."

The two rolled the steaming car inside. Jake fumbled with the dipstick when he tried to check the oil. "My goddamn fingers are numb again."

"Yeah, it's been pretty cold," the man said, his hands buried deep in his coat pockets. A plaid scarf was wrapped around his neck.

"Naw, hot or cold, my fingers and toes are numb all the time. Ever since I got back home."

"You served overseas?"

"What do you care?" Jake asked, suddenly feeling irritable.

"I'm just interested."

"I was in the Philippines," Jake said. "Then the Japs shipped me up to Mukden."

"Mukden? You must have had it pretty rough."

Jake filled the radiator with water without answering.

The man strolled around the shop, scrutinizing the swim-suit models on the walls. "How's your health?"

"You want my life story or what?" Jake said angrily, then rolled under the car.

"I don't mean to pry, it's just that I'm a doctor."

"My head feels like it's about to split open, but other than that, I'm swell, thanks."

"The drink probably isn't helping," Murray said gently.

Jake rolled out from under the car. "Look, pal, I'm doing you a favor."

Murray held up his hands. "I'm sorry. I didn't mean anything by it."

Jake stood up. "Well, you're leaking water, so you're going to have to leave her here until next week. C'mon, I'll take you home."

"We're at the corner of Cedar and Rose," Murray said as he climbed into the shop pickup. They rolled out of the garage, into the falling snow. An idea suddenly occurred to him. "Did you ever hear of a Dr. Naito?"

Jake snapped to attention. "How do you know that name?"

"I met him in Japan."

Jake gasped. "What—you mean that shithead's not in jail?"

"I'm afraid not," Murray said. The response confirmed his worst suspicions. "Tell me, did he give you any vaccinations?"

"Vaccinations?"

"You know, shots."

Jake slammed the brakes, causing the truck to shimmy gently to a stop. "Look, I said I didn't want to talk about this crap, and you keep bringing it up." He dropped his head, pinching the bridge of his nose. The conversation had brought on a splitting headache. "I can't believe that asshole is actually free."

"I'm sorry," Murray said quietly, though he knew his apology amounted to nothing. The snowflakes swirled like moths in front of their headlights. Naito, he had heard, was actually doing quite well. A good number of the Japanese scientists had won plum university jobs, all as a result of his foolish offer of immunity. When he got out of the car, Murray tried to apologize again, but the young man, lost in his thoughts, merely slammed the door and drove off.

* * *

Leo stayed in his room long after the breakfast noises subsided downstairs, typing an essay to include with his college applications. Recalling his work with the medical corps, he described the sense of purpose he felt wrapping tourniquets, and how, during those grueling hours on his knees, he had managed to dim the flash and boom of the war, at least for a while. College, he assumed, would prove equally diverting. At home, the windswept mesas were too quiet, an echo chamber for his thoughts, with only his father's bark breaking the silence, reminding him why he had enlisted in the first place.

At that moment, his father appeared in the doorway. "Why aren't you dressed?"

"I'm not feeling well this morning," Leo answered.

"I don't care how you're feeling," his father said angrily. He strode across the room and pulled the sheet of paper from the typewriter. "You need to get outside. Young men don't spend all day in their rooms. It isn't healthy."

"But I told you, I need to finish this by Friday," Leo said, startled by his father's gruffness.

His father clapped his hands twice in succession. "Out the door right now, or I'll carry you myself."

"OK, OK, I'm getting dressed," Leo said, hurriedly pulling on his pants.

Two horses were saddled outside. "I need your help today," his father told him. "Jaime has to fix a break in the south fence. A coyote got a few of the goats."

They rode into the foothills, where the January wind blew cold. As they waded through the silver-gray sage, Leo smelled lupine blown down from the forests. Up ahead, on the grassy slope, goats, maybe a hundred of them, grazed peacefully. Jaime, a pueblo man, was watching over the herd on horseback. When Leo's father whistled, the ranchero nodded and turned his horse homeward.

They tied their mounts to a nearby tree. His father had packed a lunch of roast chicken, tortillas, and beans. For a while, they ate in silence, overlooking the long valley. "I am disappointed in you," his father said calmly. He took a bite of chicken, tearing at the meat with his teeth. "But that's not important. You need to get to work and stop this nonsense. If you continue this laziness…"

"But, Papa—"

His father slapped him across the face. Though he used an open hand, the blow exploded in Leo's head. He almost swung back, but checked himself. As quickly as his feelings flared, they cooled and hardened, as he retreated inward. He went numb. Being hit by his father made him feel more loneliness than pain. He had withstood much worse, and he had survived. And he would survive this. When the Japanese guards had beaten him, he had remained passive but upright. Going limp only enraged them. He tried to remember that it wasn't him they were beating. He could have been anyone. The body was a garment, nothing more.

From this place of calm, he could do anything, even look into his father's face, which had softened. "I only want what's best for you," his father said apologetically. He never explicitly said sorry to anyone. "It's an easy job. Keep the goats in front of you."

"I won't do it," Leo said quietly.

"Don't take your eyes off them," his father continued. "If something scares them, move down the mountain."

"Find someone else to do it." Leo rose to his feet. "I'm going home."

"You're not going anywhere," his father replied, the anger surging in his voice again. "Someone has to stay up here with the animals."

Leo was already swinging his leg over the horse. He glanced at his father once more and shrugged, his heart slamming in his chest, exultant and fearful. His father's rage, no matter how long it lasted, wouldn't kill him. He was free at last. He rode briskly down the mountain, ignoring his father's call, not looking back even once.

* * *

The same skinny kid was working when Murray came to pick up his car the following week. The weather had grown extremely windy, tossing stray pieces of garbage across the parking lot. An obese man with glasses greeted him at the front of the garage, sipping from what looked like a glass of whiskey over ice. "Hey, Jake," he called. "Roll out the coupe." The young man floored the car out of the garage, then slammed on the brakes. "Goddamn you!" the big man hollered. "I told you not to do that!"

When Jake stepped out, a terrific gust of wind almost knocked him over. He wobbled, then regained his footing. "What's eating you?" he asked his boss.

"You could have killed this guy!" The heavy man took a long gulp of his drink. He shook his head, muttering as he wandered back to his office, "Damn kid ain't worth a hill of beans."

Murray climbed inside the car to get out of the cold. He rolled down the window. "How you feeling, soldier?"

The mechanic looked at him unsteadily. The wind flattened his hair along one side of his head. "I'm fine, Doc," he said, cracking a grin.

Murray could see that the young man was not fine. Though he was six feet tall, he could not have weighed more than one hundred and thirty pounds, barely enough to anchor himself against the buffeting winds. His skin was blotched with broken blood vessels; his eyes peered out from deep within his head. With his red, swollen nose, he already looked like a hopeless drunk. "How old are you, son?"

"Twenty-four," he said and stumbled in the wind. "Are we going to play twenty questions again?"

Twenty-four. Murray shuddered at the thought of his own boy looking so ragged and torn at that age. Murray wanted to tell the mechanic everything. About Ishii's deadly weapons, about the experiments he was now convinced had been conducted on soldiers like him; about the deal cut under Mac-Arthur's command. But of course he was forbidden to say anything. "Did you ever request your medical records from overseas?" he asked. The mechanic put his hand to his ear. Murray shouted over the whining wind. "Your records, did you ever ask for them?"

The young man shook his head. Conversation was out of the question in this weather. Murray clucked his tongue in frustration. He rummaged through the glove compartment for a pen and a matchbook, which he handed out the window. "Give me your phone number," he shouted. "I'd like to talk to you sometime." The mechanic squinted at him suspiciously, but scribbled something down, before Murray left him to battle the breeze.

* * *

"Give me another, Eddie," Jake said to the bartender. "The tequila tastes good tonight." He had already finished off a pint of whiskey with Bert, but the bennies made him thirsty. They propped him up, scalp tingling, in love with his own voice. He could drink and talk all night. The saloon was nearly empty, a typical Tuesday night, with only Jake, Lucy, and a table of young officers in uniform from out of town keeping the bartender busy.

"I don't like it when you drink that stuff," Lucy said, a glass of red wine in front of her. She looked pretty in the evenings, with eyes shaded in blues and greens like the feathers of a peacock. "Tequila makes you crazy."

"You love me when I'm crazy," Jake replied, and gave her a wet smack on the lips. He rapped his empty shot glass on the wood and raised his voice to get the barkeep's attention. "Hey, did I ever tell you I served under an Ed? Edward Dyess—"

"The greatest man who ever walked the face of the earth," the bartender said. "Yeah, I know."

"So you've heard of him," Jake said with a smile. Although Jake didn't like talking about the war, Dyess had become a towering figure in his memory, the one officer who had earned his respect. Word of the colonel's death had only heightened Jake's admiration. He had learned of the crash by chance, from a day-old newspaper he'd found on a bus stop bench. It was a wild story. Dyess and a few companions had escaped from Mindanao, hacking their way through the jungle until they crossed paths with a band of Filipino guerillas who delivered them to safety. After recuperating for a few months, the captain had reenlisted, and began flying training missions when his airplane crashed into a church steeple in California.

"I knew Dyess," someone said from down the bar. One of the officers had come to fetch another pitcher of beer.

He had narrow-set bright blue eyes, which contrasted with his black hair, reminding Jake vaguely of an Alaskan malamute's. He offered Lucy a smile. "We were at West Point together before the war." He motioned to his companions. "We all were."

Jake furrowed his brow. "Dyess didn't go to West Point."

The officer sniffed. "Of course he did." The pitcher of beer arrived, overflowing with suds, and the young man turned to his companions. "Hey, guys, do you remember Ed Dyess?"

"Edward Dyess," one of them said. "One of those poor bastards from the Death March. Died in a plane crash."

"A toast to Dyess, a hell of a pilot," the man with the pitcher declared as he began sloppily filling the mugs on the table. The men murmured their respects. Lucy seemed amused by them. When Jake turned to see what had captured her attention, the officer with the sled-dog eyes was offering her a glass of beer. "Come join us," he said to her before he noticed Jake glaring at him. "You're both welcome."

Jake shook his head. His jaw ached. He had been talking for hours, it seemed, days. He was shocked when Lucy sauntered over to the table, shaking her hips, the same way she had first approached him, the bitch. He followed her across the floor, hating her, but afraid to let her out of his grasp.

"So you must have been on Bataan too" the officer said to him. "Did you ever meet MacArthur?"

Jake snorted. "I wouldn't want to meet that son of a bitch." Over in Japan, Old Mac thought he was king of the world, another goddamn graduate of West Point.

"What do you say we play some music?" Lucy asked, sensing trouble. "Let's enjoy ourselves. The war's over."

"Amen," the officer said and ambled over to the jukebox. Jake's mood lightened when he heard Benny Goodman. The man could play. But then a new song began, something he hadn't heard before at the club, yet familiar. After a few bars he recognized it as the one Naito was always whistling in the infirmary. The officer sang along, his eyes on Lucy as he came back to the table with another pitcher of beer.

I don't want to set the world on fire,

I just want to start

A flame in your heart...

Jake could hear the wind sighing through the windows of the medical ward. He could hear the tap of Naito's wingtips on the tile floor, and the hiss of the Flit gun. He remembered how Larsen had held him down while that Jap bastard stuck him with the syringe. He could see the scene vividly, now that he had been reminded of it for the second time in a week. He glared at the officer.

When the prick asked Lucy to dance, and patted her ass as he escorted her to the dance floor, Jake tackled him. The two barreled into the table, sending the pitcher and glasses crashing to the floor. Suddenly Jake was fighting for his life; he was back in the infirmary, trying to gouge out the doctor's eyes. He could feel someone kicking him in the gut, but he continued to dig his thumbs into the sockets. He would fight until they killed him. He could hear Lucy screaming as they kicked him in the ribs, the shoulders, the head, then a heel broke through his teeth.

* * *

Chapter 14

Los Alamos, New Mexico

February 1947

The telephone startled Murray from his midday nap. He had been sleeping with his feet propped up on the metal desk they had given him in the basement of the laboratory. This was what he got for playing the good soldier: a microscope and some slides in a windowless office. He hadn't the strength to work more than a handful of hours a week down at Los Alamos, doing contract jobs for the nuclear crowd. "Murray?" a forceful voice inquired. "Jim Hallstrom here. How are you doing, son?"

"I'm fine," he said lightly, trying to sound alert. "Just enjoying the New Mexico sunshine."

"We'd like to get you back at Detrick soon," he said. "We're doing big things here, boy. Expanding by leaps and bounds. We could use someone with your expertise."

"I've sent my resume to at least six different department heads," Murray reminded him. "Not one has given me a call."

Fear of the Soviet Union had led to a broad expansion of the biological weapon program. Much of the budget was devoted to "covert and clandestine" operations through the Office of Strategic Services. Murray's former boss, Ira Baldwin, was studying the effects of noninfectious bacteria on large populations. The same kind of studies the Germans had performed on the Paris Metro and the London underground before the war, testing the dispersal of harmless germs through ventilating systems and industrial-sized fans. Camp Detrick's Special Operations had sprayed *Serratia marcescens* into the air-conditioning system at the Pentagon, launched vast quantities of *Bacillus globigii* from ships anchored off the coast of Hampton, Virginia, and sent fluorescent particles spewing over San Francisco, in each case, unbeknownst to the populace. The tests were no different than those Murray had carried out at Columbia University years before, yet he had never received a call.

"We'll get you all the work you need once you're at full strength," Hallstrom reassured him. "Once you're in with us, you're in for good."

"I guess after the work I did in Tokyo, I imagined something a little more exciting," Murray said.

"Say, you'll never guess who's giving a series of lectures at Dugway Proving Grounds this month," Hallstrom said, changing the subject. "Ishii Shiro. Our man from Japan. Crazy, isn't it? I thought you might want to hear what the old bastard has to say. Naturally, it's all very hush-hush."

"Ishii? But how—" Murray coughed once, then again. He was shocked. He recalled what Powell had said about shifting alliances. He had been right on every count. As a result of the arms race, Japan had already become a staunch ally, less than two years after the war. It was bad enough they forgave the emperor, now they let this murderer into the country? He was furious, but made sure to maintain his composure. "Count me in."

* * *

Leo was surprised to find Angelina sitting in the dim light of Jake's hospital room well after nine o'clock in the evening. His friend was still unconscious a day after the fight. They had beaten him badly, blackened both eyes, knocked out his front teeth. Beneath the turban of gauze crowning his head, Jake looked as frail as a toothless old man.

"Papa just left ten minutes ago," Angelina said quietly.

"Papa was here?"

Angelina nodded. "He was worried about Jake even before this happened. He wants to clean him up. Give him a job and a place to live. Get him off the liquor. You know how Papa thinks."

Leo rolled his eyes. He hadn't spoken more than a few words to the old man since their argument. "Always ready to offer a helping hand," he said sarcastically.

"I know he loves you," Angelina said. She paused, considering her words. "He's only trying to help."

"Yeah, well I don't want his help," Leo said, suddenly depressed. The hospital room reminded him of the infirmary.

"Love's easy to take for granted," Angelina said gently. "You might come to miss it if you're not careful."

Leo shrugged. At an impasse, the siblings sat in silence. They had once been close, but years had passed, and now Angelina was a wife and mother. Leo didn't quite know what to say to her. He looked at Jake breathing shallowly with his wounded mouth agape. "The Japanese used to give the men a lot of sleeping pills," Leo said. He cleared his throat. "They'd put patients to sleep in the afternoons, then do strange things to them. Run feathers under their noses. Spray stuff up their nostrils with Flit guns. Like they were guinea pigs in a big science experiment."

Angelina widened her eyes in surprise. "That's horrifying."

Leo had expected her to react with skepticism or to change the subject. Her interest encouraged him. "Oh, I saw terrible things. The doctors cut people open without anesthetic and killed them right there, cold."

His sister covered her mouth with both hands.

"Working in the infirmary, I saw all this stuff happening," he said, his voice rising with emotion, "and I might have saved somebody's life by speaking up, but I was afraid I'd be next. So now I have to live with this crap, this guilt." He grew angry. "And all I want to do is get on with my life, you know?"

Angelina gave him a reassuring look. "If I'd been there, I'd probably have died of fright."

"Nobody understands," Leo said as he looked at Jake with a new appreciation. "You couldn't know unless you went through it."

His sister nodded.

Leo cracked a smile. It felt good just to tell someone. "What are you really doing here, Angelina?"

His sister blushed and fumbled with the buttons on her sweater. When she looked up, her eyes were glassy. "Oh, I always liked Jake," she said, and began to say something more, but stopped herself.

Leo didn't press her. "Me too."

* * *

Arriving early, Murray found a seat in front near the stage. He wanted to get a good look at the man. The auditorium was stuffy and smelled of wet wool. As Murray settled into his chair, he watched the other attendees filing in. Many he recognized from years past: there was Dubos from Harvard, there was George Merck himself, flanked by a small entourage. Many retained their military bearing, razor-short haircuts, chins polished to an almost reflective shine. Murray had heard about experiments with *lysergic acid diethylamide*, planting it in cocktails to see how an individual would react. For all he knew, they could be gassing the auditorium at that very moment, and he smiled at the thought of all the buttoned-down gentlemen reduced to raving baboons. The seats were filling quickly.

A heavy-set man—Murray recognized him instantly as Norbert Fellows—emerged from the wings of the stage, followed by a young Japanese woman, and finally an elderly Japanese man. The girl he didn't know, but the regal manner of the gentleman left no doubt as to his identity. He was taller than Murray had imagined him to be, his neck stretching from the collar of an elegant black suit. A smattering of applause rose from the audience, now near capacity.

Fellows strode to the podium and cleared his throat. He had a hard, chiseled face and the shoulders of an All-American linebacker. "When I first met Lt. General Shiro Ishii a year ago in his Tokyo apartment, I never in a million years imagined that he'd be standing before you today. The pain of the war was still fresh in my mind, and to me, Ishii was a criminal." He turned to his guest. "No offense," he said, and the audience laughed. "But in the many weeks I have spent with him since then, I have been pleasantly surprised to find a friend."

Unbelievable, Murray thought, shaking his head. He wondered if anyone would dare publicly admit to a friendship with Josef Mengele, the good doctor's German counterpart.

"The materials he will present today may shock you—they certainly surprised me—with their grisly subject matter. But keep in mind that this work was done under the strains of war. Let's put aside the past, and see what we can learn from our colleagues in the East. Please give a warm welcome to our distinguished guest, Shiro Ishii."

The young woman followed Ishii to the podium, and lowered the microphone to her own height. "I'm afraid my father does not speak English very well, so he has asked me to translate for him." Ishii began to speak quietly. After a moment, his daughter assumed an authoritative tone as if she were a medium channeling the words of a spirit standing in the shadows behind her. "Dear sirs, I will begin by telling you what I always told my own men: what you are about to see will forever change your perceptions of the role of science on the battlefield. As the German scientist Fritz Haber said of chemical weapons when he accepted the Nobel Prize after the First World War, 'It is a higher form of killing.'"

A movie projector in the back of the room began to whir and light filled a screen along the back wall of the stage. A grainy black-and-white image appeared: two men attaching a cylinder to the fuselage of a two-seater airplane, then clipping a hose and spray gun to the wings. "The receptacle you see beneath the aircraft," the young woman explained, "is filled with plague-infested fleas."

The plane was shown flying low over a primitive village, where it released a cloud of white smoke. Then it was seen taxiing to a stop. As soon as a disinfection team blasted it with hoses, out came the pilot, Shiro Ishii, grinning proudly.

A light murmur of recognition rose from the audience. "This attack occurred on a Chinese village in 1940, before the United States entered the war," she said. "It resulted in a plague epidemic which killed ninety-nine people. Later, we developed a porcelain canister to hold the fleas."

A diagram of the bomb appeared on the screen, the same diagram Murray had been shown in Tokyo. The reminder of it made his ears burn.

A new scene came into view: Ishii in scrubs at an operating table. The lights glared on the pale nude body before him. A surprisingly Caucasian-looking assistant with blond hair went about preparing for what looked to be an autopsy. Ishii was shown sawing open the rib cage. Just as he was removing the heart, he shouted at someone off-camera. His daughter began to speak. "This subject had been exposed to anthrax in a crystallized form, sprayed at close range with a Flit gun. Within days, we found the bacteria had thoroughly cut off function of his lungs, resulting in respiratory failure."

The girl's detached, firsthand account sounded so convincing, as if she had actually been there. At this point, anything seemed possible. But she was so young, so sweet. Had she witnessed her father's deeds? Murray wondered. Had they discussed his work around the dinner table? Did she love him?

She went on to describe how the United States could implement her father's research in future wars. He was exploring the use of more effective vectors: spiders, houseflies, crickets. Japanese encephalitis, her father believed, would be an especially effective weapon. A team of U.S. scientists were working with his former colleagues from Unit 731 on these very issues in Japan.

At the close of the lecture, the audience members rose to their feet in applause. Ishii descended the stairs at the side of the stage, just a few yards from Murray, to answer questions, and was immediately surrounded by curious scientists. Fellows and the young woman, standing together in the wing, were now discreetly holding hands. Ishii couldn't speak English well enough to respond to the inquiries, but it didn't matter. Those encircling him appeared satisfied just to bask in his presence. Murray pressed closer, to almost point blank range. He could shoot him right now and know he had done his part for humanity.

A flashbulb popped. Ishii's cheeks were flushed from the excitement. Scratch marks, perhaps from a razor, showed beneath his chin. All Murray really wanted to do was introduce himself, to watch the look of recognition pass across the man's face. When Ishii came close enough to shake hands, Murray handed him his business card as an introduction. Ishii glanced up absently, smiled, then removed a pen from his jacket pocket to autograph it.

* * *

Murray watched the flames lick the burgers and frankfurters roasting on the barbecue. Occasionally, one of the hotdogs would split, sending grease hissing into the fire, and he would turn it with his tongs. He felt a little silly in his red-checkered apron and floppy fishing hat, but only a little. The storm that had blown through over the weekend left unseasonably warm temperatures in its wake, perfect weather, unfortunately, for Molly's father to pay a visit to see his grandson before returning east.

"Don't overcook them, son, whatever you do," Hallstrom warned Murray for the second time. "There's nothing I hate worse than a burned patty." He leaned forward in his lawn chair, his elbows on his knees. Beads of sweat glistened atop his bald crown. The temperature would reach eighty-five by midafternoon. "I tell you, I don't know how you can stand the heat out here in the desert."

They both turned their attention to Tommy, in shorts and a fire engine-red T-shirt, running around the yard with a little bow and arrow. Just the day before, Murray had played catch with him for the first time. The boy had a good arm.

"I still think you three would be happier back in Frederick," the older man said. "Better schools."

"No interest." Murray said flatly.

Hallstrom was taken aback. "You've been begging me for a job at Detrick for months. We're just waiting for you to recover.

There's plenty of work. You saw it yourself this weekend. The program is growing like gangbusters."

"What I saw this weekend was horrifying," Murray spat. "It made me physically ill."

Hallstrom chuckled. "Well, like I was saying, once you're back on your feet—"

"What do you think the newspapers would say if they heard about Ishii making an appearance on American soil, Jim?"

"The newspapers?" Hallstrom asked, confused. No one even joked about breaking confidentiality. A security breach would mean certain jail time. But soon the older man's face relaxed. "You had me there for a minute."

"I'm serious, Jim. What if I told somebody?" Murray asked. "I imagine old Ishii got some kind of honorarium for his appearance. Maybe he's on salary. Hell, he's probably making more than I do. A nice way for the department to spend taxpayers' money, I'd say."

Hallstrom chuckled nervously. "Now calm down, Murray. You're talking nonsense now." He lowered his voice and reversed course. "And besides, even if you were that stupid, you'd have no proof, son."

"Oh, I've got all the proof I need," Murray lied. He had nothing, but he wanted to unsettle his father-in-law, just this once. "I've got boxes of evidence. Did I ever show you MacArthur's pledge of immunity for those scumbags, written in his own hand?"

Molly appeared at the back door with a salad bowl. She was wearing an attractive dress of a bright floral print. "There's my princess," Hallstrom called to her, all smiles. She set the potato salad on the table and sat down beside her father with a sigh. To keep cool, she had pulled her curls atop her head. Hallstrom turned and noticed the large black pearl hanging from a silver chain around her neck. Murray almost dropped his spatula when he saw it; he had been searching for it for weeks. "Would you look at that," Hallstrom said. He tapped it lightly with his finger.

"I found this when I brought one of Murray's jackets to the cleaners," she said proudly. "I thought I'd surprise him. I didn't have a chance to get it mounted until last week."

Hallstrom gave Murray a hard glance. "That must have cost you."

Murray lifted his father-in-law's flaming burger from the grill.

* * *

Murray was in the darkroom at Los Alamos, watching fluorescent bacterium under the microscope, when someone entered unexpectedly. Though the light momentarily blinded him, he caught the outline of two figures coming in the door. "Who's there?" he called.

"No need to fear, Mr. Sanders," one said. Murray recognized the voice instantly as Naito's. As his eyes readjusted to the dim red light, his guess was confirmed. There was his former interpreter. He was accompanied by a hulking Japanese man in a sharp suit who hung back a few steps, his hands in his pockets. The guy looked like a thug.

"What are you doing here?" Murray asked in alarm. "This is a secured area."

"I have a pass, Mr. Sanders," Naito said. He was dressed in his usual finery with a bowler perched atop his head. "Don't worry, we've been approved by the proper authorities."

Murray glanced at Naito's companion: the bloated face of a boxer, nose askew, his hair slicked back in a solid, shiny mass. The two stood between Murray and the phone on the wall.

"I saw you at the Ishii conference," Naito said. "Remarkable, wasn't it?"

Murray could feel his heart thumping in his chest. The surreal atmosphere of Tokyo was coming back to him now, the inane chitchat, his guide's cat-who-ate-the-canary grin. Murray had been aware of the unreality, yet he had played along, he didn't know why. "You told me Ishii was dead," he said. "You lied to me."

Naito shrugged, chuckling. "Lie is a strong word, Mr. Sanders. It implies a desire to hear the truth."

"You looked into my eyes and said that you had never performed experiments on humans," Murray said. "I took you for a man of honor." Murray recognized the ridiculousness of the statement as soon as he said it. He had never trusted Naito. "What do you want from me?" Murray demanded, moving toward the phone, but the big man blocked his path. "I'm done playing games."

"Games are for children" Naito agreed. He motioned to his partner, who produced a flat leather case from his breast pocket. He flipped it open to reveal a bracelet of black pearls on a bed of satin. Murray noticed the man's wrist was decorated with tattoos stretching up his arm. "Mr. Kuritsu sends his thanks," Naito said.

"More bribes," Murray said, shaking his head in disgust.

"More pearls," Naito corrected him. "I'm told the one we gave you in Japan has become a charming pendant for your wife. This completes the set."

"If I had any idea…" Murray protested, but his voice trailed off. Who was he kidding? All his life he had been sleepwalking with nary a thought except to what others expected of him.

Naito continued as if Murray hadn't said a word. "Mr. Kuritsu and I have started a new company, the Japan Blood Bank, with MacArthur's approval, of course. We're hiring the best minds in science, and we'd like you to be a part of it."

The burly man placed the jewelry case on the counter and remained next to Murray, looming, his head less than a foot away from the red bulb on the ceiling. Murray could hear him breathing through his mouth. In the light, more tattoos were revealed, blue fish swimming up the man's neck from beneath his collar. He must have been covered with them.

"You could stay in New Mexico," Naito continued. "Writing, reviewing."

Murray laughed quietly to himself. "Get out of here."

"Think about it, Mr. Sanders," Naito said. "We could use a man like—"

"I said get the hell out!" Murray shouted and bolted across the room to grab the phone. "I'm calling security."

The tattooed man slapped a massive hand on Murray's neck, but Naito said something in Japanese, and he let go. They turned to leave. "Think about it, Mr. Sanders," Naito said. "You've never disappointed us before."

* * *

Leo was reading in his room when Jake appeared in the doorway, a fedora tilted raffishly on his stubbled head. He grinned at Leo's surprise, displaying a wide gap from his missing teeth. "Your pop said he'd put me up."

"I'd hope so," Leo said, genuinely pleased to see his friend. A weight had been lifted since he'd spoken of his experience at the hospital. He realized that he wasn't to blame for them, and he'd come to see Jake in a new light. What they had lived through together would mark them forever, and if his friend were ever again in serious trouble, he'd circle the world at a moment's notice. But their relationship had changed; they were no longer living in extremis, and no longer dependent upon one another. Leo neither had to play nursemaid for Jake out of guilt, nor push him away in anger. He could simply be glad that they both were still upright walking the earth.

Jake remained in the doorway, tossing a baseball into an old mitt. The hollows beneath his eyes were still dark, lending him a slightly ghoulish appearance. "What're you doing holed up in this cave?" he asked, glancing around the room, then up at the window, dotted with raindrops from a passing storm. Leo held up a book of anatomy.

"C'mon," Jake said. "Let's play some catch."

Leo glanced at the window. "But it's raining—"

"I don't care if it's snowing." Jake pulled his friend from the bed. "For old time's sake."

The rain had stopped, leaving cotton-tailed clouds in its wake. They stopped at a liquor store for a six-pack, then set out for the old sandy ball yard at the edge of town. When they got there, they found it had been converted into a parking lot, but

Jake's spirits remained high. Cracking open a can of Schlitz, he took a long swig. "Why don't we just play catch here?"

"We'll scuff up the ball."

"We won't drop it," Jake said as he backpedaled into the lot and lobbed a throw to his friend. Leo caught the ball and fired it back with mustard. Jake had to drop his beer to catch it. "Are you crazy, Leo? Look what you made me do."

"Throw it, Jake, there's a play at the plate!"

Jake flung the ball wildly, but Leo caught it with ease. He laughed and sent it back. "Don't drop it!"

"I won't!" cried Jake, extending his glove for an over-the-shoulder grab. Keeping the ball from touching the pavement became the game. They made ten, then twenty throws. On the twenty-first, the ball struck the base of Jake's mitt and rolled off. When he picked it up, he found the gravel had chewed up the leather along one side.

"I'm waiting," Leo called. A heavy cumulus cloud passed in front of the sun.

"We wrecked it," Jake said, dejected now.

Leo hopped up and down. "C'mon, throw it back. This is fun."

Jake went to the bag for another beer. "Let's take a break," he said. "My arm hurts." The sky was darkening again. A few drops splashed onto the pavement. When the rain began to come down in sheets, they found shelter under a tall cottonwood. Jake took another long drink. "There was a time when you couldn't drag me off the field," he said in apology. Leo noticed a lisp from the gap in his teeth. "But things are looking up," Jake said. "Your father said he'd put me to work."

He poked the mud with a stick. "You know, this doctor I met says he wants to talk to me about what happened over there."

"In the infirmary?"

"Something like that."

"I'd jump at the chance," Leo said, careful to temper his enthusiasm. He wanted so badly to help his friend, but undo pressure would scare him away.

"I don't know," Jake said doubtfully with a wave of his arm. "I don't see what's in it for me."

"We can disagree about what happened back at Mukden," Leo said. "We can try to forget about it. But that stuff isn't going away."

Jake nodded, intent on the hole he was digging in the mud.

"Talk to the doctor. Tell him everything."

"Just to help *him*?"

"Of course not," Leo said. "To help yourself."

* * *

Murray knew something was amiss when he pulled into the driveway and noticed the front door hanging open. Molly complained if anyone allowed the cold to come in for even a minute. More importantly, if her car wasn't in the driveway, why was the door ajar? A gust slammed it shut as he stepped onto the porch. It had been a week since his visit from Naito, and in that time someone had been repeatedly calling and hanging up. Someone either wanted to scare him or to check if anyone was home.

The house was ransacked from top to bottom. Smashed furniture, holes in the wall. "Molly?" he called. His voice had an odd, metallic ring. A breeze rattled the windows. "Anybody here?"

The family photos on the wall were smashed. Someone had cut open their mattress and pulled out the stuffing. He wandered into Tommy's room, fearing the worst, but it was surprisingly intact. Then he noticed the shards of glass on the bed. A jar had been broken. As he picked up one of the pieces, he noticed a spider crawling on it, then another on the pillow. The bed was swarming with wolf spiders. He threw the glass on the floor and ran to the bathroom to wash his hands.

The phone rang. The house felt empty, abandoned. Afraid of who would be on the other end, he hesitated before answering, then remembered it might be Molly. He had never been so glad to hear her voice. "I'm sorry we're running late for dinner, honey," she said. "Tommy and I got held up at the Pic'n Pac."

Murray pictured her standing in a phone booth, the receiver tucked under her ear so she could hold Tommy's hand. She had deplored this business he was in and never tired of reminding of his oath to do no harm. "Don't bother coming home, love," he said, trying to sound calm. "I'll meet you two at the Chinese place for dinner. I need to talk to you about something."

"But we got all these groceries...."

"That's OK," he said. A spider crawled across the counter in front of him. "I need to make a phone call, then I'll be right there. Order me a beer, love."

Off the phone, he quickly leafed through his address book. Forget confidentiality. Forget the career. They could try him for treason, for all he cared. The house was darkening with the coming of evening. He looked at his watch. It was just after nine o'clock in New York. He listened to the faintly ringing phone, five, six, pick up, goddammit. "Hello, Powell?" he asked. "This is Murray Sanders."

"Murray," the reporter said. "I was wondering when you might call."

"I'm ready to talk. I want to blow this thing wide open."

The reporter laughed. "That's what I like to hear. Now what do you have on paper?

"Don't worry about records," Murray assured him. "I've got it all in my head."

"Hmm," Powell said. He sounded doubtful. "See, without documents, it's your word against the government's. And for all anybody knows, you could be a crackpot."

"You want proof, I've got somebody I want you to meet," Murray whispered. "He's all the proof you'll ever need."

* * *

Leo insisted on saying farewell to his family up at the ranch. He gave his mother and sisters quick hugs and dashed out the door before they tried again to convince him to stay. He found his father wrestling with a bale of hay in the barn. Together they tossed it into a corner. "I've come to say good-bye, Papa," he said, brushing himself off.

His father's back stiffened. He hadn't said a word when the letters of acceptance began rolling in. He slowly removed his leather gloves. "Where are you going?" he asked, playing dumb.

"I'm leaving for California today, you know that," Leo said, making sure to hold his father's gaze. He wanted desperately to promise he'd be coming back soon, that he would return in the summers to work on the ranch, but he stopped himself, and let the awkward silence hang in the air.

His father crossed his arms and looked at Leo appraisingly. He shrugged. "Well, go make your own decisions, even if I think they're foolish."

Leo nodded, accepting the remark as the most he could expect. He reached to shake hands, and the old man pulled him close for a rough embrace.

Jake drove him down the mountain in the pickup. He had just returned from the salvage yard with the bed chock full of greasy engine parts. With a cigarette dangling from his lips, he chatted happily about the treasures he had found. Leo listened patiently, ignoring the clink of bottles under the seats. At the station, he gave Jake the journal he had kept at Mukden. "Show this to the doctor, if you ever decide to look him up," he said.

"I might," Jake said with a smile. Leo prayed he wouldn't break down in tears, ruining what he hoped would be a simple farewell. But Jake made it easy, almost pushing him onto the car after a quick embrace and a stinging slap on the back.

The coach was nearly empty. Settling into the soft leather seat, Leo took a last look out the window. Jake was flashing a gap-toothed grin up at him when a gust blew off his baseball cap, sending him sprinting down the platform to catch it. Leo laughed and shook his head. The train began to roll.

The sun was just beginning to dip behind the mountains. It was his favorite time of day.

Outside, the silver gramma grass stretched across the tableland, broken up by ground-hugging mesquite and the odd juniper or piñon. A moment later, his stomach dropped as the prairie gave way to the yawning gorge of the Rio Grande, a thousand feet below.

* * *

Jake ran his tongue along his new front teeth, a habit he'd developed since the Jimenez family bought him some replacements. His mind wandered to the fifth of Smirnoff waiting for him in a bucket of ice back at the hotel room. He didn't want to recite his tale of woe to this reporter with the round glasses, whom he knew nothing about except that the guy was supposed to be a real shit disturber along the lines of I. F. Stone. An army of typewriters clacked outside the office door. Sanders, the doctor, had convinced him to come to New York with the promise of an open bar tab, but at the moment, it hardly seemed worth this misery.

They'd been dragging the stuff out of him for an hour already: the shots, the Flit gun, the feathers under the nose. He'd told them about his long bout with dysentery and the sudden, mysterious death of Whitaker. It made him sick to see all the memories piled up before him like a tangle of old chicken bones. But Powell seemed to enjoy picking through the mess. Jacket off, sleeves rolled up, he listened, hunched over his desk, so close Jake could smell the Brylcreem in his hair. He seemed to know what to ask, as if he had heard similar stories—but he was no pushover. More than once, he'd caught Jake exaggerating. He shook his head sympathetically when Jake finished talking, then turned to Sanders. "It's a sad story, Murray, but I haven't really heard anything new here," he said. "Certainly no hard evidence of biological hanky-panky."

"How can you say that?" Sanders asked. He had been pacing the room throughout the interview, agitated, injecting questions when he saw fit. He was going to lose his job for this, he kept saying. He pointed to Jake with a look of mild disgust. "Just look at him. What more do you need?"

Powell lit a cheroot, and through the smoke, gave a quick appraisal. He shrugged, which Jake found irritating. After dumping all that garbage, the least he felt he deserved was a little recognition.

"Show him the photo," Sanders said and slapped a folder down on the desk. Jake had brought a picture of himself before the war at the doctor's request. He'd packaged it with the materials Leo had given him, and handed it over to Sanders without bothering to look at any of it.

Now studying the photo, he hardly recognized himself: the wild, sun-bleached hair, open-mouthed, laughing, the thick curve of his shoulder under a T-shirt. His teeth, so straight and white. He couldn't remember ever having such healthy teeth.

He slid the photograph to Powell. The reporter took a look and glanced up, equally surprised. "You poor kid."

"Look at yourself back then, Jake," Sanders whispered, hovering just behind him. "Look how handsome you were. How do you feel when you see that picture?"

Jake's chest felt tight. He looked out the window to the brick building across the street, where he could see a secretary filing papers. He shrugged.

"That's it?" Sanders asked. "After all that shit you've told us about, you mean to say you just don't care?"

"Leave me alone!" Jake shot back.

"Stand up," Sanders commanded. When Jake remained seated, Sanders knocked over a chair with a loud bang. "Stand up, goddammit! Stand up, or kill yourself right now! Get it over with. I'll give you the gun."

Jake rose slowly to his feet, fuming. He wanted to rip out the doctor's lungs, but something paralyzed him. Sweat poured from his armpits. He needed a drink.

"Look at yourself," Sanders said. "A shell of who you used to be. Can you look at that photo and tell me you're not angry? I gotta tell you, pal, if you don't feel something, you're already dead."

Jake clenched his teeth to keep his composure. Kindness has no place here, Dyess had told him as he struck the bottoms of Leo's feet with a bamboo pole. Survival is in the mind.

"Do us a favor and take off your shirt," Sanders said.

Jake glared at him.

"C'mon, show us your muscles."

Jake slowly undid his shirt, his fingers fumbling with the buttons. Kindness has no place here. When he stretched out his arms, Powell looked horrified, his eyes flitting over the thick white injection scars. Survival is in the mind.

"Now read what your friend wrote," Sanders said with the scraps of paper in his hand. To Powell, he said, "You wanted something in writing."

The pages were smudged with Leo's fingerprints. Jake could barely read the handwriting. It appeared to be a list:

"*30 Jan 43* Everyone received a 5 cc typhoid-paratyphoid A inoculation.

7 Feb 43 Vaccination for smallpox, British only.

19 Feb 43 Several officers have been questioned about dysentery and diarrhea."

The entries went on for pages, needle after needle jabbed into the flesh. Powell scribbled intently into his notebook. Jake kept reading. His fury kept growing.

He let the pages float to the floor. His temple throbbed just above his right eye. He was drenched with sweat, and exhausted. He slumped into his chair and took a deep breath.

The office, darker now with the setting sun, was strangely quiet. The clattering of the typewriters receded. The secretary across the street was putting on her coat to go home. Only the scratching of Powell's pen broke the silence.

"So do you think we have something?" Sanders asked the reporter.

Powell looked up from his writing, and nodded solemnly. He glanced at Jake. "You dropped your papers," he said.

"Oh, sorry," Jake replied and bent down to retrieve the scraps strewn about the floor.

"No need to apologize, soldier," Powell said. "You didn't do anything wrong."

The End

Afterword

We kept firmly to the truth in our telling of this dark chapter of America's past. Our fictional heroes, Jake and Leo, might have been any of the soldiers who fought with New Mexico's Two Hundredth Coast Artillery, many of whom fell into the hands of the Japanese on Bataan and eventually landed in Mukden. We based their stories largely on firsthand accounts of those who survived the ordeal. The depictions of Murray Sanders and Ishii Shiro, as well as the other real-life figures dotting the novel's landscape, sprang from historical investigation of their actions and characters.

The book is based on facts, and yet they are facts that the U.S. government continues to deny. While a wealth of scholarship on Japan's biological weapons program has emerged over the past twenty years, the United States government has contributed very little information. The stark fate of U.S. veterans captured in the Philippines has been treated with similar silence. This reticence is due to the sensitive Pacific partnership forged in the years following the war, when the United States began to build Japan into a bulwark against Communism. Though the Cold War ended long ago, Japan continues to play a critical role in support of this country's presence in East Asia. Thus the United States is extremely protective of its ally, to the extent that it still only tacitly acknowledges having made a deal granting immunity to those Japanese scientists who engaged in research on humans. The legacy of this agreement— and the lengths to which the United States has gone to cover it up—makes for an instructive coda to this story.

* * *

Scholars now estimate that Japan's army medical corps killed roughly ten thousand people in laboratory experiments and field trials,[1] mostly Chinese, but also Mongolians, Koreans, White Russians,[2] and some Allied prisoners.[3] In addition to Ping Fan and Mukden, the army erected facilities in Changchun and Nanking. Satellite units ranged as far as Burma, Singapore, and possibly even Manila and the Dutch East Indies, employing thousands of the country's brightest doctors and scientists.

Ample evidence suggests that Emperor Hirohito was aware of the program, though he may not have known about the human experiments. His personal seal appeared on the founding documents of Ping Fan.[4] His younger brother, Prince Mikasa, reportedly visited the facility.[5] Another brother, Prince Chichibu, was said to have attended one of Ishii's extended lectures before a large military audience.[6] Hirohito's name was also cited at the Soviet-sponsored Khabarovsk war trials of 1949, where twelve Japanese scientists confessed to having performed experiments on human subjects, including Americans.[7] They also testified that the emperor had ordered the creation of the so-called Water Purification Bureau.[8] The defendants—spared death in exchange for the information they provided—received sentences ranging from two to twenty-five years.[9] The U.S.-sponsored War Crimes Tribunal, held between 1946 and 1948, would certainly have heard similar testimonies had American authorities chosen to press the case.

Hirohito himself never stood trial for his pivotal role in the war and continued to rule Japan, at least ceremonially, until his death in 1989. The medical corps personnel were also freed from prosecution, and similarly went on to lead professionally productive lives, unencumbered by the past. Ishii, for his part, retired on a handsome government pension of ninety thousand yen.[10] There is some evidence that he gave a series of lectures at Camp Detrick regarding human experimentation, though government officials deny that he ever visited the United States.[11]

Ishii's daughter Harumi stuck by him until the end, postponing marriage until two years before he died of throat cancer in 1959. It seems that she, like many of her generation, chose to overlook the more grisly aspects of her father's life. "My father was a very warm-hearted person," she told the *Japan Times*. "He was so bright that people sometimes could not keep up with the speed of his thinking, which irritated him and made him shout. I am really proud of him."[12]

Ishii's old rival, Kitano Masaji, who assumed control of operations at Ping Fan between 1942 and 1945, officiated at his funeral. The scientist placed one of Ishii's bones under a monument erected in honor of the medical corps, called the Seikon

Tower, located in the Tama cemetery in a suburb of Tokyo. A dwindling number of former members continue to occasionally gather for reunions.

Ishii's subordinates returned to academia and the business community. Many made up the mainstream of the country's medical establishment. To name just a few:

- Dr. Ishikawa Tachiomaru, who was responsible for secreting thousands of human pathological samples, became a professor and then president of Kanazawa University's Medical School.
- Dr. Okamoto Kozo, who conducted numerous vivisection experiments at Ping Fan, became a professor at Kyoto University and director of the university's medical department.
- Dr. Yamanaka Taboku, one of Ishii's researchers stationed in Nanking, became dean of Osaka Medical School, and in 1974 director of the Japan Bacteriology Association.
- Dr. Yoshimura Hisato, who carried out frostbite experiments, eventually became president of Kyoto Prefectural Medical College. He later worked as a consultant to the Japanese Antarctic Expedition and in 1973 became the first president of the Japanese Meteorological Society. He was forced to step down in 1978, when journalists exposed his past and prompted a scandal, but he nevertheless received one of the country's greatest honors, the Order of the Rising Sun—Third Class.
- Dr. Tanaka Hideo, who specialized in the mass production of fleas, became director of Osaka Municipal

University's School of Medicine. He also received an Order of the Rising Sun in 1978.[13]

Others went on to successful careers at Takeda Pharmaceutical Company, the Hayakawa Medical Company, Tokyo University's Infectious Diseases Research Institute, Osaka's Kinki University, the Showa University of Pharmacology, and the Nagoya Prefecture Medical University. Still others moved into government positions. As the late Sheldon Harris, author of *Factories of Death*, pointed out, every director of the Japan National Institute of Health between 1947 and 1983, with one exception, had served in the country's biological weapons program. Five of the directors committed either vivisection or bacteriological experiments in the war against China.[14]

After the war, a number of members of the institute advanced their research with further experiments on humans. Two of the doctors injected a fever virus into prisoners at Fuchu Prison in 1947. They later used another strain of virus on mental patients in Niigata Prefecture, which led to nine deaths, including a suicide. One doctor from the institute allowed infants at the National First Hospital to ingest *E. coli*, which causes diarrhea and can be fatal. The doctor later published a paper on his findings, hiding his use of children as subjects.[15]

These scientists provided a wealth of information to Arvo Thompson, the real name of the lead investigator in Tokyo, who committed suicide in 1951, and his successor, Norbert Fell, whom we call Fellows in the novel. These investigations garnered thirty-five reports, eight thousand slides, complete with bone and tissue samples, twenty exhaustive autopsy reports on glanders, plague, and anthrax.[16]

Of all the experts, Naito Ryoichi (the Japanese list their surnames first) achieved the greatest success. With the active encouragement of the occupation authorities, he went on to establish the Japan Blood Bank, later renamed the Green Cross Corporation, a hugely successful pharmaceutical company led by several scientists from Unit 731, including Kitano Masaji, who served as vice president. Naito died in 1982, but his company, founded on a culture of corrupt medical practices, subsequently sold unsterilized blood products to the public during the 1980s, well aware of the risk of HIV infection. Thousands in Japan contracted the virus. As of January 2000, 493 had died of AIDS-related complications.[18]

Green Cross's chairman, a Naito protégé, was sentenced to two years in prison for criminal negligence. After reaching an agreement in 1988 to pay $216 million to the victims, the company was absorbed by Yoshitomi Pharmaceutical Industries in an acquisition estimated at $900 million.[19] Since then, a number of new cases have been filed against the company, claiming its blood products infected more than ten thousand people with hepatitis C.[20]

* * *

During the Korean War, John Powell wrote hundreds of stories for the *China Weekly Review* accusing the U.S. Army of using biological weapons on the North Koreans, an allegation that has yet to be proven with solid evidence. Much of his material was based on Chinese and Soviet Union claims that cemented his reputation in the U.S. government's eyes as a Communist provocateur. Upon his return to the United States in 1956, he was charged first with sedition, and later with treason, for his writings. The government eventually dropped its case against him in 1961.

Though he never proved his case, in 1980 Powell published the first documented story about the Japanese biological weapons program during the Second World War, based entirely on U.S. records still classified at the time. The government initially refuted the story, before conceding its accuracy. The article, published in the *Bulletin for Atomic Scientists*, remains a seminal work on the subject.

During the ensuing media uproar, Murray Sanders, after years of silence, went public with his role in the agreement that set hundreds of war criminals free. Upon his recovery from a two-year battle with tuberculosis, he ignored the siren call of biological weapons research and returned to teaching, first at the University of Miami, and later at Florida Atlantic University, where he studied degenerative diseases affecting the central nervous system. For his groundbreaking work in this field, he earned a nomination for the Nobel Prize in 1967. He eventually went blind in one eye, the result of his earlier efforts to isolate the kerato conjunctivitis virus at Camp Detrick. He spent the last period of his life exploring the restorative powers of cobra venom.[21] In 1985, four years before his death, he participated in a British documentary and a subsequent book[22] addressing the previously hidden details of Japan's biological weapons program and the American efforts to conceal it.

Sanders surely must have known that he had been deceived in Japan, yet strangely, during much of his career, he maintained a working relationship with Naito. He agreed to serve as a consultant for Green Cross and published several research papers for the company. Naito even paid Sanders a visit in Florida when the two were both old men. At Sanders' request, he brought six perfect pearls from the esteemed Mikimoto Kokichi, the Pearl King.[23] The ongoing relationship with Naito seems to belie Sanders' assertion that the original, inadequate report he produced on Japan's germ program was the result of ignorance.

To his credit, Sanders' public statements on the subject helped focus international attention on Japan's suppressed war crimes. In 1986, within months of the British documentary and book publication, Pat Williams, a congressman from Montana, convened a half-day Senate subcommittee hearing devoted to medical crimes suffered by former prisoners of war. The politician introduced Sanders at a press conference as the man who made the hearing possible. "We not only have the smoking gun, but the U.S. military officer who was there when it was fired." Sanders responded sheepishly. "I was the gun."[24]

While his statement seemed to imply responsibility for an immunity agreement, in fact the ultimate decision stretched far beyond even General Douglas MacArthur to the Joint Chiefs of Staff in Washington and possibly to President Harry Truman.[25] Final approval came only after many months of high-level discussions. Declassified documents reveal that State Department officials were keenly aware that such an agreement "might later be a source of serious embarrassment for the United States."[26] Thus, elaborate precautions were taken to suppress the entire affair.

There is considerable evidence of a cover-up. Sheldon Harris, who spent over a decade researching the subject, reported running into repeated roadblocks in his dealings with the U.S. government. The eight thousand slides of blood and human tissue turned over to American authorities mysteriously "disappeared" when they were shipped off to storage. Of the twenty human autopsy reports provided, only three remained; officials declared the other seventeen "missing." When Harris requested the notes from debriefings of the Mukden prisoners of war, the military informed him that a fire at its storage facility in St. Louis had destroyed the materials.[27]

At the Senate subcommittee hearing convened by Pat Williams, the army's archivist, John Hatcher, claimed that his extensive search through military files had produced no documents relating to Japan's experiments on human subjects. Upon further questioning, he allowed that the army had possessed Japanese-language materials seized immediately after the war. But after they languished in the National Archives for thirteen years, he explained, they were returned to the Japanese government—untranslated, unread, and, besides a few pages, uncopied. Thus he could neither confirm nor deny the claims at hand.[28]

Ultimately, the hearings came to nothing. Japanese officials have since refused to return the War Ministry records, numbering some twelve million pages. They have also declined requests to provide information on surviving veterans suspected of having committed atrocities.[29]

At the war crimes tribunal in Tokyo, only nine of the many thousands convicted were doctors, and they had conducted vivisections at an army hospital in Kyushu. None of Ishii's men were ever tried. In general, American treatment of Japanese war criminals contrasts starkly with that of Nazi perpetrators. While nearly a thousand Japanese offenders were put to death and thousands of others were given prison terms, even life sentences, few remained incarcerated for very long after Japan regained its independence in 1951. In the early 1950s, hundreds of militarists and war criminals began their lives anew. Some became involved in organized crime syndicates; others, with the financial support of the Central Intelligence Agency, went into politics, eventually reaching the highest offices of government.[30] All were free to travel between Japan and the United States as they pleased.

This is very different from the barriers erected against some sixty thousand Nazi perpetrators who were placed on a Justice Department watch list in the 1970s, prohibiting them from entering the country. Officials failed to create any such list of Japanese nationals, allowing men like Naito, for example, to bring Sanders a string of pearls. It was not until 1996 that the Justice Department finally created a similar list of sixteen Japanese individuals (adding seventeen more the next year), including many of the same doctors spared prosecution fifty years before.[31]

The Justice Department has withheld the names on this list, "the disclosure of which would constitute a clearly unwarranted invasion of personal privacy."[32] Only one individual has been refused entry since the list went into effect, and ironically, that was Shinozuka Yoshio, a former surgeon, who had agreed to give a series of lectures detailing the activities he witnessed at Ping Fan.[33]

The inclusion of doctors and scientists on the list, even at such a late date, is a tacit admission that it was an immunity deal that spared these men from prosecution. In 1998, Eli Rosenbaum, director of the Justice Department's investigative unit, wrote to Rabbi Abraham Cooper of the Simon Wiesenthal Center that they possess documents that "confirm that Ishii and his colleagues received immunity from prosecution and that, in exchange, they provided a great deal of information to U.S. authorities."[34] Never before had a law enforcement official made such an explicit statement.

In 2000, a federal Interagency Working Group was created to reopen the books on Japan's wartime past, similar to a task force charged with reexamining Nazi atrocities. Unlike its predecessor, however, the sponsoring legislation lacked key language that would have allowed it to override the 1947 National Security Act, a law that allows intelligence agencies to withhold information on the basis of "personal privacy," and other exceptions, including anything "that would seriously and demonstrably impair relations between the United States and a foreign government."[35] Though the subject matter is over fifty years old and almost all the players long dead and buried, U.S. intelligence agencies have taken full advantage of these loopholes to limit the scope of the investigation.[36]

When asked about the limitations of the Working Group, the chair of the investigative panel remarked, "The legislation never would have passed without them."[37] Yet the working group assigned to study Germany's wartime record was granted the authority to set aside the protections enshrined in the 1947 National Security Act. From that project, historians uncovered new documentation showing that the government smuggled Nazi war criminals into the United States to use in intelligence channels during the Cold War.[38] When it comes to the country's staunchest ally in the East, it seems that historians must play by a more restrictive set of rules.

* * *

This reluctance to air all the facts has undercut the efforts of former prisoners of war seeking recognition for the abuses they endured at the hands of the Japanese. Public officials, for instance, continue to adamantly deny allegations that American prisoners were used in medical experiments during their captivity in Manchuria. They have stuck to this position even in the face of recent research by historians showing that a team of Japanese scientists visited the prison camp at Mukden and dispensed "inoculations," an often-used euphemism for toxic injections.[39]

If, during his investigation following the war, Murray Sanders was unaware of these occurrences, his immediate successors certainly heard allegations of such criminal conduct. Documents show that intelligence agents suppressed at least four reports indicating that Americans were, in fact, subjected to medical research. As further evidence began to emerge in 1947, records reveal that officials in Washington agreed to "the recommendations of [General MacArthur]...that all information obtained in this investigation would be held in intelligence channels and not used in 'War Crimes' programs."[40] The decision still reverberates today in the limitations forced upon the Feinstein-sponsored working group.

These facts have surfaced thanks only to persistent investigators like Greg Rodriquez, Jr., who has devoted his life to the collection of documents on behalf of his father, a Mukden survivor. If not for others like Linda Goetz Holmes, author of the book *Unjust Enrichment*, the public may never have learned of the roughly eleven thousand prisoners of war who died at sea when the Japanese tried to transport them in the "hell ships" to slave labor camps in Formosa, Korea, Japan, and Manchuria. In violation of international law, the ships bore no markings indicating the presence of prisoners of war, and, in fact, several sank under American bombings and torpedoes.[41]

In contrast, the government's reticence would suggest that it considers these events—and perhaps even the men who suffered them—unsuitable for public consumption. Thus after his heroic escape from the prison camp at Mindanao and safe return home in 1943, Captain Edwin Dyess was thwarted in his efforts to tell the story of the Bataan Death March. The *Chicago Tribune* battled with the State Department for nearly five months before it received permission to publish his revelations. As Dyess's biographer noted, "Official reluctance, indecision, resistance, and actual hostility in high places all contributed to the lengthening of the fight."[42]

The contributions of Dyess and his fellow captives have gone largely unacknowledged. In the face of an overwhelming enemy, the fighting forces in the Philippines held the islands for three months during a crucial period when the United States needed to recover from the shock of Pearl Harbor. More importantly, they probably averted a Japanese invasion of a defenseless Australia. After years of silence, the survivors are finally able to reflect on their experiences, which they do at annual reunions of the American Defenders of Bataan and Corregidor. While many signed waiver forms prohibiting them from discussing their war years, once their story became public in the 1980s, they no longer saw reason to honor that commitment. Before then, few realized the significance of the Japanese guards spraying Flit guns in their faces. Though investigators had sufficient evidence to suspect Japan's doctors of malfeasance, no one asked the men upon their release whether they had endured medical experiments.

Men like Jake and Leo suffered repeatedly, first as soldiers, then as captives, then as slave laborers, then as civilians. Many suffered from alcoholism after the war; a few committed suicide. The Veterans Administration, unaware of the unique nature of the abuses inflicted on them, turned away many soldiers who could have benefited from counseling and more sophisticated medical attention.

The government paid soldiers who had been in captivity one dollar for every day of "missed meals," and $1.50 for "each day they were forced to perform labor and/or were subjected to inhumane treatment."[43] Most received close to the maximum $3,100 available; officials are quick to point out that in today's terms the award would be worth approximately $23,000. Nevertheless, it fell far short of what the men felt they deserved.

The question of compensation remains a thorny issue. In exchange for Japan's pledge of unconditional support in the Cold War, the 1951 Peace Treaty with the United States absolved the country and its nationals of any further financial obligation to its victims, though the Japanese economy was already rebounding. Veterans have recently taken to suing companies like Mitsubishi and Mitsui, which forced them into slave labor during the war. Still, the litigants have met with resistance, not only from the Japanese government but also from the State Department, which has filed several court briefs in defense of the Japanese corporations, insisting that the Peace Treaty settled all claims. A federal judge has heeded the State Department's advice and dismissed a large consolidation of the cases, declaring that the treaty had exchanged "full compensation...for a future peace."[44] In 2002, the Court of Appeals upheld the decision.

Others have lobbied Congress for a one-time, tax-free stipend of $20,000 to the veterans or their extended families. Outside the United States, many Allied countries have taken this approach, including Canada, England, Australia, and New Zealand, which paid their veterans compensation ranging from twelve to fifteen thousand dollars.[45] Even Switzerland and the Isle of Man, mere footnotes in the war, recently paid their veterans for Japan's atrocities.[46] Germany, for its part, has voluntarily distributed $80 billion in reparations to the victims of Nazi persecution. As of 1993, Japan had spent roughly $27 billion."[47]

Like the skulls and thighbones unearthed in 1989 at the site of the Army Medical College in Tokyo where Ishii began his career, the crimes committed more than fifty years ago continue to haunt us. In the Zhejiang province of China, villagers still suffer from an ailment known as "rotten leg" syndrome, the persistent effects of glanders poisoning during the war. In the United States, veterans have taken their case to the Supreme Court, less for money than the desire to bring the truth to light. Until the government agrees to present an accurate account of its complicity in the blood pact, the wounds will continue to fester.

Endnotes

1   Ralph Blumenthal with Judith Miller, "Japan Rebuffs Requests for Information," *NewYork Times*, 4 March 1999.

2   Sheldon Harris, *Factories of Death*, rev. ed., (NewYork: Routledge 2002), 49.

3   "U.S. Prisoners of War and Civilian American Citizens Captured and Interned by Japan in WorldWar II:The Issue of Compensation by Japan," Report for Congress, 22 August 2002, 19.

4   Harris, *Factories of Death*, 192.

5   Ibid.190.

6   Ibid.

7   Ibid. 318.

8   Ibid.

9   Ibid. 321.

10 "The Issue of Compensation by Japan," Report for Congress, 22.

11 Harris, *Factories of Death*, 325.

12 Peter Williams and David Wallace, *Unit 731: The Japanese Army's Secret of Secrets*, (London: Hodder and Stoughton, 1989), 298.

13 Ibid. 287–292.

14 Harris, *Factories of Death*, 338.

15 Ibid. 338–339.

16 Ibid. 276–277.

17 Harris, *Factories of Death*, 344.

18 Ibid.

19 *Japan Today*, 24 March 2002.

20 Interview with Peggy Sanders, 2002.

21 Williams and Wallace, *Unit 731*.

22 Interview with Peggy Sanders.

23 Jeanne McDermott, *The Killing Winds: The Menace of Biological Weapons*, (New York: Arbor House, 1987), 138.

24 Harris, *Factories of Death*, 279.

25 Harris, *Factories of Death*, 302.

26 Harris, *Factories of Death*, xv.

27 Harris, *Factories of Death*, 161.

28 Blumenthal, "Japan Rebuffs Requests for Information," *New York Times*, 4 March 1999.

29 David Kaplan and Alec Dubro, *Yakuza: The Explosive Account of Japan's Criminal Underworld*, (Massachusetts: Addison Wesley Publishing Company, 1986).

30 Ken McLaughlin, "U.S. Bars 16 Japanese as War-Crimes Suspects," *San Jose Mercury News*, 4 December 1996.

31 Japanese Imperial Government Disclosure Act of 2000, Section 703, Requirement of Disclosure of Records.

32 Michael Zielenziger, "Refused Entry, 'War Criminal' Says U.S., Japan Avoiding Truth," *San Jose Mercury News*, 2 July 1998.

33 "The Issue of Compensation by Japan," Report for Congress, 22.

34 1947 National Security Act.

35 Mark Fritz, "Bill Could Hamper Investigation into U.S. Knowledge of Japanese Atrocities," *Los Angeles Times*, 26 October 2000.

36 Interview with Steven Garfinkel.

37 "Bill Could Hamper Investigation," *Los Angeles Times*.

38 Linda Goetz-Holmes, "Unit 731 and Experiments on American Prisoners of War," *Report to the Nazi War Crimes and Japanese Imperial Government Records Interagency Working Group*, 2002.

39 Harris, *Factories of Death*, 278.

40 Linda Goetz-Holmes, *Unjust Enrichment*, (Mechanicsburg, Pennsylvania: Stackpole Books, 2001), 33.

41 William Edwin Dyess, Charles Leavelle, ed. *The Dyess Story: The Eye-Witness Account of the Death March from Bataan and the Narrative of Experiences in Japanese Prison camps and of Eventual Escape*, (New York: G.P. Putnam's Sons, 1944), 11.

42 Holmes, *Unjust Enrichment*, 138.

43 Judge Vaughn Walker, U.S. District Court, Northern District of California, "World War II Era Japanese Forced Labor Litigation," 21 September 2000.

44 "The Issue of Compensation by Japan," Report for Congress, 32.

45 Ibid.

46 Ibid. 31.

ABOUT THE AUTHORS

Lee Brandenburg has been a longtime student of American history. Having completed two tours of duty in the U.S. Army, both as an enlisted man and an officer, he has always held a great interest in the fate of those who served their country, and has attended reunions of the American Defenders of Bataan and Corregidor. He is also co-author of *The Captive American: How to Stop Being a Political Prisoner in Your Own Country*, and author of *The Powerhouse Entrepreneur: Wealth and Success Though Creative Action*. He lives with his wife and family in northern California.

Matt Isaacs has worked as an investigative journalist since 1996, writing for *Diablo Magazine*, the *San Francisco Examiner*, the Center for Investigative Reporting, the *SF Weekly*, and the *Bay Guardian*. He lives with his wife and two children in California.